"Who do you think you are, anyway?"

"My name's Dashiell."

"As in Dashiell Hammett? The famous detective writer?" Liz rolled her eyes. "I suppose that would explain the trench coat and the fedora. Do you think you're a private eye?"

"Let me come inside and I'll explain."

"Give me one good reason why I should."

Dash concentrated on producing a quick miracle, so she'd believe in him—and he could keep her out of danger. His brilliant revelation was accompanied by a swelling chord of heavenly sound, the sweetest music in the galaxy. Then he explained, "It's like this, Liz. I'm an angel."

Liz gasped. Her curling brown hair seemed to be standing on end. Her complexion paled beneath the tan. A shiver made her shoulders tremble.

Dash frowned. Was the woman simply taking it well…or didn't she believe him?

Dear Reader,

The word *angel* conjures up chubby cherubs or wizened old specters, not men who are virile and muscular and sinfully sexy. But when you enter the Denver Branch of Avenging Angels, you'll meet some of the sexiest angels this side of heaven!

Whenever there's injustice, the Avenging Angels are on the case.

Last month, author Margaret St. George brought you the first irresistible angel in *The Renegade*. Now, well-known author Cassie Miles brings you *The Impostor!* Cassie's created a sexy, trench-coat-clad P.I.—who just happens to be an angel, too!

I know you'll love Dashiell—and all the Avenging Angels coming your way now through May. Don't miss any of this superspecial quartet!

Regards,

Debra Matteucci
Senior Editor & Editorial Coordinator
Harlequin Books
300 East 42nd Street
New York, NY 10017

The Impostor
Cassie Miles

Harlequin Books

TORONTO • NEW YORK • LONDON
AMSTERDAM • PARIS • SYDNEY • HAMBURG
STOCKHOLM • ATHENS • TOKYO • MILAN
MADRID • WARSAW • BUDAPEST • AUCKLAND

In memory of Cynthia Bergstrom Climp.
Too soon an angel.

ISBN 0-373-22363-3

THE IMPOSTOR

Copyright © 1996 by Kay Bergstrom

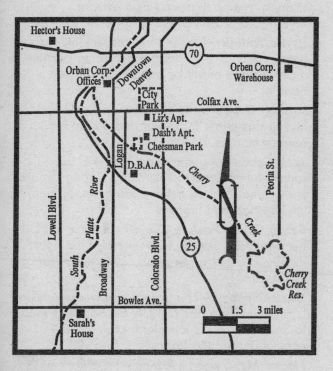

CAST OF CHARACTERS

Dashiell Divine—He's tall, dark and very strange. His background as a private investigator hasn't prepared him for this case.

Liz Carradine—Looking for excitement, she's ready for a career change, but being partner to a private eye might be more than she can handle.

Agatha Orben—The elderly victim of a mysterious crime that went undetected for several months.

Jack Orben—Agatha's son inherited the successful company OrbenCorp Coffee Imports. Though he's not an astute businessman, he likes the prestige and money.

Sarah Orben Pachen—Agatha's niece tended her while she was ill, and inherited the house. Finally, she has a gorgeous home to die for or to kill for.

Gary Gregory—The accountant whose passion is rose growing has recently become engaged to Sarah. Was his long-term plan to gain control of the inheritance?

Hector Messenger—A man with a dark and dangerous past, he buys raw coffee beans in exotic locations. His skill at working a deal might have gotten him into trouble.

Sister Muriel—The hardworking nun counsels the Orben family and inadvertently becomes pivotal in solving the case.

Chapter One

The first thing Dashiell saw was legs. Long, sleek, tan stems under silky black running shorts. She was something, really something. If he could have gotten her out of the jogging shoes and into a pair of high heels, Liz Carradine might be one classy-looking dame.

Despite the evening drizzle, she slowed to a walk, breathing hard after her run around the Big Lake at Denver's City Park. She stopped, braced those amazing legs and tossed her head, sending a ripple through the brown ponytail atop her head. She glanced toward the east, then the west where the front range of the Rocky Mountains was invisible behind a curtain of gray September dusk. Again, she looked around and frowned.

She sensed his presence, Dash thought. That was good. He liked a woman who was alert. Not only beautiful, but smart, too! This Liz Carradine might be the perfect contact inside OrbenCorp Coffee Imports.

He turned up the collar on his trench coat and stepped from the shadows of a spreading elm tree. His footsteps crackled through a blanket of yellow autumn leaves as he approached her. "Dangerous time to go for a jog," he offered.

"What?"

Though she was startled and backed away from him a step, he sensed no fear in her wide-set, pale blue eyes. Gently, he repeated, "It's almost dark. Kind of a dangerous time to be out running."

"Not for me. I can take care of myself."

Though she spoke with as much bravado as a punk carrying heat, he knew she didn't have a gun. There was no place in that skimpy little outfit to hide a weapon, not unless she had a switchblade stashed in the heel of those clodhopper running shoes. Why did women wear those things, anyhow?

She glared hard at him. "Don't even *think* about trying anything."

"Wouldn't dream of it." He smiled, just a little. This feisty little kitten had no idea who she was talking to.

"Are you laughing at me?"

He was amused. But laughing? "No. But I'm interested, precious. If I was up to something, how were you planning to defend yourself?"

"I'm not your precious."

As Dash reached into the breast pocket of his trench coat to pull out his Camels, she sprang into a karate stance.

He held up the cigarette pack to show her he wasn't going for a weapon, but she didn't relax. A Ninja broad, huh? As if a chop to the windpipe could stop him. "Listen," he said as he struck a kitchen match with his thumbnail and fired up his smoke, "all I want to do is talk to you, okay?"

"Keep away from me," she threatened. "Don't make me hurt you."

She reversed her position with a swift motion, and he admired the play of muscles in her well-toned thighs. Wow! Dash inhaled deeply. He just couldn't get over those legs. "Much as I like your... attitude," he said, "we've got some business to discuss. It's about Orben-Corp.'

"How do you know where I work?"

"I know your name is Elizabeth Carradine. I know your job is secretary to Jack Orben."

"Executive assistant," she corrected. "I'm an executive assistant to the president of OrbenCorp Coffee."

"Right. I knew that." What he didn't know was if she could be trusted. That was what he had to figure out. "Anyway, Lizzie, I think we're on the same side."

"And which side is that?"

As a rule, Dashiell wasn't inclined to discuss the eternal merits of good and evil. He'd never been much of a philosopher. He preferred action. "I'm on the side of the angels. Now, let's go sit on that bench by the lake like a couple of civilized beings, and we'll talk turkey."

He started toward her.

Without hesitation, she gave a high-pitched yell. Her foot lashed out. Her hands slashed, smacked and slapped.

Before Dash was aware of what was happening, he was sitting on his butt in the dirt beside the path, and she was sprinting like a fleet and graceful gazelle toward the Seventeenth Avenue side of the lake.

"Okay, Lizzie." Dash stubbed out his cigarette and rubbed his chin where she'd left the imprint of her sole. "You wanna play rough?"

In the blink of a mortal eye, he became lighter than air and soared through the gray mists. With one stroke of his unseen angelic wings, he was at the edge of the park, standing beneath the diffused light of a streetlamp. He leaned against it, pulled down the brim of his fedora. His match flared with sulfurous flame, and he lit another cigarette as she came running toward him.

"You!" She jumped a few steps backward, whirled and stared at the far side of the lake where she'd whacked him. When she turned around, her blue eyes were wide as china saucers. "How did you—"

"All I want to do is talk."

"No way."

Her slender eyebrows pulled in a determined scowl, and she started running again. About a hundred yards away, she paused at the curb of Seventeenth Street, waiting for a break in the traffic.

This time, Dash didn't bother to move. He formed his thoughts into words and wished them toward her in a suspended bubble that popped just over her head, spilling his thought. "Wait up, Liz. I need five minutes of your time."

"No!"

He heard her shout over the rumbling splash of the traffic. This was one stubborn woman. A tough tomato. A hot-tempered tamale. Geez, what did she want? He'd gone to the trouble of performing two minor miracles, and she was unimpressed. What made her so suspicious? He might have to rethink his plan. Using her as a contact on his current assignment might be trickier than he had anticipated.

Liz darted into the street. The pavement was slick, and she stumbled. Went down on one knee. In her haste to rise, she slipped again and sprawled flat on her stomach across the double yellow line.

Down the street, in the dusk, the red light changed to green. Two cars revved and rolled toward her prone figure. From the opposite direction, more traffic rumbled and splashed across the dark, wet pavement. Even if the drivers saw her, they might not be able to brake in time.

"Get up," Dash shouted. *Where was her Guardian Angel?*

Watching her, he held his breath. An uncharacteristic sensation clenched in his chest. Fear. He hadn't felt fear in a very long time. In slow motion, he saw the oncoming headlights approaching her. Given time, he might have been able to stop them, but that would cause a pileup. The cars were so close. She had to hurry. She had to save herself. "Move, Liz!"

She was up. On her feet. Staggering, she made it to the far side of the street where she dodged between two parked cars. She was okay. A little bruised, but okay.

Dash breathed a prayer of relief. If anything had happened to her, he would have blamed himself. He should have known better than to approach a lone woman. Though she hadn't seemed frightened of him, he'd startled her, made her careless.

It wouldn't happen again. To avoid further mishap, he waited until she'd limped across two more busy streets. When she stood outside her place and fitted the key in the lock, he materialized again. "Liz, may I come in?"

She turned and glared. "You've got a lot of nerve."

He couldn't deny it.

"Did you see what happened?" she demanded. "You almost got me killed."

He shrugged. Dash knew, from experience, that there were fates worse than death. "Let me explain."

"Oh, I think I understand. You're some weirdo who lurks around in the park in a trench coat, getting your kicks from scaring women."

"That's not true. You've got me wrong, all wrong."

She pushed open the door to the renovated Victorian mansion where she had an apartment on the third floor, but before she went inside, she turned to him. "How did you get across the park so fast after I hit you?"

He would have lied if it was possible. That was one of the problems with being an angel. There was no sinning allowed. Whether he liked it or not, he was stuck with a couple of unbreakable commandments. So he winced and told the truth. "I flew."

"Sure you did." She stepped across the threshold. "Who the hell do you think you are, anyway?"

"My name's Dashiell."

"As in Dashiell Hammett? The famous detective writer?" She rolled her eyes, then chuckled. "I suppose that would explain the trench coat and fedora. Do you think you're a private eye?"

"Let me come inside and I'll explain."

"You've got to be kidding!" She muttered, "You pop up from nowhere and scare me half to death. Then, you want me to invite you inside?"

"That's about the size of it, precious."

"You're crazy!" She stepped inside the doorway to a tiled foyer.

"Wait!"

"Give me one good reason I should."

Though Dash had always preferred the direct, simple approach without the celestial fireworks, there were occasions when a small dose of flash and dash could save a lot of time. This was one of those occasions. Liz Carradine was a hard sell, and it was going to take an extreme measure to get past her suspicious nature.

"Here's my reason," he said.

Dash issued forth with a burst of luminosity. The explosion lasted only for an instant. Prolonged exposure to the full force of his radiance would have blinded her. His brilliant revelation was accompanied by a swelling chord of heavenly sound, the sweetest music in the galaxies. A hard breeze rocked against her as he offered a glimpse, a quick impression, of feathers. Pure, glowing, pearly white feathers. Wings.

Then the street was silent and dark again.

''It's like this,'' he explained as he stuck a Camel in the corner of his mouth. ''I'm an angel.'

Liz stood and gaped, backlit by the glow from inside the entryway. Her curling brown hair seemed to be standing on edge. Her shoulders trembled. Her complexion paled beneath the tan, causing the sprinkle of freckles across the bridge of her nose to stand out in sharp relief.

He thought, all in all, she was taking it well.

She closed her mouth with a snap, shook her head in disbelief and stared at him. ''Tell you what, Dashiell—''

''Call me Dash.''

''I'll call you gone,'' she said. ''If you're an angel, I'm Ivana Trump!''

She slammed the door in his face and he was left out on the street.

If he could have felt the chill, he probably would have shivered. Never before, in his years and years of angelic existence, had he ever encountered such a bullheaded dame. Most humans were knocked for a loop by a total radiant manifestation. Most humans fell to their knees and tried to kiss the hem of his trench coat. But not her, not Liz. Talk about your doubting Thomasina!

He stared at the carved oak door and beveled glass of the Victorian mansion where she had her apartment. That door had slammed hard. Inside, he imagined her stomping up the stairs, mumbling about weirdos.

Working with her was going to be a challenge, but she was still his best source at OrbenCorp. He'd have to try again. He'd have to convince her. A challenge, he thought. Might be fun. Grudgingly, Dash acknowledged a certain respect for this feisty little number with the great gams.

When he turned around, Dash came face to face with the sleaziest-looking Guardian Angel he'd ever seen. Her celestial robes were bordered with fake leopard skin and fitted tight. Her lipstick was red enough to stop traffic. She had big, blond hair and bigger bazooms. She laughed at him, then winked. "So, you're the famous Dash from the Denver Branch of Avenging Angels. I've heard of you."

"Sorry I can't return the compliment, cookie."

"You can call me Cherie." She rested her fist on her hip and stuck out her bosom. "I'm the original hooker with a heart of gold. As you know, some of us do make it to heaven."

"Are you supposed to be the Guardian Angel for Liz?"

She fluffed her hair. "That's right."

"You're doing a lousy job, babe. Liz almost got killed in the traffic on Seventeenth Street. Where were you?"

"It's not my fault. I got distracted," she said brazenly. "There was a party in one of the bars on Seventeenth and I dropped by. Out of nostalgia, you know. I used to love parties. Besides, I knew nothing would happen to Liz. Nothing ever does. I've never been Guardian Angel for somebody who's so boring. She's got no vices to speak of. All she ever does is work and read and jog and watch the tube." She gestured for him to come close and whispered, "She hasn't been with a man for three years."

Dash found that hard to believe. No men? This nineties sensitivity stuff was getting out of hand if a snappy number like Liz Carradine wasn't getting dates. He frowned at Cherie. "You wouldn't lie, would you?"

"No way, Dash. I'm an angel." She arched one painted eyebrow. "You sound like you might be interested in Lizzie. Tempted?"

Dash didn't even dignify her comment with a reply. He knew the rules, and lust was one of the seven deadlies.

"My, my," Cherie said, "this might be fascinating. The well-known detective Avenger falling for a human?"

"Knock it off, Cherie. You know better than that."

"Do I?"

It was too bad that Liz got stuck with this floozy for a Guardian. On the other hand, Cherie's lack of interest in her duties as a Guardian might work to his advantage.

Over the years, he'd done a lot of negotiating with the Guardians, and it was always a drag. With them, it was whining about one thing or another. Nervous Nellies. They were always complaining to the Avengers. *Don't do that. It's dangerous.* But he could tell that Cherie was different. She'd welcome some excitement.

Slinking close to him, she batted her eyelashes. Her scarlet fingernails creased the lapel of his trench coat. "Say, Dash, you think you could do anything about getting me reassigned? I'd be a great Avenging Angel."

He suspected the only reason she wanted to be an Avenger was so she could once again take tangible physical form instead of being invisible to all but other angels. And he had to agree that it was a shame to waste all her spectacular artifice on angels. He hooked his arm through hers. "Let's talk."

LIZ CARRADINE watched from her upstairs bay window as the man who called himself Dash strolled down the street, talking to himself. Dash, as in Dashiell Hammett, who was one of her favorite mystery authors. Dashiell Hammett, who had written *The Thin Man* and *The Mal-*

tese Falcon. Was that his real name? More to the point, how did he know her? How did he know where she worked?

Painfully, she lowered herself to the window seat. Her right knee was scraped raw from when she fell on Seventeenth Street, and the palms of her hands were bruised. She'd been lucky to get out of the way before the traffic had come squealing down upon her. Shuddering, Liz realized that she'd been about five seconds away from being road kill.

On the street below, she saw Dash pause, straighten his shoulders and gesture emphatically. The man was severely neurotic, and that really was a shame because he wasn't bad looking. He had a broad set of shoulders under that ridiculous private-eye trench coat, and he must be in excellent shape because he'd gotten across the park before she did. He hadn't even been breathing hard—in spite of his nicotine habit.

She continued to observe as he talked to himself and lit another cigarette. Then he held the cigarette, butt out, and it puffed all by itself. The ember tip glowed red in the darkness. A wispy smoke ring appeared. It was as if someone else, an unseen person, was taking a drag of Dash's Camel.

Liz rubbed her eyes. Was she as crazy as he was? Was his nuttiness contagious?

Or maybe he really was an angel, capable of strange and wondrous miracles.

"No way," she said aloud. This angel craze had definitely gone too far. Liz was a very down-to-earth person, and she wasn't even sure she believed in celestial beings. Even if there were such things as angels, they didn't wear trench coats and talk like somebody doing a bad Humphrey Bogart impression.

Still...she couldn't explain that flash of light, like a lightning bolt that touched down right there on her doorstep. And she'd heard music—a single beautiful chord that sounded and vanished more quickly than thunder. For an instant, she'd felt warm and safe, somehow protected, enveloped in a beautiful, luminous cocoon of the softest eiderdown.

The sensation lasted for the merest second, only the blink of an eye, but the feeling was remarkable. What was it? What natural phenomenon had caused the light and the sound? She was reminded of the description given by people who had near-death experiences. They talked about a tunnel of pure white radiance. An encounter with the angels?

As she watched, Dash turned his head and looked at her. He raised his hand, still holding the cigarette, and waved.

Though his lips did not move, she heard his voice as clearly as if he'd been standing right beside her. He said, "Here's looking at you, precious."

THE NEXT MORNING, Liz walked stiffly through the reception area at the downtown corporate office of OrbenCorp Coffee. Though she'd bandaged her scraped knee, the injury felt hot and stinging beneath her loose linen slacks. Liz wouldn't have minded a bit of sympathy, but the perky new receptionist didn't bother to look up from the phones as she waved a cheery good morning.

Nor did Jack Orben pay the slightest attention to Liz's halting gait. He strode past her in the corridor, studying the morning newspaper. Absently, he said, "Good morning, Liz."

"Hi, Jack."

She watched his back as he pushed open the door to his plush corner office. Loudly, Liz cleared her throat, hoping to attract his notice. It took an effort to stop herself from exhaling an agonized moan. That would have been excessive, perhaps even pathetic, as a bid for attention.

Jack pulled his nose out of the newspaper and scowled in her direction. "Liz? What's the matter with you?"

"I'll survive." But she exaggerated her hobble. "Last night, when I was jogging, I stumbled and—"

"Big day today," he said. "Hector's in town. Oh, that reminds me, are you coming to Sarah's dinner party tonight?"

"I really hadn't planned—"

"Of course you are. You're practically family, and Sarah's counting on you."

"But I'm really not feeling well." Liz blessed her injury. If a scraped knee could give her reason to escape one of Sarah Orben Pachen's tedious dinner parties, the pain was worth it. "Yesterday, I almost got killed on Seventeenth Avenue. So I won't be able to make it to the dinner tonight."

"Sure you will," Jack said. "Call Sarah this morning and let her know if you're bringing a date. And I'll be out for most of the day with Hector, so you carry on around here. Thanks, Liz."

He pivoted and went into his office.

"You're welcome, Jack," she said to the closed door. Never mind that she was hurt. Never mind that she'd been accosted last night by a man who thought he'd flown across City Park, a man who dressed like a latter-day Humphrey Bogart and had told her—with a completely straight face—that he was an angel.

Though she wasn't a whiner, Liz had expected a little more compassion from her co-workers. A friendly "How

are you?'' would have been nice. Or "Could I help you?"
But no. Never.

She was utterly taken for granted. Good old Liz, always on time, always doing her job, always overlooked.
As far as OrbenCorp was concerned, Liz was a function,
not a person. She was the indispensable administrative
assistant to Jack Orben, the company president and CEO
since his mother passed away six months ago.

Slipping into her narrow office right next to Jack's, she
slammed her briefcase on the desktop.

Almost ten years ago, she'd started here, fresh from
college and full of ambition. She'd expected to rise swiftly
through the ranks of the small family-owned company,
which seemed favorably placed in the burgeoning market
for exotic coffees. Ultimately, she hoped to become a
buyer, traveling in Central and South America with occasional forays along the Pacific Rim. She was hired, after all, for her training and ability in languages.

And now? Ten years later? She was nothing more than
a glorified lackey, racing to cover Jack's lack of business
acumen. He was a terrific sales promoter, suave enough
to do his own advertising appearances on television. But
when it came to the daily transactions necessary to keep
the business rolling, Jack couldn't be bothered.

Limping around her desk, she yanked open a file
drawer and dug inside until she found the accounting
folder with the latest buy-sell comparison figures.

"Busy day," she muttered. Hector Messenger, the
buyer who had the job Liz coveted, was in town.

To Jack, Hector's presence meant a prolonged lunch,
a dinner party at Cousin Sarah's and a nightcap afterward. Hector, like Jack, was divorced, and the two of
them were infamous for their business carousing.

To Liz, Hector's arrival meant something altogether different. She'd been comparing figures on the purchases OrbenCorp had made on raw and processed coffee beans versus the prices paid by other companies for virtually the same product. It seemed to her that over the past several months Hector had been contracting for eight to twelve percent more than OrbenCorp's competitors. He had some explaining to do.

"Good morning, Liz."

She glanced up. Hector Messenger stood in her doorway. He was a short, swarthy man in his mid-fifties who considered himself to be a sharp dresser. Too sharp for Liz's taste. The knife-edge creases in his trousers were too emphatic. The blue stripe in his gray wool blend suit shone overly bright. The collar of his shirt was open one button too low. He was one of those men who always wore jewelry—a couple of rings, a heavy gold wristwatch and two necklaces, a St. Christopher medal and a gold locket.

With a nod, she acknowledged his presence. "How are you, Hector?"

"Not bad. And yourself?"

"I'm miserable," she said. She straightened and shoved the file cabinet drawer closed. "I stumbled last night while I was jogging and scraped my knee."

"Any stitches?"

"No."

"A sprain?"

"Not really." Liz shrugged. "Okay, it's not a serious, life-threatening injury. But it still hurts."

He flashed his toothy white grin. "I am so sorry."

Was that sarcasm? She knew that Hector, during his peripatetic world travels, had been in tight situations in several Third World nations. He'd witnessed revolutions. According to the rumor mill, he'd been a mercenary before he joined OrbenCorp. Once, he was almost kidnapped. His job could be dangerous.

And still Liz wanted it. She wanted to be a buyer, a world traveler. She hungered for the excitement.

"Please sit down, Hector." Suppressing her limp, she went behind her desk and eased into the chair behind it.

"Sorry, Lizzie, I can't stay. Gotta do my first cup of coffee with the big boss."

"I need to verify some figures with you," she said. Liz knew very well that Jack wouldn't mention Hector's overpayments on beans. Jack would be thoroughly delighted that Hector, his playmate, was back in town—no matter how much Hector was costing the company. Therefore, as always, the unpleasant confrontation was left to Liz. She started, "I've been studying the contracts from last quarter and—"

"Later," Hector said. He strode the two paces it took to cover the space in her cubicle-size office and held out his fist. He opened his fingers, displaying a set of fancy silvery earrings. "These are for you, Liz."

She plucked them from his hand. They were huge and shiny, a lacy design with silver teardrops that would dangle to her shoulders. There was no way understated Liz would ever wear heavy, gaudy earrings like these. Dryly, she said, "Gosh, thanks."

"When I saw them, in a market in Cartagena, I thought of you."

She wondered why. If Hector had ever spared more than a quick glance in her direction, he would have noticed that she never wore jewelry like this.

"Put them on," he said.

"I think not. I'll save them for a dress-up occasion." Like Halloween, she thought. "Now, Hector, I'm sure you have a few minutes, and we really need to discuss these amounts."

"Please put on the earrings. Come on," he cajoled. "Let yourself go. You're a very attractive woman, Liz. Come on, let your hair down."

She patted the sleek French knot that held her long brown tresses in place. "I like my hair this way."

"So do I. Hey, don't get me wrong. I'm not criticizing. Lizzie, I'm old enough to be your father, and my advice is meant in a fatherly way. I've known you for seven years now."

"Eight," she corrected. She vividly recalled the day Hector had been hired and the position for buyer had been filled. Liz had been promised the next opening. When? Sometime in the twenty-first century?

"Eight years," Hector repeated. "That's a long time."

"Extra long when you're stuck behind a desk."

"That's what I mean, Liz. I'd like to see you put some more fun in your life. Take some risks. Loosen up."

"Sorry, I'm not a loose woman."

He chuckled. "See you later. Tonight at the dinner party."

"Wait!"

But he was gone, marching down the short corridor to Jack's office. She heard the two men exchange hale and hearty greetings, which, she knew from past experience, would be followed by a couple of raunchy jokes and a lot of backslapping. What a couple of jerks! Hector and his fatherly advice could go right straight to hell. She ought to take her information about his overpaying directly to the head of accounting. Gary Gregory watched over every OrbenCorp penny with the avidity of an obsessive-compulsive hawk. If he suspected Hector was paying too much for beans, Gary would go through the ceiling.

She listened to the loud masculine laughter that emanated from Jack's office. "Damn."

Ten years at OrbenCorp was an eternity. When would she get her chance? How long could she cling to the slender thread of hope that someday Hector would move on? And when that time came, would Jack give her the job, or would he look for another good old male buddy?

Liz drew back her arm and flung the ghastly earrings toward the light switch beside her open office door.

A hand reached out and caught them. Smoothly, he stepped inside and closed the door behind him. "Remember me?"

How could she forget? It was Dash, the lunatic. Today he wasn't wearing the trench coat, but his double-breasted suit had a distinctive thirties cut to the trousers, and he still had the fedora on his head.

Her eyes narrowed suspiciously as she glared at him. "What are you doing here?"

"Like I said yesterday, I need to talk to you, precious." He stood on the other side of her desk. "And I wanted to find out how you were. You took a hard fall last night."

Finally, someone was concerned. "It's just a scrape," she said. "No big deal, but it hurts every time I bend my knee."

"Can I take a look at it?"

"No! Not unless you're a doctor... as well as being an angel."

"I'm sorry, kiddo. I feel responsible."

"Well, you should. It was your fault that I went running out in traffic." As soon as she spoke, she felt petty.

"Forgive me?" he asked.

His coffee-colored eyes twinkled with a soft, gentle light. For some unfathomable reason she felt she could trust him. "Okay, Dash. I forgive you. Now, would you please leave my office?"

"I hope and pray you'll feel better."

"What an odd thing to say!" And yet, almost instantly, her aches lessened. She relaxed. The clenched fist of anger in her chest eased.

He shrugged his broad shoulders. "Hey, precious. A little prayer never hurt anybody."

"Oh, no, you're not going to start in on that angel stuff again, are you?"

"No, I'm not." He winked. "Meet me in fifteen minutes at the bakeshop on the corner and I'll buy you a cup of java."

"Coffee? You're offering me a cup of coffee?" She raised her eyebrows. Not only was he a crackbrained loon who seemed stuck in a bad impression of Bogie, but he was also unobservant. This was OrbenCorp, one of the leading processors and packagers of coffee in the country. Asking her out for coffee was like carrying ice cubes to Antarctica! "If there's one thing we have in this office, it's coffee."

"But you're shy on privacy, doll face. And I need to talk to you alone."

She gestured to the walls of her office. "Isn't this alone enough?"

"The walls have ears," he said cryptically.

"I really don't have time to play these games with you, Dash. I mean, why all the secrecy? What's the big deal?"

"Murder," he said.

He dropped the earrings onto the center of her desk and left the room.

Chapter Two

Murder? Was Dash serious or was he seriously deluded? Liz stared at the closed door of her office and wondered. Murder. That would explain his whole cloak-and-dagger demeanor. Maybe Dash really was investigating a murder case—just like Humphrey Bogart as Sam Spade.

A tickle of excitement started in the back of her throat, and instead of clamping down in a frown, her lips twitched into a grin as she contemplated the unusual thrill of a murder investigation. Wouldn't that be a switch from her regular, dull routine? A murder! But who?

Though Dash might be crazy, Liz had to find out.

She grabbed her purse and left the office, pausing in the receptionist's area to wait for the peppy blonde behind the desk to simultaneously complete the transfer of a phone call and the application of her hot pink lipstick. She was also reading a magazine and drinking coffee. This little bundle of energy was named Becky, and Liz had hired her only three weeks ago.

Though Becky's only qualifications for the job were attractiveness, a willing attitude and a sincere love of coffee, she was working out well. Her all-American-cheerleader look complemented the bright decor of the front office.

She snapped her mirrored compact shut. "Hi, Liz. What can I do for you?"

"There was a man who just came through here. Did he leave his full name?"

"A man?" Becky hefted her coffee mug. Judging by her hyperactivity, this had to be her fourth or fifth shot of straight French roast for the morning. "I didn't see anybody."

That was impossible! Everybody had to come through the front reception area. "Becky, he just came into my office. Not more than five minutes ago. A man. A little over six feet tall. Dark gray suit and white shirt. He was wearing a fedora."

"A hat? Nope, I didn't see him." The corners of her freshly colored lips pulled into a frown. "Was it important?"

"I hope not. Listen, Becky, I'll be out of the office for a couple of minutes. Take messages for me, okay?"

"You got it."

The phone rang, and Liz slipped out through glass doors with the words OrbenCorp Coffee stenciled in gold. She headed for the elevators.

Down on the street, she rounded the corner of the downtown Denver skyscraper where OrbenCorp had their offices on the fourteenth floor. The bakeshop, called Chez Muffin, was tucked into the retail first floor. The menu offered berry muffins, croissants and coffee in a very clean setting with blond wood tables, cane-bottomed chairs and a mural of the Eiffel Tower on the wall. Dash in his fedora and dark suit looked out of place with his shoulders hunched, his expression dark and the ever-present Camel stuck in the corner of his mouth.

He didn't really look like Humphrey Bogart, Liz thought. Dash was too tall. His features were too symmetrical to look dissipated. Still, the coolness in his manner suggested the great Bogie in his prime. As she approached him, Liz couldn't resist quoting a line from one of Bogie's most famous movies. She gestured toward the mural on the wall and said, "We'll always have Paris."

"Huh?"

"You know, like Bogie said to Ingrid Bergman. In *Casablanca?* It's my guess that you're a major Humphrey Bogart fan."

"Yeah, I like the Sam Spade movies, but I never much cared for that romantic tripe. That's not my style."

"So you're a tough guy, huh?"

She took the chair opposite his. In his hand, he cuddled a steaming extra-large mug of coffee, which, she judged by the aroma and color, was a rich Sumatra blend. Liz ordered Colombian, in honor of Hector's ghastly Cartagena earrings.

When she spoke again, she focused on the business at hand. "You mentioned a murder."

He placed a finger across his lips, indicating that she should keep her voice down. "You know, precious, this is a lousy joint for a clandestine meeting."

"*Au contraire.* I think it's very nice."

"Too nice," he muttered, taking a long drag off his cigarette. "In the old days you could get an honest cup of joe and a doughnut at any greasy spoon. Not these French pastry puffs."

"Well, you picked the place. So if the ambience doesn't please you, that's too bad."

"Right you are, cookie."

"Now then, Dash," she said, nudging him back to the subject. "Who's going to be murdered?"

"It's already happened."

"Somebody at OrbenCorp?"

"That's right."

Her mind raced through the possibilities. Though she wasn't closely involved with the daily business at the warehouse and processing facilities, Liz couldn't recall any reports of violent deaths. "Who?"

"Agatha Orben."

"You can't be serious! The woman was almost eighty. She'd been ill, and she passed away from a stroke in her sleep."

"Take my word for it. Agatha Orben was murdered."

"No, I can't believe that." Liz shook her head in denial. All of a sudden, the idea of murder wasn't so much fun. Quietly, she said, "I don't *want* to believe that someone killed Agatha."

"You liked her," he said. "I'm sorry, Liz. I'm not real good at this comforting stuff."

But when she glanced up from her coffee and looked into his dark eyes, she found a startling depth of compassion. At this moment, he seemed utterly sane, and he radiated an aura of sincerity, a true understanding of the deep sorrow of loss.

Stubbing out his cigarette, he reached across the table and held her hand. His fingers massaged her knuckles, and she felt strangely at peace.

"Tell me about Agatha," he said.

She hesitated. Why should she confide in him? It didn't serve any purpose. And yet, why not?

Liz started, "Agatha and her husband founded OrbenCorp nearly twenty years ago. That was back in the days when cappuccino and latte were considered exotic beverages. From what I understand, the start-up was difficult, but they persevered. That was Agatha's trademark, you know. She never gave up. When she believed in a cause or in a person, she dedicated her time, her

money and her efforts. She was generous but tough, un-
relenting when she had a point that she wanted to make.''

Liz had admired the old woman's attention to detail and
her perfectionism. After her husband passed away, Agatha had single-handedly built OrbenCorp into a company worth reckoning with.

But the constant stress had taken a toll. About a year
ago, Mrs. Orben's health began to fail. She deteriorated
quickly, requiring bed rest. When she died six months ago,
no one had been surprised. ''She died a natural death,''
Liz said. ''Her doctors did everything they could. Frankly,
Dash, that's why I can't believe what you're saying. Agatha was a wealthy woman. She had the best care money
could buy.''

''Poisoned,'' he said. ''Right under the doctors' noses.''

Liz shook her head. Murder wasn't the sort of thing
that happened to people like Agatha Orben. On the other
hand, Agatha had never been ill before last year. She was
vital, full of energy. ''Supposing this is true—''

''It's true, all right. I never lie.''

''But why? I simply can't imagine that anyone had a
reason to harm her. She was a good person. Everybody
liked her.''

''Did they?''

Liz considered for a moment. There was the time, a
couple of years ago, that Agatha had discovered her son,
Jack, using company funds to finance the purchase of his
new Mercedes. Agatha had chastised Jack, humiliated
him in front of the executive staff and insisted that he return the car. Jack had been furious, but certainly not angry enough to kill his own mother.

''Think about it,'' Dash urged. ''Even if Agatha was a
saint, there are reasons for murder. Agatha was wealthy.
A lot of people benefited financially from her death.''

"Jack inherited the company. And, of course, there's Sarah. She inherited big." Sarah Orben Pachen, the niece who had lived with Agatha, had been left the house and most of the furnishings. At the time, it seemed right. Sarah had cared for her aunt when Agatha was ill. "But I always had the impression that Sarah liked Agatha and was grateful to her."

"And they never argued?"

"Well, of course they did. Agatha was difficult at times." Reluctantly, Liz admitted, "Maybe she wasn't a sweet little old lady with homemade cookies and doilies. But murder? Who would do such a thing?"

"Don't know, precious." He squeezed her hand and released it. "That's why I need your help."

Slowly, Liz lifted her mug and took a sip. The brew was fresh and excellent, another fine Orben coffee. "Why are you interested in this, Dash? Who told you Agatha was poisoned? Where are you getting your information?"

"You might say that a little birdie told me." Dash shifted uncomfortably in his cane-bottomed chair. He was avoiding the truth, stretching the boundaries of angelic behavior. But he couldn't risk losing her attention at this point, and that was exactly what would happen if he laid it out straight and true as the road map to hell.

Besides, Dash knew he was right, dead right, about the fact that Agatha had been murdered. The old lady herself had relayed her story—complete with enough detail to merit consideration—to the Denver Branch of Avenging Angels.

Newly deceased and in the process of earning her halo, Agatha had stormed into the office demanding that their best operative take on her case. Dash was the best. That wasn't pride talking, just fact. He got the assignment.

"Why do you care?" Liz demanded.

"It's my job. I don't take it personal, if you know what I mean. All I care about is justice."

"That's rather abstract." She cocked an eyebrow. "Justice?"

"The scales of justice." He held out both hands, palms up, to illustrate. "You gotta have balance. You can't let the evil in the world outweigh the good. Or else—" He dropped his left hand below the tabletop and shot the right hand up. "Evil reigns supreme. Humanity takes a nosedive, plunges into chaos. Got it?"

"Colorful metaphor," she said. "And so, I assume, you're here to bring justice to the world. Like Superman?"

He'd told her before that he was an angel, an Avenging Angel who did his bit to keep the balance, but she wasn't buying that line. He shrugged and said, "It's my job."

When she confronted him directly, he saw a disturbing glitter of excitement in her blue eyes. That eagerness worried him. All he wanted from her was an introduction to the main suspects and some of the history of Orben-Corp.

"Your job, eh?" Her voice was cool but challenging. "So let me get this straight. First you tell me that you're an angel. Now you seem to be hinting that you're some kind of cop or detective."

He neither confirmed nor denied. He wasn't misleading her on purpose, just allowing her to draw her own conclusions.

"You are, aren't you?" She smiled too broadly. "A real private eye. I'll be damned!"

"I hope not."

"Well, that explains everything. That's how you knew who I was and where I worked. You're investigating the death of Agatha Orben."

"You got that right. I'm investigating. And I need your help, precious."

"Who hired you? Was it Jack? I know he was broken up by his mother's death, but I never would have thought Jack had the gumption to hire a private eye. So, who?" She waved her hands as if to erase her question. "Never mind. That was a silly question. I know you can't tell me. Client confidentiality, right?"

"I'd rather not spill the beans. The less you know, the better."

She took another taste of her coffee and studied him across the rim of her mug. "I can't believe I'm talking to a P.I. named Dash. This is like something out of a pulp novel."

"There's a dinner party tonight," he said. "At the former home of Agatha Orben, which was inherited by Sarah Orben Pachen, a niece of the dead woman. I want you to take me to the party as your date."

"Okay," she agreed readily. "What else?"

"That's it. You introduce me around, and I'll do the rest."

"But I could really help." She leaned forward, avid and confidential at the same time. "I've been around these people for ten years, Dash. I've seen them argue and make up. I've seen them get divorced. If you're looking for someone to investigate from the inside, I'm your woman."

"I don't work with a partner."

"But this is perfect. Nobody notices me. Around OrbenCorp, I'm invisible."

He shook his head. He couldn't believe that a long-stemmed beauty like Liz could fade into the woodwork. Even in those trousers, she was an eye-stopper. She was the kind of dame that kept herself wrapped so tight a man couldn't help but want to untie the ribbon and open the package.

A man, a human, earthbound man, would feel like that, Dash reminded himself. He had no right to even be thinking what he was thinking. He wasn't a man. Lust wasn't in his repertoire. "How's the leg?" he asked.

She raised her leg. Carefully, she stretched it, pointed her toe and flexed her knee. There was only a twinge of pain. "It's a lot better." It hadn't bothered her since she'd left the building. Sheepishly, she thought, all she needed was some sympathetic attention and her injury went away. "Thanks, Dash."

"For what?"

"Being kind enough to ask."

"Don't peg me wrong. I'm not a nice guy."

"Maybe you're more gentle than you think." She rose to her feet. "I should get back to the office now."

"Tonight," he said, tossing back the dregs of his coffee. "I'll stop by your place at six-thirty. You drive."

"Sure. I'll be ready."

"Wear a dress, sweetheart. It's a shame to cover up those legs."

Liz smiled. Wear a dress? That was the second unwanted fashion tip she'd heard today. First Hector and his awful earrings. Now Dash. "Tell you what, I'll wear a dress, if you'll do something for me."

"Shoot."

"When you're around me, I'd like for you to cut back on your smoking."

He grumbled, "Yeah, yeah, okay."

"Also, I'd appreciate if you'd drop all this 'sweetheart' and 'precious' business. I do have a name, you know."

Wryly, he said, "And you'd appreciate that."

Though his expression was impassive and calm, she sensed his intensity. It was as if he was playing along with her, allowing her to have her way. Yet his arrogance was perfectly natural—he was just like a private eye ought to be.

"I'd like to be called by my own name," she repeated. "If you don't mind."

"Not at all. I can't promise that I won't slip from time to time, but I'll try to call you...Elizabeth."

His voice seemed to echo. His tone had as much substance as a physical caress. The way he spoke her name in his smoky baritone sent a shiver up and down her spine.

"Elizabeth," he repeated. "I'll see you tonight."

She nodded once and left Chez Muffin. Outside, the sun seemed brighter in the skies. Though she solemnly regretted that the investigation would center around the death of someone she had cared about, the idea of sleuthing was undeniably exciting. Detective stories were among her favorite fantasies, and she couldn't wait to get started.

She walked briskly. Her limp was gone, and she knew that she was taking the first long strides toward an adventure that would change her life forever.

DASH PAID for their coffees and left the bakeshop. Outside, he lit a cigarette and inhaled deeply. *Cut back on his smoking? Who did she think she was?* He'd been sucking down unfiltered Camels since he took on the duties of an Avenging Angel in the 1930s. He didn't need to worry about addiction. And hazardous to his health? That was a laugh and a half.

He was an angel. His health was always perfect. Though he was capable of sensory feeling, his physical body required zero maintenance. He needed neither food nor drink to stay alive.

There were benefits to being a celestial entity, and he liked his work as an avenger. He was good at it. He had an aptitude. His instincts perfectly suited the job. When he'd been assigned, he took to detective work like a bloodhound to the scent, like a priest to his prayers, like a moth to a flame.

Nobody—with the exception of St. Michael himself—told Dash what to do. Until now.

And now, in one conversation, he'd agreed without a struggle to cut back on his Camels and to make his vocabulary more politically correct.

Because of *Elizabeth*. What was it about her that got to him? First time he saw her, she'd kicked his butt.

He stood on the street corner, smoking, and considered. He liked the way she looked, the way she was put together. Dash had always been a connoisseur of the female form. He admired women, their shape and form and the way they moved. Women intrigued him, but he never got involved. Lovely as they were, dames were trouble. With a flick of their pinkie or a flutter of their eyelashes, they could send a guy spinning. Dash had always kept his distance.

But Liz was different. She was like a rosebud about to blossom. When he touched her hand in the bakeshop, he had felt life, vibrant life, pulsing beneath the surface of her skin. She could turn out to be a really great broad. All it would take was a small bit of nurturing.

But that wasn't his job. He wasn't a Ministering Angel or a Guardian. He was a warrior, an Avenger.

"Hey, handsome."

He turned and spotted Cherie, the sleazy Guardian Angel, sitting in a parked convertible with the top down. She crooked her index finger and beckoned to him.

He sauntered over to her and leaned against the shiny red fender of the car. Though Cherie was invisible to everyone but him, she looked right at home in the passenger seat of the classy automobile. Her fake leopard-skin trim contrasted nicely with the sleek black leather interior.

"A word of advice," she said. "Don't."

"Don't what?"

"I saw how you were looking at her. I've been around the block more times than the St. Patrick's Day parade. And I know carnal sin when I see it."

"You're wrong." He took a drag on his cigarette. Mindful of the fact that there were people all around who couldn't see Cherie, he spoke in a low voice from the corner of his mouth. "I don't lust."

"Come on, baby. You can't fool me. I was a hooker. I know what lust looks like. And what it sounds like. You couldn't keep it out of your voice when you spoke her name." In a mocking tone, she whispered, "Elizabeth."

"Don't worry about me." Dash pushed himself from the car and strolled away from her. "See you around."

Cherie fell into step beside him. "What's it like, Dash? What's it like to have a physical body again? I mean, have you ever, you know, done it?"

"Done what?"

"Made love, you idiot."

"No way," Dash informed her. "You know the rules. We're angels. We don't swear. We don't lie. We don't lust."

"But you avenging types have gotten around one very big restriction. The biggest, in fact. You guys get away with murder."

"You're wrong, doll. It's not murder. We take vengeance. It's exactly precise. We follow orders from the higher authority."

"Have you ever wreaked vengeance? Ever killed a person?"

He didn't reply. For him there was no pleasure in death.

"Have you?" Cherie demanded.

Dash had been on assignment in Nazi Germany, at the heart of darkness where evil raged virulent and strong, corrupting good men and abetting those whose souls were already lost. He shook off the dark memories of those days when the light of justice shone so dimly that the flame was almost extinguished. "Not much call for the flaming sword these days. We get justice the usual way, through the legal system."

"And how do you get satisfaction? A manly satisfaction?" She gazed at him with knowing eyes. "What do you do about that yearning? You've got a body. You've got to be feeling it. But you'd better not try anything with Liz."

"Some Guardian Angel you are! I thought you wanted her to try out some earthly pleasures. You were upset because she hadn't been with a man in three years."

"A man, Dash. Not an angel. I don't even know what happens when an angel and a human do it." Her full lips pouted. "It's an interesting thought, but I really don't want Liz to get hurt."

"Neither do I." But he felt a strange tension when he thought of Liz. These were sensations that were better forgotten or suppressed. He knew the rules. Still…maybe he ought to take himself off this case.

As soon as the thought crossed his mind, the beeper in his pocket went off. He was being called to the office.

He waved to Cherie. "See you around, babe."

Faster than the speed of light, he flew to the Denver Branch of Avenging Angels. In his wake, Dash left rustling autumn leaves and a softly swirling cloud of dust. He touched down outside an old brown brick building on Logan Street. Dash tipped back the brim of his fedora and sauntered inside. No matter what turmoil he felt inside, he kept his cool. He was Dashiell, the best detective of all the Avengers.

Inside the offices, the decor reflected a genteel, slightly worn charm. The dark wood wainscoting and antique furniture were cozy, but Dash tried to spend as little time here as possible. He was an old-fashioned man of action, not a desk jockey who did his investigations on a computer screen. Dash preferred to work on gut instinct.

A couple of the other Avenging Angels waved a greeting and called out his name. Dash nodded to the handsome, fiery young angel named Kiel. The kid always seemed to be brooding, and Dash could tell that he was only a step away from trouble.

A curly-haired young man sat at the grand piano. As Dash strode across the richly figured Oriental carpeting, the angel plunked out a tune, "As Time Goes By." *You must remember this, a kiss is . . .*

"Knock it off," Dash said. The music reminded him of Liz, of the shimmer in her eyes when she'd quoted *Casablanca* lines to him.

Dash hurried up the stairs to the second floor, where a balcony overlooked the large front room. Before entering the office of Angelo, who supervised this branch, Dash lit a Camel. It wasn't that he wanted a cigarette, but his habit annoyed Angelo, who was a stickler for the rules and regulations surrounding angels. Angelo was a bug on vices.

Dash strolled into the supervisor's inner sanctum, enveloped in a pungent cloud of smoke.

"Cute," Angelo said curtly. Then, uncharacteristically, he grinned. "I understand that you've promised to cut back."

"Maybe."

"Oh, no, you promised that woman, and angels honor their promises." He chuckled. "She's a handful, Dash. You'd better watch out or she'll domesticate you."

"Fat chance, buster. All I need from Liz Carradine is an intro to the suspects and some background."

Angelo gestured to the computer screen in front of him. "When are you going to step into the 90s? Why not use the technology available?"

"I don't work like that." He knew that Angelo couldn't argue with his methods. Dash's success rate in solving the crimes assigned to him was one hundred percent. "Why'd you call me to the office?"

"The boss wants to see you. St. Michael is waiting in the corner office."

Dash nodded and left. To most angels, a meeting with St. Michael, the patron of cops, was cause for fear and trembling. But not for Dash. He and Mike went way back.

Dash strode through the open door and closed it behind him. For an instant, when he faced the saint, Dash was overwhelmed by the power and glory of his presence. Mike had a glow about him, a nimbus. He could disguise it when he went out in public, but here—among the angels—he didn't bother.

When he spoke, his voice rumbled like thunder. "Dashiell," he said. "You're having doubts about this case."

"It happens, Mike."

"Not to you. You're one of my best operatives. A natural investigator with a clear sense of justice."

"Might be best," Dash said, "if you pull me off the case."

"They say temptation is good for the soul." He fixed Dash with a burning glare. "Is it evil that tempts you?"

"Evil? No." He didn't think of Liz as evil. Not in any way. "It's the woman. Elizabeth Carradine."

"Ah, the temptress."

"That's not it. She's a good person. A little bit lonely. A little sad. But she's not a victim. She's a tough cookie."

"Women can be a problem," Mike said. "I'd like to lift your burden, Dash, but there is…Agatha. She refuses to allow me to reassign this case."

Dash raised his eyebrows. Where did Agatha Orben get this kind of pull? She must have some big connections upstairs.

St. Michael waved his hand and a form materialized in the chair opposite his desk. Dash recognized Agatha Orben from her last visit to the office, but she was different now. The first time he'd seen her, she was bent and stooped, an aged creature. Now her spine was ramrod straight. Her bearing was regal. She was almost beautiful.

She turned to Dash and said, "You are the best detective in the Rocky Mountain region. I'm well pleased that you have been assigned to solve the mystery of my demise. Have you made any progress?"

"Not much." He smiled. "You're looking sharp, Agatha."

"Thank you. I'm so delighted that the good works I did on earth have made a difference. I was never quite sure that they would, you know. In any case, that's not why I did them.''

"She's a good soul," Mike said. "One of the best. And we're very unhappy about the fact that she was murdered.''

From their prior conversation, Dash knew roughly how the murder was done, and he knew that Agatha had left behind a tangible clue that could lead to conviction for the perpetrator of the crime. But nobody—not even Agatha—knew the murderer's identity. In this case, none of their otherworldly abilities could help. There are dark crevasses in the human heart that are invisible even to angels.

Agatha turned her head and stared at Dash. Her gaze was firm, unwavering. Her voice was dulcet, yet imperial. "Is there a problem?''

"Liz Carradine," he said.

"Oh, no, Dash. You're on the wrong track. Liz is a wonderful girl. She never would have hurt me.''

"She's not a suspect," Dash said. "And I agree with you. Liz is pretty wonderful.''

"Oh." Agatha packed a wealth of innuendo into that single syllable. "You're attracted to her. Well, I can't say that I'm surprised. She's charming, intelligent and lovely. I don't know how you could avoid being interested.''

"Don't play matchmaker with an angel, lady.''

Dash knew what happened to angels who broke the rules. They got removed from their choice assignments and shipped to lesser positions, like guard duty for the Cherubs. He shuddered to think of that consequence. All those little kids. All those heavenly diapers. "I want off the case.''

"But you're the best," Agatha said. "I want you.''

But he didn't want to take the risk. "There's something else," he said. "Liz wants to play detective with me. This could be dangerous for her. I want out."

He turned to St. Michael, who rolled his eyes toward the ceiling and sighed. "Where's the wisdom of Solomon when you really need it?"

"What's it going to be?" Dash asked.

He knew that Mike wasn't one of those philosophical saints who pondered ethics and weighed alternatives. St. Michael made quick decisions from an unerring sense of right and wrong.

St. Michael looked him straight in the eye and said, "You stick to the case, and you solve it. That's your job, Dash."

Dash bobbed his head once. He didn't like Mike's decision, but he knew better than to argue with the boss. Dash had his orders, and he had to make the best of them. Take the lemons and make lemonade.

He pivoted, almost military in his bearing, and strode toward the door. "See you around, Mike. Nice talking with you, Agatha."

"Dash!"

He paused, his hand on the doorknob. "What is it, Mike?"

"Be careful. You know the consequences for lust."

"To tell you the truth, it's not lust I'm worried about." Dash turned slowly. He faced the saint and the elegant elderly lady. "Liz Carradine is one gorgeous female. No doubt about that. But I've been around beauties before. Movie stars. Socialites. Women with perfect faces and hourglass figures that knock your socks off. But I've got willpower. You know me, Mike. I'll never take the fall for some dame."

"Then what's the problem?" Mike inquired.

Dash frowned and shook his head. He couldn't put his feelings into words. They didn't make sense.

"I know what it is," said Agatha. "His attraction to Liz isn't carnal. It's pure. Maybe even good. I do believe Dashiell is falling in love."

She had the nerve to sound pleased about it.

Chapter Three

Liz paced in the confines of her office. The distance was exactly seven steps from file cabinet to file cabinet. As never before, she felt trapped in this small cubicle on the fourteenth floor of a downtown skyscraper. The space had never felt so claustrophobic. The air had never tasted so stale. When Dash had spoken of murder, investigation and private eyes, she'd caught a whiff of adventure, and she longed to inhale deeply of the fresh, rich atmosphere beyond the scope of her ordinary life.

He'd said that he never worked with a partner.

Well, she'd just have to change his mind!

She paced, turned and paced again. All her life, she'd done the sane and sensible thing, hoping that someday, someone would notice and give her a chance to fly. No more waiting! Liz didn't intend to spend another ten years hanging around while someone else decided whether she was capable of handling a challenge. She was capable, dammit! And her patience was gone.

Seven more steps. She could be a private eye—a great private eye! She was intelligent and well-organized. And she most definitely had the ability to creep through various situations without attracting attention to herself. The invisible woman, she thought. So average it was painful.

But Dash had noticed her.

She stopped and rested her arms on the file cabinet.

Dash had noticed. He'd cared enough to ask about her injury, and when he'd taken her hand, she felt the most incredible warmth emanating from him. They had connected. In some strange way, she felt close to him. Her mind easily conjured up a picture of his face, his eyes, his hands. A private eye. Imagine that!

She resumed her pacing, back and forth, wearing a rut in her carpet. With each step, her curiosity grew. Who did Dash work for? Who had hired him? Why did he tell her that crackpot story on the night he accosted her in the park about being an angel? He must have been joking. But why? He must have thought she'd be spooked by the idea that he was a private eye. But an angel? Why, why, why?

She paused to stare through her narrow office window, a mere eighteen inches wide, at a limited vista of the distant, snowcapped front range of the Rocky Mountains. If he was going to convince Dash that she could be his partner in crime-solving, she needed to stop skittering back and forth like a gerbil in a cage. She needed to organize her thinking.

Sitting behind her desk, she pulled out a fresh yellow legal pad and made a note across the top in the precise penmanship that Sister Elaine had praised so highly when Liz was a straight A student at Holy Cross grade school.

Liz wrote, "Premise—Agatha Orben was murdered. Method—poison."

Was such a thing possible? Given the teams of highly paid, sophisticated doctors who had attended Agatha, how could poison go undetected?

Liz reached for the Rolodex atop her desk, flipped to D for doctor and dialed the office number for Dr. Clark

Hammerschmidt. During the six months Agatha was ill, Liz had spoken to dear old Dr. Clark a number of times. He was a homey, white-haired guy, fussy about his patients and full of gossip. Most of his conversations with Liz had revolved around how on earth they could keep Agatha from charging out and working until she dropped.

The receptionist at Dr. Clark's office informed her that the doctor was busy but would call back as soon as possible.

As Liz replaced the receiver, she wondered if she should have gone to see Dr. Clark instead of settling for a phone call. In a telephone interrogation, she would miss the important visual clues of body language. She wouldn't notice if he shifted his eyes or hunched his shoulders. On the other hand, a personal visit would surely arouse suspicions.

Being a detective would be a whole lot easier, she thought, if Dash had agreed to help her instead of making a dorky suggestion that she ought to wear a dress tonight so he could get a better look at her legs. She could have used some on-the-job training.

When the phone on her desk rang, she jumped and answered quickly, "Hello?"

"Liz? This is Dr. Clark. How's everyone at Orben-Corp?"

"Fine." *Except that somebody here is possibly a murderer.*

"No illness?" the doctor inquired. "I saw Jack a few weeks ago for a checkup, and he was in good shape."

"Was he? Oh, good." She vaguely recalled that it was time for Jack's annual physical, a requirement for the company insurance.

The doctor continued in his folksy manner, "And I hear Sarah and that fellow from accounting are getting married."

"Really?" Liz hadn't known about that. "You mean Gary Gregory?"

"I think that's his name. Gary." Dr. Clark paused. "What about you, Liz? Any special man?"

She hesitated. Did Dash count as a special man? She probably ought to say he was even if he wasn't, because she was taking him to Sarah's dinner party. Tonight, he would be impersonating a date and—

"Liz?"

"Yes, I'm seeing someone."

It felt good to say that. For once, she wouldn't have to endure the sympathetic tsk-tsk of a kindly, well-meaning acquaintance.

"Wonderful!" he said enthusiastically. "Anybody I know?"

"Probably not."

"I wish you the best, dear. Now, why did you call? What's on your mind?"

"I was just thinking about Agatha." *What questions should she ask?* "Kind of remembering, you know."

"That's good, dear. It's important to process your grief. At least, that's what psychiatrists tell us."

"When she first got sick," Liz said. "It was a flu, wasn't it? Upset stomach. Vomiting."

"I really don't remember all her symptoms." The kindly old doctor sounded slightly impatient. "Why?"

What should she say next? How should she ease into the subject without raising suspicion? "Of course, Agatha didn't die from flu symptoms, did she?"

"Her heart failed. Happened in her sleep. It was a peaceful death." He cleared his throat. "What's this about, Liz?"

"Oh, gosh, I don't know."

She cursed herself for handling this conversation so clumsily. She could almost hear the doctor writing her off as a hysterical female, a woman caught in the throes of PMS. This detective business was harder than she had thought it was—there wasn't enough time to think things through. She had to react, go on instinct.

"I need to go now," the doctor said. "Say hello to everyone for me, and try not to worry too much."

"Was Agatha poisoned?" Liz blurted.

There was a silence on the other end of the phone, and Liz held her breath. Why had she said that? It was a huge mistake. A clammy, nervous sweat broke on her forehead. She was handling this so badly!

Then Dr. Clark chuckled. "Why would you think that?"

"Well, Agatha had always been healthy as a horse, and then she failed so suddenly."

"She was almost eighty, dear. These things happen."

Having made the initial goof, Liz blundered on, "Supposing she had been poisoned—"

"She wasn't. Now, let's have no more of this nonsense."

"You must have run blood tests," she said.

"My treatment procedures are none of your concern."

"But you did run tests, didn't you? You must have checked for poison. I was just wondering what kind of poison would produce the symptoms she suffered from? I mean, I know she was taking high blood pressure medicine. Is it possible that she had a reaction to something else?"

"I don't appreciate the tone of this conversation. Not at all, young lady. I did everything I could for Agatha."

"I wasn't suggesting malpractice." *What was he afraid of?*

"I certainly hope not. Now, I have to go. Liz. I suggest you get counseling to deal with your grief."

"Thank you, Doctor," she said meekly.

She hung up the phone and groaned. This private-eye stuff was hard. On her yellow legal pad, she wrote, "Dr. Clark says no poison."

But he'd never answered her question about blood tests, and he seemed angry that she'd asked. Had he been remiss in the thoroughness of his treatment? Had Agatha's very expensive care been given short shrift because of her age?

She flipped to another page and began writing. Her pen paused, mid-stroke, as she sensed presence in the room. Though she hadn't heard the door open or close, someone was here. Surreptitiously, Liz peeked through the fringe of her eyelashes.

No one was in the room.

In her mind, she clearly heard Dash's voice. "What have you done?"

"Dash?" she whispered.

There was a swift rap on the door, then Dash pushed it open and strode inside. One glance told her that he was angry, very angry. His eyebrows were pulled down. His lips were a thin, straight line, and he led with his jaw.

As he paced the same route she had followed—the only route possible in her fourteenth-floor cubicle—he seemed to have sparks flying from his heels, but there was a darkness all around him, as if a thundercloud had invaded her office.

He tore off his fedora and dragged his fingers through his short-cropped hair. This was the first time she'd seen him without his hat, and she stared. He looked different, much younger. His hair was a deep, rich mahogany brown.

He halted on the opposite side of her desk, stuck his hat on his head and stood there, waiting for her to speak first.

"What?" Liz bolted to her feet. "What's the problem?"

Still, he said nothing. His eyes glared. They shone like dark, molten coals.

His words echoed, though his lips did not move. "What have you done?"

For the first time, she realized that Dash could be a dangerous individual. Yet Liz would neither back down nor apologize. She'd had ten years of waiting, and now, with adventure within her grasp, she wouldn't let go without a fight.

She jabbed a finger at him. "You're not going to intimidate me, Dash. I have as much right as you to investigate."

He inhaled sharply. "Look here, sweetheart—"

"Liz. My name is Liz."

"I don't want you involved in this. I don't want to see you get hurt."

"For heaven's sake, Dash. I only talked to Dr. Clark Hammerschmidt, and he's a kindly old doctor. He wouldn't kill a fly."

"You don't know that."

"He's a sweet old man. He's like Wilford Brimley. He's Marcus Welby, M.D. Dr. Clark wouldn't kill Agatha."

"Don't talk to anybody else."

"Are you giving me an order?" She felt the blood rush to her face in a sudden flush. "How dare you tell me what to do?"

"Until we learn differently, everyone is a suspect. Do you understand?"

"I suppose so, but—"

"Elizabeth!" This time, he spoke her name like a whip cracking. "Promise me. You won't talk to anyone else."

She stood up to him. Though his rage was formidable, her furious energy protected her. After years of frustration, her will was strong. "I can take care of myself."

The fire within him seemed to roar louder than a furnace. White-hot rage emanated from him, surrounding him like a halo. Then he blinked. A muscle in his jaw twitched. He seemed to physically contract, as if he were reining in his energy. The flames were banked and under control. He said only one word. "Please."

"All right." She readily agreed, not wanting to continue this battle of wills. "I won't do any more investigating on my own. Not until tonight."

He pivoted and left her office with the door standing open.

Liz sank down in the chair behind her desk. She was breathing hard. The blood surged through her. The vein in her temple beat hard as a jackhammer, and she massaged that spot with her fingertips. *Calm down.*

Leaning her head back, she inhaled deeply, expanding her lungs until her rib cage hurt. She needed more breath. It was as if Dash had sucked all the air from the room, as if the fire of his anger had burned away all the oxygen.

She exhaled in a prolonged gasp, forced herself to relax.

Strangely, she'd felt no fear in his presence. In spite of his ferocity, it had never once occurred to her that he might hurt her. His motives were good. He wanted to protect her.

And even in this stormy battle, there was a silver lining. Dash had said *we.* He'd said, "Until *we* learn differently." That wasn't the way a man without a partner talked.

Slowly, a smile curved her lips, and hope flickered within her. Whether he knew it or not, he'd begun to think of her as a cohort, as someone he could confide in. Already, she'd found a chink in his armor.

LIZ LEFT WORK EARLY—partly because there was nothing going on and partly because she wanted to get in half an hour of jogging before she got ready for the dinner at Sarah's.

She changed quickly into her shorts, T-shirt and running shoes. Though she dressed her scraped knees with salve, she left off the bandages so the air could soothe the last remnants of pain. Loosening up, she trotted the six blocks to the Big Lake at City Park and began her circuit.

Running always seemed to help her think, and she had a lot to consider. There was a list of suspects she'd come up with. And the niggling thought in the back of her mind that she made too many mistakes in her conversation with the doctor. What would happen if she expanded her circle of interrogation? Accusing her co-workers of murder probably wasn't a good way to advance her career at OrbenCorp.

As she ran, her brain chugged through the several gears. Who killed Agatha? Was she poisoned? Above all, she thought about Dash.

There was something elemental about him. He was like a force of nature—like wind, fire and air. Earlier today, when he was angry, he seemed to have stepped from another time and place, blazing with fiery, passionate heat. In the coffee shop, when he touched her hand, his grasp was as gentle as dew on a lily.

However, Liz reminded herself as she circled the far end of the lake, Dash was also very weird. He'd claimed to be an angel. And his real profession, private eye, wasn't exactly defined by the parameters of stability.

No matter who or what he was—she was anxious to see him again tonight. His presence would make dinner at Sarah's bearable.

Her pace was slower than usual, and a couple of other afternoon joggers passed her. Liz slowed to a walk, then started her second lap around the lake. Gradually, she became aware of someone behind her, and she turned to look. There was a man dressed in a baggy black nylon running suit. He was about thirty yards behind her on the running path, so his features were indistinct. And he was wearing a black knit cap.

Liz faced forward again. The cap was unusual, but not too much so. There was a brisk wind this afternoon. The man in black was probably just another city dweller out for some exercise.

And yet she sensed danger, an aura of menace that caused the muscles in her back to tense. She picked up her pace, hoping to outdistance him before she headed toward home.

When she looked again, he was still following at the same distance. Apparently, he had imitated her speed.

Though she told herself she was imagining the threat, that it was purely paranoid to worry about a jogger, she couldn't help thinking of danger. Dash had been so certain there might be jeopardy. What if he was right?

She slowed again and cautiously glanced back. The man who followed kept his distance. Surely, he wouldn't try to attack her here in the park. There were witnesses all around. But if he trailed her to her home, she might be in trouble.

What should she do? She couldn't keep running forever.

Liz veered toward Seventeenth Street.

When she looked back, the man was still following.

Instead of crossing the street, she kept running along the curb. Usually, there were police cars patrolling. But now? Nothing! The traffic was even lighter than usual.

When she'd faced Dash, she'd felt no fear. But now, the black-clad jogger instigated a dark terror in her heart, a premonition. Who was he? It made sense that he might be one of the suspects she'd considered. If he was someone she knew, he'd stay far enough away that she couldn't make out his features. But who?

She might stop right now and face him. Then she would know who had killed Agatha. But that was a terrible risk.

He might flee from her. He might run up beside her and feign surprise that they were both on the same jogging path. Or he might hurt her, might eliminate her. It would be easy, she thought. He could run up beside her, jam a pistol in her face and fire before anyone had a chance to react.

Finally she spied a police car waiting at the stoplight. She ran toward the vehicle, waving her arms. Gasping with the exertion of her run, she shouted for help.

The driver turned on the lights and glided to a stop at the curb beside her. The uniformed officer got out of his car. "What's the problem, ma'am?"

"That man is following me." She turned and pointed. "He's a suspect in a murder and he's—"

He was gone. Vanished among the gold-leafed trees and autumnal foliage.

Chapter Four

At six twenty-five that evening, Dash strode along the sidewalk on the street where Liz lived. He regretted his outburst of anger this afternoon. Usually, he had better control. But when he'd sensed that Liz was in danger, that she'd placed herself in jeopardy by playing private eye, he couldn't help the power surge, the raw instinct of rage.

One thing was dead certain. She was off the case.

He needed this investigation to be over. Tonight, at the dinner party, he would glean useful clues about the murder of Agatha Orben. He'd keep his wits about him. He'd be cool as ice. Yeah? Sure! He'd be cool if he could stop thinking about Liz.

Elizabeth. The sound of her name ricocheted in his brain like a bullet from a forty-five.

Spending time with her was more dangerous than facing a room full of crooks. In her smile, she had the power to knock the legs out from under him. With a flash of her bright blue eyes, she could turn his tough-guy attitude to mush.

Dash couldn't let that happen. Not for her. Not for himself. He went inside the foyer and pushed the bell for her apartment. Through the intercom, she told him to come on up.

This was it, Dash told himself, he was going up there and laying down the law. No more investigating. But when she opened the door to her third-floor apartment and he saw her, Dash felt like he'd been belted by a roundhouse right from the heavyweight champ. She was a knockout.

She wore a simple black over-blouse and a short skirt that flirted above her knees. Black tights. High-heeled shoes. Her long brown hair tumbled past her shoulders in graceful, shimmering waves. She looked soft. She smelled good.

Dash had had more than a lifetime to practice self-control, but he was melting faster than a snowball in hell. "Hi, precious." He paused. "Elizabeth."

"Come on in for a minute, Dash. I have something I want to show you."

When she turned, her hair rippled enticingly, and his fingers itched to touch that hair, to glide through that silky texture. He'd been tempted before, but it was nothing compared to this. The welling desire in his angel heart was almost painful.

He braced his hands against the doorframe. Holding back with all his strength, he fought the magnetic pull she exerted without even trying. "We gotta go. I got a job to do."

"That's what I'm talking about." She swirled away from him, almost dancing, delicate as a moonbeam. "Five minutes won't make any difference."

Full of apprehension, he stepped inside her apartment. Like the rest of this renovated Victorian mansion, her rooms on the third floor had kept the charm and lost the cobwebs. The ceiling was high. The dimensions were gracious. There was a front bay window and a window seat. The south wall had two more arched windows. The walls

were white. In southern light, her houseplants flour-
ished.

The place looked like her. Light, airy and clean. A beige
and blue patterned rug decorated the gleaming wood
floor. The furniture was simple. Framed prints and
paintings hung on the walls. A glance at the titles on her
bookshelf showed him that she liked the same mystery
fiction he preferred. She had the collected works of
Dashiell Hammett in hardback.

There was a small kitchen behind a clean counter. In the
dining area was an oblong, light wood table beneath a
stained-glass lamp.

Through an open door, he could see into her bedroom
where there was a brass bed and antique dresser. From her
bathroom, he smelled the fragrance of her perfume.
Apart from a couple of flowery feminine touches, he
wouldn't have minded living here himself.

He cleared his throat. "Nice joint you got here."

"It suits me. Everybody tells me I ought to buy a house
because it's a good investment, but I like this apartment.
I'm not ready to settle down into a house. Not just yet."

He went to the bay window and looked out at the faded
pink skies of a Rocky Mountain sunset. The yellow autumn leaves of a cottonwood tree shivered in a breeze. In
here, it was safe and warm. Homey.

Sometimes Dash missed the reassuring pleasures of
domestic life. A dinner on the table. A soft bed.

He didn't have a place of his own, except for a closet in
the basement of the Avenging Angels offices where he
kept the same wardrobe he'd conjured together in the
1930s. As a spiritual being, he didn't need an apartment.
When he was on the job he worked twenty-four hours a
day. Other times, he relaxed into invisible limbo. Sometimes he allowed himself the sheer pleasure of angelic

perfection, soaring on his giant wings into the cosmos, touching the edge of the Milky Way, then descending through the atmosphere, luminous as a falling star. Sometimes he rested in a church on the front pew, lying on his back and looking up at the marble statues of saints who never laughed and never moved. If people on earth believed heaven was that static, so bereft of vitality, why would anybody want to go there?

During the infrequent times he wasn't on a case, he returned to the heavenly realms for contemplation and renewal. Dash frowned. He hadn't enjoyed that respite in a long time. He needed a vacation, but Dash was good, the best detective in the Rocky Mountain region, and he was always in demand. As the millennium approached, there was a lot of evil in the world.

He rubbed his forehead. Though he didn't experience pain and headache in a mortal sense, there was a heaviness around him. Weighing him down. He needed a break. Maybe that was why he felt so tempted. He'd been too close to humanity for too long.

Liz stood beside him. "What's wrong, Dash?"

"I've got to make this clear, precious, before we go any further. You're not working with me. It's dangerous."

"Okay," she said, easily.

Too easily, he thought. He studied her falsely innocent expression, and he knew she was lying about her intentions. Humans could get away with that. Sometimes, he thought, mortals had all the advantages. "I mean it, Liz."

"And I heard you. I don't want to be in danger." This afternoon in the park had convinced her of that. Even though she might have been imagining the threat, her fear had been very real.

Liz would have to rethink her ideas about becoming a private investigator. She wasn't giving up on the plan, but she would proceed with extreme caution. "However," she said, "I really wouldn't be in any kind of peril if you'd tell me what to do."

"No."

"Oh, come on, Dash. Take me under your wing. At least tell me what a private eye does."

"Most of the work is boring, digging through other people's garbage for dirty little secrets. And you're always hanging around with the bad guys. There's a high sleaze factor."

"Not this time," she said. "All the people from OrbenCorp that I consider to be suspects aren't sleazy."

"Why? Because they have bankrolls and estates?" His lips thinned, exactly like Bogie's, and he said, "Money's no guarantee of purity, sweetheart."

"But they're not Mafia hit men or gangsters. I don't think of people at OrbenCorp as being bad because I know them."

"All murderers are evil."

"Evil, Dash? Isn't that rather a dramatic description?"

"I don't know another word for it. A murderer steals the most treasured possession the victim can own—earthly life. Murder is an offense against God and nature."

He seemed to be surging toward anger again, that intense elemental rage she'd seen in her office, and Liz wanted to derail him before he got started. "You're absolutely correct. On the other hand, this particular murder—a well-planned poisoning—isn't typical of a psycho or a serial killer."

"They could still be that."

"What do you mean?"

"If the murderer is threatened, they will kill again."

She thought again of the jogger in the black suit. Had he been pursuing her? Why? All she'd done was talk to Dr. Clark and suggest the possibility of poisoning.

Frowning, Liz realized that her chat with the kindly old doctor was tantamount to announcing her intentions over a loudspeaker. Dr. Clark was a terrible gossip. She wouldn't have been a bit surprised to discover that he'd tracked down Jack and told him she was having a nervous breakdown. Or he might have called Sarah. Or, if she considered every possibility, Dr. Clark himself could be the killer.

"This is complicated." She sighed, wishing there was some infallible method for telling when someone meant to do you harm. She'd give a lot to know whether the man who was following her in the park was an innocent jogger or...something else.

Should she be frightened? Should she forget it?

"A penny for your thoughts," he said.

"They're not worth much more than that." She definitely wasn't going to tell Dash about the incident in the park. Every instinct warned her that he wouldn't react well. He'd probably lock her in her apartment and post an armed guard outside her door. "Okay, Dash. When you're on a case, how do you know which suspect is the killer?"

"I *don't* know. Not until I've got proof." He smiled ironically. "Too bad we aren't in Biblical times. Then we'd have the mark of Cain branded across a murderer's forehead. We could tell."

"But now, everybody is innocent until proven guilty. Which is as it should be. It's not right to condemn people on a suspicion. And nobody deserves to be branded. After all, nobody is all, one-hundred-percent bad, are they?"

"There are some." Dash had seen the cold face of evil—sheer, horrible, unredeemable evil. A soul that was not only lost, but had purposely turned away from good.

"How can you tell when somebody is completely bad?"

"Instinct." He shrugged. "The shrinks call it psychosis. They say somebody's a sociopath, that they're disturbed, they can't tell right from wrong. But it's worse than that."

"How?"

"Think of evil as a flame. Everybody has an occasional spark."

"Even you?" she teased.

"That's right, precious. Even me." As an angel, he knew better than to violate the code. But when it happened, when he gave in to the impulse to tell a lie or to swear, the consequences were disastrous. Like immediate karma.

"So, what do you think happens when the spark gets out of control?"

"It feeds on wrongdoing. A person does one evil deed, then another and another until the flame becomes a holocaust. The fires consume every bit of good, and all that's left is a charred, deformed shard of obsidian coal." He clenched his hand into a fist. "No light can penetrate the surface. An evil person has no pity, no generosity, no forgiveness, no love."

Evil was hard to explain to a mortal, but she was nodding as if she understood.

"You catch my drift?" he asked.

"Not entirely." Brightly, she continued, "By the way, I made a list of suspects."

"Why?"

"If we're going to figure out who killed Agatha—"

"Hold it right there, sweetheart. You're not hearing me. We? *We* aren't doing anything. *I* am investigating. By myself. I work alone. Always have, always will. Got it?"

"Sure, of course. But this list might save you some time." She went to a writing desk beneath a window and picked up a lined yellow legal tablet. "These are just the people I know from OrbenCorp. Agatha's circle of acquaintances was much wider than this. She worked with a lot of charities."

"I know," Dash said. That was why she got the heavenly red carpet treatment. "She had a good heart."

"Anyway," Liz said, "I came up with fourteen names, then I narrowed my list to four. Want to hear?"

"No."

"First off," Liz said, utterly disregarding him, "there's Jack. I know he's my boss and it's disloyal to accuse him, but he did inherit the whole business when his mother died. And that could have been a motive."

Dash didn't want to be sucked into her line of patter, but he couldn't help pointing out, "Jack was pretty much running the business, anyway."

"Ah, but he and Agatha had a major disagreement. That was about a year ago. Jack wanted more budget for a grandiose promotional campaign, and his mother refused. Then, Jack had negotiated for a private plane for the company. It was a twin engine Cessna, which, he said, could be used for flying Hector around the world to buy beans. Agatha pointed out the obvious fact, that it would take days for Hector to make those flights in a small plane. Plus, maintenance and upkeep on the aircraft was too expensive. Again, she refused. Jack was furious."

Dash was interested. This was all good information. "Okay, precious, here's the deal. You give me this inside dope. Then you step out of the picture. Back off. Understand?''

''Sure.'' Her smile was as sweet as strawberry taffy and as counterfeit as a three-dollar bill. ''Want to hear more? I can fill you in while we're on the way. You drive.''

She reached into her purse, fished out her keys and tossed them to him.

Dash looked at the array of keys on a round gold ring and frowned. He didn't drive. Why bother with cars when he could get where he wanted to go with a couple of swoops of his angel wings?

But Liz was already halfway out the door. ''Come on, I'm parked out in back.''

On her way down the rear staircase, she continued with her list. ''My favorite suspect is Hector Messenger. But I'm probably prejudiced because I'd love to have his job and I hate the way he pats me on the head and disregards everything I say.''

''Hector?'' Dash hadn't even considered him as a suspect. ''The buyer?''

''Here's why,'' she said. ''I discovered a discrepancy in the last quarter between the price Hector was paying and the prices other coffee brokers got for the raw beans. There might be some kind of payoff going on.''

''And you think Agatha might have known about it?''

''Before she died, she suggested that I start comparing prices.''

''It's a motive,'' Dash conceded as they descended the last flight of stairs leading to the rear exit. ''But Hector's out of town a lot. On the road. How could he poison her?''

''I guess it depends on how the poison was administered. Do you have any idea how it was done?''

He did, but that wasn't info he intended to share. Some facts were too dangerous for her to know. Dash stepped through the door to the small parking lot.

"Here's my car." She stepped to the passenger side of a little red Honda Civic, about five years old. "I'll give you directions. It's easy to find the house."

The last time Dash had been behind the wheel of a car was in the 1950s, and that was a tank-size Chevrolet. How was he going to get out of this situation without losing face?

He fitted the key in the lock and opened the door, but before he climbed inside, he said, "I forgot. I need to pick something up. At a drugstore."

Unaccustomed to even telling a little white lie, he stammered over the words.

"No problem." She smiled at him across the roof of the car. "We can stop on the way."

His tongue stuck to the roof of his mouth. Why didn't he just tell her the truth? He couldn't drive. But that seemed like such a pitiful admission. He was supposed to be a private eye. How could she believe he was an investigator if he couldn't even manage a vehicle? "You go ahead. I'll meet you."

"But we're supposed to be on a date. It won't look right if we arrive separately." Firmly, she said, "We'll stop on the way."

He entered the car and reached across to unlock her door. Then he tried to adjust the seat. There had to be a button somewhere. He groped at the edges of the bucket seat.

"Here." She reached between his legs and pulled a lever. "Push back," she instructed.

He did, and the driver's seat shot backward. Now he couldn't reach the pedals on the floor, and she still had her arm between his legs.

"Adjust it," she said.

"Adjust what?" He almost groaned. She was so close that he could smell the fragrance of her shampoo.

"The seat, silly."

After a little more fumbling, he felt comfortable in the seat—distinctly more at ease when she removed her arm and leaned back in her own bucket seat. The dashboard was full of dials and switches, but everything was labeled, and he managed to get the key in the ignition and the car running. Fortunately, it was an automatic transmission. He wrestled the gearshift into D for drive and lurched ahead.

Though Liz jolted forward in her seat and gave him a curious look, she said nothing.

He tapped on the gas pedal and pulled into the alley behind the house. Too fast! He tromped on the brake. Both his hands gripped the wheel. He grasped a button on the spoke of the steering wheel. The horn honked.

"What are you doing?" she asked.

"Checking everything out." He turned the wheel, maneuvered carefully between trash cans and bins.

At the mouth of the alley, she instructed, "Turn right."

As he eased into the street, swinging wide, he heard the squeal of brakes in front and behind.

"Geez, Dash! Watch where you're going!"

He muttered under his breath about infernal machines and satanic inventions. If ever an angel had wanted to curse, Dash did right now.

By the time they got to the second corner, he was beginning to get the hang of driving. He pressed down on the accelerator and rolled along the street at a speed that was slow motion compared to his flying.

But Liz gripped her legal pad with white knuckles. Tersely, she said, "Slow down."

"We're barely moving."

"I said for you to slow down, buster. And I mean it! I don't know what kind of high-performance car you're accustomed to driving, but this is a Honda and I'd like to keep it in one piece."

He practiced keeping pace with the other cars, stopping and starting and looking far ahead to anticipate hazards. He found himself grinning. Once he got accustomed to being surrounded by this hunk of metal, the challenge of driving was enjoyable. He darted from one lane to another. He couldn't imagine why he hadn't indulged himself in driving before now.

"Please, Dash. I hate to be a passenger-seat driver, but I wish you'd use your signal."

What signal? None of the buttons or gears seemed to be labeled as a signal.

"Turn left at the light," she said. "And I'd really appreciate if you'd use your turn signal."

"Got it." He flicked a lever beside the steering wheel. The windshield wipers dragged across the glass.

"Here." She unfastened her seat belt and leaned across him to manipulate a lever on the other side of the steering wheel. "Okay?"

He saw a little green arrow on the dashboard to indicate a left turn. Interesting.

"Well?" She stared at him expectantly.

"Well what?"

"We need to turn at the next corner. Get in the far left lane."

She couldn't mean that. If he got all the way over, he'd be driving straight into the path of oncoming traffic. He whipped into the farthest lane that he deemed safe. Again, from behind, he heard the screech of brakes and a honking horn.

He grasped the button on the spoke of the wheel and honked back, delighted with the Klaxon sound.

"All right," she said sternly. "Now we stay on this street for about five miles. Don't speed."

"Got it."

Again, she consulted her notes. "Another suspect from the office is Gary Gregory, the head of accounting. He and Agatha were always fussing at each other about one thing or another. Once, at an executive board meeting, she discovered that he hadn't made a charitable contribution she'd instructed him to make, and she read him the riot act."

"Sounds like a typical office squabble," Dash said. "Not a motive for murder."

"Maybe not," she said. "But I was sitting right next to Gary, and I could see the notepad in front of him."

"I don't get it, precious."

"All the time that Agatha was chastising him, he was nodding amiably, but he was scribbling obscene doodles and notes, one of which said, Die, You Old Witch." Meaningfully, she added, "That's witch with a B."

"But what's his motive?"

"Greed. Power. Gary works with the money, and he's pretty much autonomous. There could be some funny business with the accounts." She pointed to the far right. "There's a drugstore. Let's stop so you can pick up what you need."

Dash had forgotten his excuse for not driving. His little white lie. Now he was stuck. If he admitted that he was lying before, then he'd have to say why, then she'd wonder why he didn't drive, then he'd have to tell her that he was an angel who flew, then . . . "Okay, I'll pull over."

He'd found a space and parked before he realized he had another problem. Money. Dash always picked up petty cash for expenses at the office before a case, but his wallet was slim. He hadn't expected to need much, and now he was going to have to purchase something.

Of course, if the going got tough, he could always conjure up a hundred-dollar bill. But that wasn't his way. Apart from the flying, Dash tried to follow the restrictions of mortal behavior. To catch a mortal criminal, he had to think like a mortal.

He climbed out of the car and went around to open her door for her, but Liz had already gotten out. She checked her wristwatch. "We ought to hurry."

"Sure. This will just take a minute."

Inside the small drugstore, he scanned the shelves for something that was cheap and looked like a necessity. There were shelves and shelves of merchandise, ranging from sacks of fertilizer to perfume.

Liz pointed. "The pharmacy is over there, if—"

"Sure." He set out in that direction. There were medicines for headaches, stomachaches, itches and smelly feet. A pleasant-looking woman sat behind a counter and smiled at him. "Can I help you?"

His gaze lit on an open box to the right of the cash register. It was filled with foil-wrapped disks that were marked one dollar each. Dash picked one up. "I'll take this."

"All right." She turned to the register beside her and rang up one buck and tax.

Dash pulled out two singles, the only cash he had in his wallet, and paid.

He turned to see Liz standing beside him. Her blue eyes snapped wide. "A condom, Dash?"

At that moment, Dash knew that an angel could blush.

"I don't believe it," she muttered. "You had to stop to pick up a condom? An emergency condom?"

He tucked the foil-wrapped disk into his pocket with the receipt. There wasn't a single thing he could say to ease his embarrassment. This moment, he knew, was the karmic payback for telling that little white lie. Hesitantly, he mumbled, "You never know when you'll need one."

"Well, I can guarantee that you won't need one tonight unless you have a hot date after you take me home."

In the parking lot, she held out her hand for the keys. "I'll drive."

Without protest, he handed over the keys. Dash felt like a prize chump. Usually, he was super competent. But today? Super klutz was more like it. What was it about her that caused him to be so clumsy?

In contrast to his driving, she handled her little car smoothly, talking as they went. "The last of my four suspects has got to be Sarah Orben Pachen. She'll be our hostess tonight."

"I know that."

"Oh, really?" She stopped for a red light and turned toward him. Archly, she said, "After your presumptuous purchase at the drugstore, I'm not sure what else you might have forgotten."

"Come again?"

"You might not remember that this isn't a real date. I'm just helping you on a case."

Helping him? Dash ignored her inference. "Why would you suspect Sarah? She's a niece, right?"

"Right. The rest of her family lives in Seattle, I think. But Sarah wanted to stay in Denver after her husband died. That was about three years ago. She moved in with Agatha."

"Did they get along?"

"I suppose so. As well as two women who have nothing in common could get along. Agatha was a hardworking businesswoman who spent her spare time with worthy causes. And Sarah? Well, she's a first-class shopper. I'm sure she's memorized every inch of the Cherry Creek Mall."

"So, what's her motive?" Dash asked.

"Money again. As you also must know, Sarah inherited the house from Agatha. That's pretty obvious, as motives go, because this is a fabulous estate. And, from what I understand, Agatha stipulated that after her death, Sarah was supposed to turn the house into a shelter for battered women."

"Has she?"

"Not as far as I know. Also," Liz said, "I've heard that Sarah and Gary Gregory might be getting married. They might be in this together."

She'd driven into the exclusive Littleton area and eased her car into a space opposite a lavish home in the English Tudor style. "Okay, Dash. What's your cover story? What should we tell the people inside?"

"It's best if we stick as close to the truth as possible. We'll say that you and I met while you were out jogging. This is our first date."

"What about an occupation? You can't very well say that you're a private investigator."

Or an angel, he thought. "Tell them I'm a philosopher."

She shook her head. "These are business people. They'll want to know how you make a living."

"Being a philosopher," he said steadily. At least, it was close to truth.

"Okay," she conceded. "How about a last name?"

Dash had run into this problem before, and he had a standard name he used. "Divine. Dash Divine."

She nodded. "Let's go."

Before she could open her car door, he caught her arm. "Listen, sweetheart. I want to apologize. For the condom, you know. I wasn't planning to put the moves on you."

She turned her head and confronted him. In the settling dusk, her smile seemed to glow. "Why not?"

He hadn't expected that response. "Because," he said.

"Do you find me unattractive?"

"Not a chance, precious. You're the tastiest little cupcake I've seen in two lifetimes."

"Cupcake?" She chuckled.

"A hot tamale," he said. "A cool tomato."

"I'm a woman, Dash. What do you think of me as a woman?"

He inhaled a deep breath and spoke the truth from his angel heart. "Beautiful."

She leaned toward him. Holding his face in her slender hands, she kissed him squarely on the lips. Pure sensation flooded his physical body. He had not been kissed, not like this, since he gained his solid form as an angel. Never.

He'd never been this close to any human being. Dash felt like he was going to explode. He reveled in the slight pressure of her mouth on his, the warm whisper of her breath against his skin.

When she leaned away from him, he looked into her face. Her eyes were warm. Her lips were soft. And her flowing hair shimmered. Her loveliness surpassed any miracle.

"Beautiful," he said.

Chapter Five

She never should have kissed him. Before their lips met, Liz had known she was making a mistake. In that split second, when she held his face in her hands and looked into his eyes, she'd known that she was opening the door into a mysterious world of brilliant hopes and dangerous passions.

But she'd kissed him anyway. Taken the risk. And now there was no turning back.

Though her bruised knee no longer hurt, she walked slowly along the winding flagstone path that led to the carved oak double doors of the house that now belonged to Sarah Orben Pachen. Dash walked behind her, but she could feel his presence all around. She breathed him in on the crisp autumn night. She tasted him on her lips.

The kiss had been an impulse. She'd wanted to embarrass him the same way he'd embarrassed her when he purchased the condom. And she'd wanted to pay him back for insinuating that he hadn't really been thinking of seducing her tonight. Surely he had. Why else make an emergency stop at a drugstore? And what if he did try to seduce her? What would she say?

Yes. Her heart whispered the answer to a question that had not yet been asked. *Yes.*

Crazy. Making love with Dash was absolutely crazy. There was no sort of relationship with him. He was a private eye, for goodness sake. He drove like a maniac. His conversation meandered off into archaic contemplations of good and evil that were, to say the least, unusual. Then there was the way he dressed, in trench coat, fedora and double-breasted pin-striped suit. He certainly wasn't the kind of guy she could take home to meet her mother in St. Louis. He wasn't appropriate.

Why, then, did she find him so appealing? And why, oh, why had she kissed him?

At the doorstep, he reached around her to press the doorbell, and his shoulder inadvertently brushed against her back. She quickly moved away. And so did he! It was almost as if he were the shy one, as if he wanted to avoid physical contact with her. But how could that be? He'd marched right up to the pharmacist and bought a condom. Talk about mixed signals!

Sarah flung wide the door to welcome them with open arms. As always, she was overdressed in abundant jewelry and a flowing blue caftan shot through with silver threads. Her flaming red hair shone with unnatural golden highlights. But she was so unrepentantly glamorous that Liz had to forgive the tacky excess.

In her melodious alto, Sarah intoned, "Liz, darling, you look marvelous. And is this your date?"

No, Liz thought, *he's a puppy and he followed me home.* "Sarah Pachen, I'd like you to meet Dash Divine."

As he shook hands with Sarah, Liz wondered if Divine was his real name or another of his bizarre connections with the angels.

The only person who had arrived before them was Gary Gregory, head of accounting at OrbenCorp and possible fiancé of Sarah. When Liz introduced Gary and Dash, the accountant asked the obvious question. "What do you do for a living, Dash?"

"I'm a philosopher."

"And you make a living doing that?" Gary tittered like a bird. With his shock of pale blond hair, sharp features and long legs, he always reminded her of an egret. "Philosophizing?"

"Kierkegaard did," Dash said. "Not to mention St. Thomas Aquinas, Nietzsche or even Plato."

"But it didn't work too well for old Socrates. He was the one who drank the hemlock, wasn't he?"

"The poison elixir," Dash said in a level voice. "Hemlock's an interesting plant. An innocent-looking herb, kind of like parsley. Lethal parsley."

"Well, I wouldn't want to garnish my dinner with a sprig of that," Liz said brightly. She guessed that Dash was leading the discussion toward poisons, and she tried to help him along. "I'm sure Gary knows all about hemlock and parsley. Gardening is one of his hobbies."

"More than a hobby," he said coolly. "Last year, I created a species of blue rose that's named for me. The Gregory rose."

"Tell me about it," Dash said.

Gary didn't smile. He never smiled, not even when he tittered. But he was obviously pleased to be asked about his gardening. His upper lip protruded over the lower in a beaklike grimace, and his thick blond eyebrows lifted to the upper edge of his black glasses frames. "It's all in the splice," he said. "An exact grafting. And patience, of course. Waiting for nature to take its course."

"Ever want to hurry things along?" Dash asked.

"Constantly. But it doesn't do a damned bit of good. At least not when it comes to plants."

"And people? Ever want to hurry them along?"

"People are easy. But plants? To offer a modest example, the Gregory rose required four years of painstaking effort. I started with a deep scarlet..."

Liz had heard this story before, and Gary's words faded to blah-blah-blah in her mind. She tuned in for the finale.

"...a power failure, and I almost lost every rose in my greenhouse. It was hell."

"Roses are hard to grow," Dash said. "Lots of potential for bugs and disease. What kind of pesticide do you use?"

"All natural. Organic. I modify my own special..."

Liz was ready to shift topics or conversation partners, but there wasn't much alternative. Nobody else was there.

She missed Agatha. The house seemed empty without her. Gary's words echoed hollowly in the spacious front room. The only major decorating change since Agatha's death was a proliferation of lush, healthy houseplants. There were blooming cactus and hanging ferns and numerous flowers—a mock orange, azaleas, fragrant gardenias and roses. Was Gary moving in? Liz remembered it was Dr. Clark who said Sarah and Gary were planning to be married.

Sarah emerged from the kitchen with drinks for Dash and Liz. Coffee, of course, was the beverage of choice at any gathering of Orbens. Liz's had been laced with Irish Cream. Dash took his coffee straight and black.

While the two men continued to talk about flowers, Liz drew Sarah aside. "I heard a rumor. About you and Gary."

"Really?" Sarah fluttered her eyelashes. "From who?"

"Dr. Clark Hammerschmidt said you and Gary were getting married."

"That old busybody! I went to see him last week, and he's so nosy. He was supposed to keep it a secret."

In her head, Liz added one and one together. Sarah had been to see the doctor. And she was getting married. The total was...three. "Oh, my God, Sarah, you're not pregnant, are you?"

"Certainly not. I'm not a giddy teenager." In a low voice, she confided, "Gary and I have been seeing each other for over a year. And he's going to move in here as soon as we finish construction on the greenhouse in the back. He's worried about moving his roses, of course."

"Of course." That wasn't Liz's idea of a grand passion, when the roses came first, but Sarah seemed content. "I guess that congratulations are in order."

"Please don't say anything yet. I haven't told Jack." She shuddered, and her dangling earrings jangled. "I don't think he's going to be pleased. He keeps telling me to be careful around men, that they're all after my inheritance."

Silently, Liz agreed. Gary was an accountant. Despite his blooming passion for roses, he always kept a close eye on the bottom line. Some of his attraction to Sarah had to be the money.

Gary waved Sarah to him. "Would you please come here?"

"Yes, dear." Instantly, she was at his side.

"Dash wants to see the Gregory rose," Gary said. "Would you fetch one of the small pots from the solarium? And do be careful not to bruise it, Sarah."

She darted from the room with an eager-to-please rustle of her caftan. As soon as she had obediently vanished into the depths of the large house, the doorbell sounded. Since Liz was closest, she went to answer.

Jack and Hector, looking like a couple of naughty boys on a bender, stood shoulder to shoulder. Jack had obviously been drinking. His bleary smile and bloodshot eyes portended a potentially difficult evening, because Jack was a cantankerous, opinionated drunk.

"Hi, Lizzie," he drawled. "You look real pretty tonight."

"Thanks, Jack."

"That's my Lizzie. You're my right-hand man, aren't you?"

Usually in this sort of situation, Liz would protect her boss. She'd make sure that Jack was safety tucked away until he could sleep it off. And Hector was looking at her as if he expected her to take care of things.

But tonight was different. She wasn't here as the right-hand man. She was here with Dash, and they were investigating the murder of Agatha Orben, a woman who had not deserved to die before her time.

Liz figured that allowing Jack to crash through the evening in his loose, drunken state might provide a catalyst toward solving the case. She held the door wide. "Come on in, boys."

Jack swaggered past, bellowing his greetings.

Hector paused beside her. "I'm sorry, Liz. Jack got a little out of hand. Help me with him. We'll get him upstairs into one of the bedrooms."

"Actually, Hector, it's after five o'clock, and I'm no longer on the job. If Jack wants to get stinking drunk and make a fool of himself, that's not my problem."

"But I'm counting on you."

"Don't," she said.

She turned away from him and proceeded into the living room, where she guided Jack into trouble. Face-to-face with Gary, she said, "So, Jack. Have you heard about Sarah and Gary?"

"What about them?"

"I promised not to tell." She looked toward Gary, and Jack's woozy gaze followed. "Gary? Do you want to break the news?"

"Not yet."

"What's going on?" Jack demanded.

"Go on, Gary. Tell us." Evilly, Liz confided to her boss, "Gary has already started construction on a greenhouse in the backyard."

"Here?" Jack leaned close to Gary, head of accounting at OrbenCorp. "You're building a greenhouse in my mother's backyard?"

"Knock it off, Jack." Gary's beaky nose thrust forward. "You don't need to be so damned territorial."

"I'm what?" He wavered on unsteady knees. "I'm a terrier? You think I'm a dog?"

Hector inserted himself between the two men. "Not a terrier, Jack. Territorial. You know, protecting your boundaries." Glowering at Gary, he added, "It was a compliment. Right?"

"Take it any way you want."

Liz observed the interplay through a detective's eye. Among these three men—all of whom she considered to be possible murderers—Hector, though the shortest in stature and the oldest, was obviously the most dangerous. His piratical appearance, enhanced by the gold necklaces, radiated machismo. He had an assurance that the other men lacked. And, as she studied him, Liz sensed an aura of world-weary tragedy, as if his coal black eyes had seen too much.

Had one of them been the black-clad jogger in the park? Though their physiques were different, it was really impossible to tell. The nylon running suit had been too baggy, and her pursuer's hair had been covered by the cap. If only she'd paused to see his face, she might have known. But if she had confronted the jogger, would she be here tonight? Safe, alive and breathing?

Muttering, Jack swaggered toward Dash. "I don't believe we've met."

"Dash Divine. I'm Liz's date."

Hector raised an eyebrow as he looked at Liz. "You're full of surprises tonight."

"Why would you say that?"

"I don't think I've ever seen you with a date before. You're always quiet little Liz, working hard and steady. Maybe you have a secret life."

"Maybe I do," she said. "Maybe I'm not even a loyal Orben coffee employee. Maybe I'm a spy for Folger's."

Jack wheeled around and confronted her. "Liz? You brought a date? What about me?"

"We've never dated, Jack." He never even noticed her, walked past her in the office as if she was a piece of office equipment. "There's no call to be territorial about me."

"But you're my gal," he said. "Everybody knows that. Mother always said that someday I was going to open my eyes and see what a treasure you are. Remember how she kept pushing us toward each other?"

"Yes, I do." But Liz never had been romantically inclined toward Jack. Not that he lacked physical appeal. Quite the opposite, in fact. Jack Orben was a good-looking man who was toned at the health club and tanned on the golf course. He'd aged handsomely to his mid-thirties. His thick brown hair was untouched by gray. But she'd never thought of him as a boyfriend

Besides, in her ten years at OrbenCorp, she'd always been one of the guys, and Jack had taken her for granted. Even after his divorce three years ago, he hadn't ever asked her out on a date. They usually ended up together at these family or company dinners, but for socializing, Jack always had some gorgeous blonde hanging on his arm.

"You're so pretty, Lizzie." His speech slurred. "A treasure."

Possessively, Dash stepped beside her. "She's precious, all right."

"What the hell do you think you're doing?" Jack stuck out his jaw pugnaciously.

"Keeping an eye on Liz, my date."

"You're making a mistake. She's mine."

Hector tried to mediate. He placed a restraining arm around Jack's shoulder. "Let's calm down, gentlemen."

"But she's my girl," Jack said. He drew his hands into fists. He glared at Dash and Gary, as if trying to determine which one of them he should slug first. Apparently, the decision was too much for him, because he turned to Liz. "You are, aren't you? My girl."

"I'm nobody's girl, Jack."

"She's a lady," Dash said, moving closer to her. "And this lady is with me."

When he clasped his hand around her waist, his touch was gentle but firm. He was being overprotective, and Liz's usual response would be to slap his hand away and firmly announce that she could take care of herself. But, somehow, Dash's attitude wasn't in the least offensive.

"Wait a minute," Jack said. "Who the hell do you think you are?"

Gary Gregory stepped into the circle. "He says he's a philosopher."

"Philosophize this." Jack took a wild swing with his clenched fist.

His blow connected with Dash's cheekbone, and Liz felt the force of it reverberate through his body. But Dash was unshaken. He carefully removed his hand from her waist and stepped aside. He looked at Jack. Then Dash turned the other cheek.

Dash pointed to the other side of his face. "Go ahead, punk. Let me have it."

Jack swung again, landing a hard jab at the jawline.

Despite Jack's drunken state, it was a good, hard hit, but Dash didn't even stagger.

It was Jack who winced with pain, cradling his fingers against his chest. "Damn, I think I busted a knuckle."

Catching hold of Jack's loosened necktie, Dash yanked him to within a few inches of his face. "Listen to me, Jack. You got two free shots. But that's all. Touch me or Liz again, and you'll regret it."

Jack shoved ineffectually. "Let me go."

"You can dish it out, huh?" Dash released his grip. "But you can't take it."

Walking slowly and carefully, Sarah appeared in the room. In clarion tones, she announced, "Behold, the Gregory rose."

Dramatically, she held out a pearly white planter with a small rosebush inside. There were two blooms and four buds. All were a pale shade of lavender blue.

Dash broke the uncomfortable silence. "Very beautiful," he said.

"Yes, it is." Sarah's smile was bright. She was oblivious to the events that had occurred in her absence. "Remarkably beautiful. The Gregory rose."

"Hey," Jack said, "I've seen that pot before. It belonged to my mother."

"You're right," Sarah said. "I found it when I was packing up some of Agatha's knickknacks." She turned to Hector. "How nice to see you."

"And you." He bowed slightly.

"I swear, Hector, you get more handsome with every year that goes by. Those South American climates agree with you." She carried the rose to the mantel and gently set down the china pot before turning to Hector. "You're half Spanish, aren't you?"

"Yes."

"And your ex-wife was from Bolivia?"

"Colombia," he corrected. "She's returned there."

Liz glided into the circle of their conversation. Hector was her favorite choice as a murder suspect, and she wanted to get as much information as she could about his schedule. "You've been to Colombia a lot recently. That was where you got my earrings, wasn't it?"

"Cartagena. Yes."

"It must be handy to have family there. You have a son, don't you?"

"He's seventeen."

"Lives with his mother?"

"Yes."

A darkness descended over Hector's features. He was clearly uncomfortable with this topic. Therefore, Liz pushed harder. "Do you ever have a chance to visit your ex-wife and her family when you're in Colombia?"

"No, I don't."

"Stop it, Liz," Sarah chided. "Of course Hector doesn't visit his former wife. I don't see my ex, either. Although I'd be delighted if he moved to another continent." With a shrill gaiety, she laughed as if she'd said something terribly witty. It was obvious that the tone of this dinner party was discord, and Sarah seemed to be trying her darnedest to cheer things up. "I'll go get the hors d'oeuvres."

It was Dash who gallantly stepped forward. "I'll help."

In the spacious kitchen, he complimented Sarah on the house.

"I can't take credit. The furniture and most of the artwork belonged to Agatha. She was a great supporter of the arts, you know."

She handed him a platter with soft cheese and crackers deliciously arrayed. And she continued to talk. Nervously, Dash thought.

"Unfortunately," Sarah said, "Agatha had no concept of good art. She'd buy because she wanted to support the artists, not because she appreciated their work. A generous woman, very generous."

"An easy touch," Dash hinted.

"In the art world, they don't call it that. They said that Agatha was a patroness. An angel."

Dash smiled. Liz didn't realize how true her words were. Agatha Orben had, indeed, entered the angelic realms.

"And have you taken up being an angel where Agatha left off?"

"Heavens, no. I don't have anywhere near enough money for Agatha's charities. All I have is what she left me—this house and the cash needed for upkeep."

Dash wondered if the upkeep was enough to finance building a greenhouse for Gary.

"I don't really own this place," she said. "I can always live here, but—according to Agatha's will—the house will become a shelter for battered women."

"A shelter, huh?" Though Dash wholeheartedly approved of this plan, he didn't imagine that Gary Gregory would be too thrilled. "When's this supposed to happen?"

"Someday. But there's a legal problem with zoning. The neighbors don't like the idea." She scooped up another tray, piled high with strawberries, kiwifruit and grapes. "And the neighbors have enough money to block the shelter for years. Gary says it may never happen."

"Convenient for him," Dash murmured under his breath. "So, what's the deal with you two? Getting hitched?"

"After dinner, I'll make an announcement."

Sarah led the way into the front room, where she forced the predinner socializing to a new level of innocuous chitchat about the weather, fashion and the latest movies.

When Sarah was finally ready to arrange them around the table, Liz stepped close to Dash. In a low voice, she said, "Gary Gregory has moved way up on my list of suspects. I think he was after the house. He's already acting like this place belongs to him."

Dash agreed. "He got his meat hooks into Sarah before Agatha died. Which means he was probably hanging around here all winter, like a bad case of the flu."

The timing was right, Dash thought. Agatha had died a year ago, after an illness of six months, which was when the poisoning started with small doses.

But Dash didn't feel a clear sense of guilt from Gary. Or from anyone else in the room. None of them was innocent. Of that, he was sure. But he couldn't pick a murderer from this crew. With the exception of Liz, everybody looked guilty as sin.

Halfway through the main course, when Sarah's persistent lightheartedness began to lag, he turned to her and asked another leading question. ''Apart from the green-house, are you doing any other renovations?''

"The only major change is that I've converted Agatha's old bedroom into a computer room." She shuddered delicately and touched her fluffy red hair. "I simply couldn't stand to leave it the same. She died in that room, you know."

"You nursed her for a long time," he said.

"Forever."

There was a flicker of sadness in her eyes, and Dash couldn't tell if Sarah was mourning her late aunt's death or if she was regretting the time she spent in caretaking.

He knew one thing for certain. Agatha had left a clue in her room. She'd told him about the object. And now it was gone.

Dash knew it was gone because his first order of business when he took on this case was to venture into this house, invisibly, to search. There wasn't a trace of the little statue Agatha had described.

"Did Agatha have antiques in her room?" he asked.

"Nothing of real value. The knickknacks were sentimental and practically worthless. Gifts from her late husband. Little presents that Jack had given her when he was a child. Photos. That sort of thing. I had to sort through all of it and decide where it would go."

Dash pretended confusion. "What do you mean?"

"Well, I couldn't very well sell it. Much of the stuff I boxed up and put into storage in the attic. Then I parceled out several items to people who were close to her. As remembrances. You know, to friends and family."

Internally, Dash groaned. The statue could be anywhere.

Sarah continued, "I was amazed by the number of people who wanted a memento. Agatha was more well-loved than I ever realized. I'm ashamed to say that I'd always thought of her as being difficult, extremely impatient."

"The kind of lady who knew her own mind," Dash suggested.

"Absolutely. And woe to him who disagreed with her." She leaned toward him and touched his arm conspiratorially. "We had arguments. I was frankly astonished when she left me this house."

Dash sensed that she was lying. "Not even a hint, huh?"

"Well, maybe a hint. We talked a lot about the battered women's shelter. I must have told her a hundred times that the people in this neighborhood would never allow this house to be used that way."

"Why not?"

"Well, it's not that these people aren't concerned about society's ills. They'd be delighted to contribute to a shelter in downtown Denver. But nobody in this neighborhood believes that charity begins at home—or even in the house down the street." She shook her head. "It's as if they believe battering is solely the problem of the poor."

"And how do you feel about that?"

"Oh, let's not chat about this. It's such negative energy. You know what they say. Never mix dinner with politics or religion." Sarah drew back into her role as proper hostess. "How long have you and Liz been dating?"

"Less than two hours."

"Lovely." Her gaze encompassed the whole long table, and Sarah seemed satisfied that her party was going well. "Liz is a charming person."

"Precious," he concurred. Unfortunately, Liz was taking her self-appointed mission as a detective too seriously. From snatches of her conversation with Hector, who was seated at her right, he heard a number of blatantly leading questions.

After she served dessert, Sarah stood at the head of the table and cleared her throat. "I have an announcement. Would you all please listen."

Liz leaned toward Dash and whispered, "Here it comes."

"Gary and I . . ." She paused. "Well, I guess there's no good way to say this but to come right out and say it. Gary and I are getting married."

Jack's heavy silver fork clattered onto his dessert plate. He looked like he was going to choke on his key lime pie. "What?"

"We've been dating for over a year. It's not like this is a total surprise, Jack."

He pushed away from the table, scraping the bottom of his chair legs on the hardwood floor, and he glowered at Gary Gregory, who remained seated, peering through his thick white-blond eyebrows.

As she watched, Liz had no idea what was going to happen next. She'd known these people for ten years, but they were like strangers to her. Though Jack had been drinking wine with dinner, he'd had enough time to sober up. His behavior couldn't be blamed on alcohol.

"That's very interesting," Jack said. "Congratulations, Gary. You've finally figured out a way to get your hands on all my money."

"Don't, Jack," Sarah pleaded. "Try to be a good cousin for me, okay? This isn't about money."

"Then what is it? True love? Don't make me laugh." He stalked away from the table. "Well, I guess I'd better start claiming the stuff around here that belongs to me."

"But, Jack, I want you to be happy for me."

"Shut up, Sarah!" He was standing by the mantel, staring at the Gregory rose. "I want this pot back."

"Don't be silly. It's not valuable."

"It belonged to my mother, and it's mine. Bad enough that you got the house and the furniture. The rest of this stuff belongs to me."

"Well, all right." Sarah bobbed her head docilely. "Whatever you say."

"I want it now," Jack demanded.

He grabbed the pot from the mantel. With one yank, he pulled out the rose by its roots and flung it against the fire screen.

"No!" Sarah cried.

Gary was out of his chair. "You bastard!"

Without another word, Jack tucked the white china planter under his arm and strode through the door, leaving it open.

Hector followed, mouthing his thanks for a delicious dinner to Sarah, who had collapsed in a sobbing heap at the head of the table. To Liz, Hector said, "I'd better catch him. He's in no condition to drive."

Liz wouldn't have cared if her boss crashed himself into a tree and died in a flaming gasoline explosion. But Hector was right. Jack could endanger other motorists. "See you tomorrow."

Gary was the next to depart. He'd gathered up the battered rosebush in a piece of plastic and was heading for the door. "Maybe I can save it. I've got to repot immediately."

"What about me?" Sarah peered through wet eyelashes. Her mascara was running. She looked dreadful. "My heart is breaking. Jack's the only family I'm close to."

"We knew he wasn't going to take it well. But he'll get over it," Gary predicted. "And so will you."

"Hold me!" She reached toward him.

"Sorry, hon. I have my hands full. I have to take care of this little plant. It was one of my best specimens, you know."

He whipped out the door and pulled it shut behind him.

Liz and Dash were left with the weeping Sarah. An uncomfortable situation, at best. Liz took a deep breath. "I'm really sorry. Can I do anything to help?"

"No."

Beneath the blue caftan, Sarah's shoulders were shaking.

"A cup of tea? Or coffee?" Liz offered.

"I never want to see coffee again. I hate OrbenCorp and everybody in it." She lifted her head. "Just get out. Both of you."

"I'll call tomorrow," Liz promised as they stepped out into the cool September night.

On the porch, Dash paused to light a cigarette, and she didn't even think of objecting. Liz almost wished she had a smoke of her own, something to calm the nerves.

"That was fun," Dash said. "What do you people do at company picnics? Line up and throw knives at each other?"

"I never would have expected these kinds of outbursts." She shook her head. "I really miss Agatha. If she'd been here, the whole thing would have been different. Damn, this really makes me want to catch the person who murdered her."

"Forget it," he said. "You got me introduced to these people, and that's all you need to do, sweetheart. Now you're off the case."

"No way. You really need my help."

He looked into her shining blue eyes. It was a temptation to agree, to give himself a reason to spend more hours in her company. But he said, "No."

"But I have a perfect in. They all know me. They won't think I'm investigating."

"Seems to me that I've solved a lot of cases." Hundreds of crimes over many, many years. "And I never needed help before."

"But this is different. Agatha died over a year ago. The trail is cold."

"You don't get it," he said. "This isn't a parlor game. Somebody here committed murder. And they'll kill again to save their worthless hide."

"I can take care of myself."

She sounded like she was pretty sure of herself, but Dash knew she'd never really been threatened. A karate chop and a tough attitude wouldn't stop a bullet.

He exhaled a breath of smoke and looked around the neighborhood. The cul-de-sac was silent. The houses were graciously separated with spreading lawns that had begun to lose their green for winter.

And he wondered. Why had Agatha wanted to place her battered women's shelter here? Why had she left Sarah in charge of the house and therefore in charge of the project? He wondered aloud, "You think Sarah is going ahead with the shelter?"

"I thought you didn't want my help."

"You're right. Forget I said anything."

"Before tonight, I would have said yes. Sarah seemed committed to fulfilling Agatha's wishes. But with Gary in the picture, I'm not so sure."

He wanted to ask her opinion of Hector. Dash liked the way Liz thought. But he kept his silence.

When she opened the driver's side door to her car and slid behind the steering wheel, he kept an eye on her long, graceful legs, which were well displayed beneath her short skirt. Long stems, he thought, like a rose. He admired the way she looked. His feelings weren't lust, he rationalized. He was merely appreciating a specimen of feminine beauty.

He climbed into the passenger seat and turned toward her.

Liz stared at him with wide eyes. "I'm afraid the decision has been taken out of our hands. I'll have to be in on this case with you, Dash. There's no choice."

"What are you talking about, sweetheart?"

"My list of suspects, the notes I made on that yellow legal pad."

"Yeah? What about it?"

"Somebody took it out of the car. It's gone."

Chapter Six

Dash was seriously rattled. He slouched in the passenger seat, not noticing the high-class suburb or scenery as they drove toward the main streets that led to town and Liz's apartment.

He'd blown it. These were the kind of cheesy mistakes a rookie would make. Not him. Not a seasoned pro like Dash. How could he have messed up so badly? Not only had he alerted Agatha's murderer to his investigation, but he'd put Liz in danger, set her up in front of the killer like a duck in a shooting gallery.

"Lighten up, Dash. At least we're on the right track."

"What?" He stared at her elegant profile, noticing the way her nose turned up prettily at the tip and hating himself for noticing. His admiration for her had blinded him, causing him to botch this case. "What are you talking about?"

"The murderer must be one of the people at the dinner party. Like my list. Jack, Hector, Gary or Sarah." She pulled up at a stoplight and glanced at him with dancing eyes. "It's one of them. I can't think of any other reason they'd steal the tablet from my car."

"Let me get this straight, precious. You think this is good news?"

She replied, "You bet. In one day, we've limited the suspects to four. That's pretty good."

He couldn't believe her enthusiastic tone. When she grinned, she looked ten years younger, and she was grinning right now. She was as perky as Nancy Drew in her red roadster.

He spoke slowly, weighing every word with ponderous gravity. "This is dangerous."

"I know. I understand." She chuckled. Actually chuckled! "But it is kind of exciting."

He flung himself back in the bucket seat and folded his arms across his chest to keep from grabbing her and shaking her until she comprehended. This wasn't funny. She could be the murderer's next target.

"The question is," she said, "who stole my list?"

"No questions, Liz. You're off the case."

"Here's what I think," she blithely continued. "The person who took the notebook had to be somebody who was parked outside. And that eliminates Sarah. It was somebody—Hector or Jack or Gary—who happened to notice his name on the pad while he was walking to his own car."

"A coincidence?" He shook his head. "If there's one thing I've learned in this business, there are no coincidences."

"What other explanation could there be?"

"Don't take Sarah off the list. She and Gary could be in it together."

"Okay." She nodded.

"And it could be somebody, anybody, else. They could have followed us, waited until we went inside and searched the car."

"Like who? Dr. Clark, maybe?"

"I don't know."

Dash hated to admit how badly he'd mangled this case. All he had wanted from her was an introduction to the main suspects. Instead, he'd dragged her into the spotlight.

He took a deep breath and laid out the most likely scenario. "Here's what probably happened. Tonight, at dinner, we did something or said something to trigger the killer's suspicions. The killer went to your car—on purpose—to look for a clue that might tell them that you and I were investigating."

"And they found the notebook."

"Bingo."

"Why take it? Wouldn't it be smarter not to let us know?"

"Pride." How could he explain the arrogance of evil? "After somebody successfully commits a crime, they're proud for being so smart. But they can't tell anybody. So they drop hints, give warnings."

"Like when a criminal returns to the scene of the crime?"

"You got it, sweetheart. They took the notebook as a threat. When we came to this dinner party, it was like we'd laid out a chessboard with a lot of clues. Now the murderer is sitting on the other side, his face in shadow, making his moves."

"Or her moves," she corrected. "Sarah might be the murderer."

"Given the method of the poisoning, she's the most obvious choice."

"And what exactly was this method?"

Dash uncoiled his arms and gestured emphatically. "I can't tell you that!"

"Well, I don't see why not."

"I work alone."

"Not this time, Dash. Whoever picked up that notebook knows me, knows my handwriting. They'll assume I'm investigating, whether I am or not."

"So?"

"So I might as well investigate."

She guided her little car into the parking space behind the Victorian mansion where she had her apartment on the third floor. Earlier tonight, Dash had noticed the charm of the place. Now he saw the shadows and the danger. "What kind of security have you got in this joint?"

"The front and back doors lock automatically when closed, and only the people who live here have keys. There are eight of us in the house. The front entry is, as you know, an open foyer to the street, then there's a buzzer system to let people through the locked door to the main house."

"So, anybody can buzz the door open?"

"Unfortunately, yes. We try to check, but sometimes people get careless."

Plus, Dash noted, there was a cellar with windows behind bars that looked impressive but could be removed with a Phillips screwdriver. And there was a trellis that climbed to a second-floor balcony. The trim around the windows and the fancy brickwork at the corners of the house offered handholds and footholds for a climber. He muttered, "Might as well be living in a treehouse. Would it scare you if I said somebody could get in here easy?"

She pondered for a moment, then shook her head. "I wouldn't be frightened. I have a gun."

"That's just swell," he said tersely. "Ever fired it?"

"I've done target practice. I bought the gun about five years ago when we were having a lot of robberies in the neighborhood."

"Ever fired at another human being?"

"Of course not." She slipped out of the car and hurried toward the rear entrance, flipping her keys to find the right one. She fitted it into the lock and opened the door before she turned to him. "Good night, Dash."

"I'm coming upstairs with you. I want to make sure there's nobody hanging around in your apartment."

Though she muttered about his being overprotective and not needing his help, she didn't refuse. Briskly, she walked down the hall to the front stairs, then up to the third floor where she unlocked her door. Dash stepped in front of her. "I'll go first."

She rolled her eyes. "Is this precaution really necessary?"

"I hope not."

He eased inside and turned on the overhead lights. Her apartment was quiet, empty. Though his angel sensitivity told him that no one was there, he made a show of checking the kitchen, bathroom and bedroom before returning to her. "It's clear."

She stepped across her threshold, but left the door open. "Thanks for seeing me in. And now, good night. It's after eleven, and I need to be at work tomorrow by nine."

"I'm staying."

"Don't get any ideas. You're not going to have a chance to take that condom out of your pocket. Not tonight."

"Get your gat, sweetheart."

"My what?"

"Your gat, your rod, your piece."

She cocked her head to one side, obviously puzzled, and he clarified. "Your handgun?"

"Okay, sure."

When she emerged from her bedroom, gun in hand, he was glad to see it was a thirty-eight caliber. At least she wasn't running around with a little derringer popgun. He snapped, "Point it at me."

"Why?"

"I want you to see what it feels like. Aim at my heart. Come on, do it like you mean it."

Though her hand held steady, her eyes flicked nervously. "I don't like this."

"When you shoot a man in the chest, the flesh explodes. And the blood doesn't trickle, it gushes. Slippery and wet, it's the goriest red you've ever seen."

Her hand trembled.

"In spite of what you've seen in the movies, somebody who's been shot doesn't fold to the floor all nice and neat. They might lurch. Might scream. Might even manage to shoot back."

In two strides, he crossed the hardwood floor and took the gun from her hand. "I'm almost a stranger. Blowing me away would be easy. Whoever murdered Agatha is somebody you know—somebody you know real well. You think you could shoot them?"

"If I had to." Her chin lifted defiantly.

"Would you hesitate? Would you wait that one extra second to think about it before you pulled the trigger?"

Quietly, she said, "I'm not sure."

"One second is the difference between life and death. One extra second, and you could be dead. Do you really want to take that chance?"

"But what can I do? The murderer already knows I'm investigating."

"Here's what you do. Don't go to work tomorrow. Take sick time, take a vacation. Get out of town. Stay with friends. Don't leave a forwarding address."

"You want me to run away and hide?"

"I want you to be safe." He had to convince her. "Please, Liz. Be reasonable."

"Of course, you're right." Turning away from him, she paced across the room, picked up one of the pillows on the sofa and plumped it. Then she fussed with another pillow, picked an invisible piece of lint off the coffee table. "I could stay with my sister in Atlanta. I haven't visited in quite some time."

"It's best," he said.

"Sane and sensible. That's me." With a sigh, she sank down on the beige-striped sofa. Sitting cross-legged, she gathered a pillow against her chest and slowly, slowly lowered her head. She seemed to be deflating. Her spunk and defiance faded. Her hair spilled over her hands.

When she looked up, her blue eyes were moist, but she wasn't crying. Her words were matter-of-fact, resigned. "All my life, I've been safe. I've always been such a good girl—so dull that I bore myself."

With total honesty, he said, "There's nothing boring about you, precious."

"But do I have the courage to face a killer? Could I pull the trigger on a gun? I don't know. Do I have the savvy to track down the person who murdered Agatha? I don't know that, either. But I hate that somebody could get away with it. That murder shouldn't have happened. Her life should not have been cut short. When I think about her suffering, it makes me want to scream. Do you understand?"

"Yes."

"Please, Dash, let me help you. Let me work with you. I want to avenge Agatha's death."

"Leave it to me, sweetheart. This is what I do."

"But I'd be good at solving crimes. I'm organized. I'm smart. I want to do this for myself. Really want to. I want to feel passionate about something. Please, Dash. I've got to live, I've got to take some risks before I get old and shriveled and die in my sleep."

He was torn. Dash wanted to give Liz the chance she wanted, but he couldn't allow her to march wide-eyed and innocent into extreme peril. It wasn't her job. It was his. Danger was his profession, his calling. He was a warrior, seeking justice against overwhelming odds.

He sat beside her on the sofa. Gently, he stroked her long, silky hair, offering solace and wishing he could take her into his arms and hold her until the disappointment went away. But he didn't trust himself to touch her. It would be too easy to ignite her fierce passions.

"I'm sorry, Liz. If you got hurt, I'd never forgive myself. Tell you what, sweetheart, if it's risks you want, I'll take you bungee jumping when this is over."

She slapped his hand away. "Don't you dare patronize me."

"I didn't mean to—"

"That's exactly what you meant to do." She was on her feet, glaring at him. "You open the door on an exciting world and let me look inside, then you tell me that I can be a cheerleader while you do all the fun stuff."

"The fun stuff? Like tracking down a killer?"

"I could do it," she asserted. "I'd be a good private eye."

"Why?" He gestured toward her bookshelf. "Because you've read all the stories?"

She threw the pillow at him. The fire in her eyes told him that he was lucky she didn't have the gun in her hand at that moment. "Get out!"

"Hang on, precious."

"I'm not your precious!"

"You're not going to investigate on your own, are you?"

"It's none of your business." Stiff-legged, she stalked to the door and threw it open. "Good night!"

He stood. He couldn't have bungled this any worse. Dredging up a confidence he didn't feel, he said, "We'll talk tomorrow."

"Out!"

How could her eyes, which had shone with such appealing light, be so cold? How could her soft, petal-like lips be set so hard? She looked like she could bite off his head.

Dash stepped into the hall. The door to her apartment slammed behind him.

With a sigh, he allowed a cloak of invisibility to shroud his presence. He might be able to crack this case right now if he flew to each suspect's house and searched for the yellow legal tablet. But he shouldn't leave Liz alone. Not now. The killer might be inspired to come here. Where was Cherie, the Guardian Angel, when he needed her?

THE NEXT MORNING, at precisely nine o'clock, Liz whipped into her office at OrbenCorp headquarters and waited impatiently until the caffeine-perked blond receptionist got off the phone.

"Good morning," Liz said. "Is Jack in?"

"Not yet."

"Or Hector?"

"Nope."

Liz really hadn't expected to find them there. The male executives seemed to feel no guilt about coming in late after a night out. To the receptionist, she said, "I'll be in Gary Gregory's office. Page me the minute either Jack or Hector come in."

"Is something wrong?"

"Wrong? No, not at all." Liz forced a smile. In order for her plan to succeed, she needed to return to her former position of nonentity. She needed to glide unnoticed through the offices until the moment she could unmask the killer. "Nothing wrong." She fluttered her hand. "I'm just a little tense this morning."

"Too much coffee," the receptionist said sagely. "You should switch to decaf."

In her office, Liz opened her briefcase and took out the computer printout that showed the figures for Hector's purchases of raw beans, then she took her list comparing those prices with those of their competitors. Documentation in hand, Liz swung down the hall toward accounting. She nodded to Gary's secretary, "Is he in?"

"Honey, he's always in."

With her usual office politeness, Liz smiled a greeting to the three bookkeepers, seated in a row at their desks. In their white shirts, dark neckties and conservative haircuts, they looked like mirror-image clones. They were modern-day Bob Cratchits, slaving away at their computers. As one, they raised their right hands and waved. "Hi, Liz."

"Good morning, guys."

She pushed open the door to Gary's inner sanctum and strode inside. Though his floor space was nearly as large as Jack's, the head accountant's office seemed crowded. There was a wall of dog-eared accounting and investment books. Two computers hummed in simultaneous harmony. Stacks of computer printouts and manila folders covered every spare inch of horizontal surface. And, of course, there were roses.

Five miniature rosebushes in varying states of bloom were scattered around the office. The place of honor on the windowsill was occupied by a specimen that was similar to the Gregory rose, but it was a very dark blue, almost black. Ominous, Liz thought.

In the midst of this chaotic domain sat Gary Gregory. On the desk in front of him was a yellow legal pad.

Liz stared at it. Was that her notebook? Had Gary left it right there as a taunt?

She remembered how Dash had compared the murderer to a chess player, making his dark and clever moves until...checkmate! But how could Gary Gregory be a cold-blooded killer? He looked like a big, goofy bird with his shock of straw-colored hair, black-rimmed glasses and pointy nose.

He said, "If you've come to ask about my rose, the prognosis isn't good. The bloom was severely traumatized."

His rose? How could he be talking about a plant when she was investigating a murder? Still, Liz pretended concern. "Sorry to hear that. But right now, I need to talk to you about Hector."

"The wild man of the expense account." He reached to the corner of his desk and picked up a massive folder. "He reports everything in Spanish with pesos, then he expects reimbursement. I've told him a thousand times that we deal in American dollars and cents."

"Is he padding his expenses?" She moved closer, trying to get a look at the yellow tablet.

"Padding? Not as far as I can tell. But he surely does include every damned taco and plantain."

On the top sheet of yellow paper, she saw a list of figures and notes in Gary's chicken-scratch handwriting. But several pages had been flipped over. She still couldn't tell if it was her notebook.

"Well?" Gary demanded. "What about Hector?"

She leveled her gaze, watching his expression for a reaction. "Agatha told me something before she died."

His Adam's apple bobbed up and down. He scowled. "Agatha? That's morbid! Why would you mention Agatha?"

"Why not?"

"Well, she's dead. She's a decomposing corpse. A human compost heap, you know." He shuddered. His feathers were definitely ruffled. "I don't like to think about death. Although some people say that bones make the best fertilizer. There was a little old lady who used to win every flower show, and people swore that she buried body parts in her flower beds to feed the blooms."

"Body parts?"

"Cats and dogs . . . I presume."

"How organic," Liz said.

"And what did Agatha tell you?"

"She suggested that I make a habit of comparing the figures for Hector's purchases of raw coffee beans with the prices paid by our competitors. I've found that we're often paying more."

She spread the sheet that came from Gary's accounting computers on the desk. "Here's what Hector paid." Then she tossed down the comparison she'd done. "Here are the competitors' figures. As you can see, OrbenCorp has been paying eight to ten percent more during the last quarter."

"I'll be damned," Gary said. He snatched up the two sheets of paper. His eyes darted between them. "And he did this after Agatha's death. When he knew she couldn't check up on him. That swine!"

He leaped up from behind his desk. Pacing with his hands clasped behind his back, his head pecked forward with each step. He looked absolutely furious, and Liz was taken aback. Geez, you would have thought it was Gary's own personal money instead of OrbenCorp funds.

"There might be an innocent explanation," she said. "I haven't had a chance to talk with Hector."

"I scoff at his innocence. His best excuse is incompetence." He returned to his desk and grabbed the two sheets. "Here's proof. Looks to me like Hector's taking a payoff."

Gary's reaction was so extreme that Liz found herself in the position of cautioning rather than accusing. "Let's arrange a conference today with Jack."

"Why bother?" He flapped his long, skinny arms. He shouted, "Jack would let Hector get away with murder."

The word hung between them. Murder. Liz felt a prickling up and down her spine. It was as if Gary was giving her a coded message. Murder. What was he telling her?

"Sorry," he said, pushing his glasses up the bridge of his beaklike nose. "I get frustrated at times. Jack knows nothing about the finances. As long as his salary is paid, he couldn't care less about the juggling act I have to perform to turn a profit month after month."

"I don't understand. I thought OrbenCorp was solidly in the black."

"We are. We are." It sounded like the belated cry of a wounded bird. "Sorry, Liz, sorry. Of course we'll conference." He went behind his desk, perched on the edge of his chair and spread the crumpled sheets of figures in front of him. "Can I hold on to these?"

"Sure, I have a copy."

"Good. Was that all?"

Wasn't that enough? "I guess so." She went to the door. When her fingertips touched the knob, she turned. "What did you think of my date last night?"

''The philosopher? He seems . . . okay.''

Gary was staring so intently at the figures she'd given him that nothing else in the world existed for him.

She left without another word.

When Liz returned to her office, she shoved aside the morning's work, flipped through her Rolodex to find Sarah's number and picked up the telephone receiver. Though Sarah was the only suspect who couldn't have stolen the legal tablet from her car, she couldn't be scratched off the list. Especially since, as Dash had pointed out, Sarah had the best opportunity to administer poison to Agatha.

Dash! An infuriating man! The thought of him caused her to forget what number she was dialing. She hung up the phone and took a breath. Last night, she hadn't been able to get to sleep because she kept thinking of him. It was almost as if he was there, in her bedroom, watching over her and unnerving her.

She wanted to hate him for treating her like a helpless bimbo he could placate with a promise of bungee jumping, but she couldn't. He had changed her life. Because of Dash, she was investigating a murder. Due to his interference, her ordered life had careened in a brand-new direction.

She was different.

Though she might be in danger, she liked the feeling of urgency that inspired her to investigate. Her actions had a renewed sense of purpose. She wasn't just a secretary anymore.

The files in her office, the sales charts, the computer printouts and the correspondence on which she had focused her attention eight hours a day seemed utterly void of meaning when compared with the horrifying injustice of Agatha Orben's murder. Could Liz ferret out the murderer? There were very few facts to draw upon. Dash had been closemouthed about the actual details, other than to say she was poisoned and had left behind a clue. A tangible clue, he'd said. And what was that? What was the object? Would she know it if she saw it?

First things first. Liz dragged a fresh legal pad across her desktop and began to make notes. Across the top of the page, she wrote, Gary Gregory.

What about Gary Gregory? He had reacted strangely when she mentioned Agatha. And he had a legal tablet, just like this one, on his desk. What else had he said? *Jack would let Hector get away with murder.*

Liz tapped her pen on the desktop. Did Gary know something? Maybe he was blackmailing Jack or Hector.

She wrote, "Blackmail" and "Tablet." Then she carefully tore off the sheet, folded it twice and filed it in her purse next to her handgun.

And now for Sarah. Liz had two reasons for contacting her. First, to get her reactions and hope she might inadvertently drop a clue. Second, Liz wanted to get back in the house and search for the mysterious clue Dash had mentioned.

She wrote Sarah Pachen across the top of another sheet of yellow legal paper and dialed the phone number. "Hi, Sarah. I wanted to thank you for dinner last night."

"Thank you, Liz." Her throaty voice was decidedly cool. "Now you've fulfilled your polite obligation. Goodbye."

"Wait! I'm sorry about what happened last night. Jack was way out of line." Though she didn't say it, Liz also thought that Gary's response was cruel and inappropriate.

"You don't think I should marry Gary, either, do you?"

"It's really none of my business."

"God, when I think of how I've treated you people as friends, I feel like such a fool. Nobody at OrbenCorp has ever liked me. They just put up with me because of Agatha."

"Gary likes you."

"Not as much as his damned roses. I told him that this morning when he called. He has some major apologizing to do."

"I agree," Liz said. "I was just wondering. You and Gary have been dating for quite some time. What did Agatha think of him?"

"She wanted me to be happy." Her voice cracked slightly. "Oh, Liz, I never appreciated her when she was alive. Now I miss her so much. She knew everything about me. She was the only one I could truly confide in."

"Agatha was an amazing woman," Liz said sincerely. "Which reminds me, Sarah, I have a favor to ask."

"What else is new? Everybody wants something."

"I really would like something to remember Agatha by. Some kind of memento."

"Something valuable, no doubt."

"Certainly not. I was thinking of a photograph, a picture of Agatha that was taken before she got sick."

"For goodness sake, Liz, all the photo albums have been packed up and stored in the attic. It's a tremendous bother for me."

"I'll go through everything. This afternoon?"

"Today's not convenient."

"Please, Sarah. I promise not to get in the way. This afternoon? Say at about one o'clock."

"Well, I have another meeting with the people from the battered women's shelter, but it's here at the house. I suppose I could open up the attic for you."

"Thanks, Sarah. I'll see you then."

Liz hung up the phone and smiled. Compared to yesterday's clumsy conversation with Dr. Clark, her interrogation of Sarah had gone extremely well. In spite of what Dash thought, she was getting better at this detective stuff.

She made a couple of notes under the heading Sarah. "Angry at Gary. Insecure. Loved Agatha. Regrets her death? Battered Women's Shelter."

Again, she tore off the page and stashed it in her purse.

She glanced up and saw Dash standing in her doorway. In his hand, he held a bouquet of daisies.

Chapter Seven

With the pitiful bunch of flowers clenched in his fist, Dash looked so sheepish that she almost forgave him on the spot. But then she remembered his patronizing arrogance. Even if he was here to apologize, she wouldn't let him off the hook easily. Her gaze was arch, aloof and chilly as an iceberg.

"Yes?" Liz said.

"I want to talk to you."

"Make it fast. I'm a little busy. You left me with a great deal of unfinished business."

"I left you?" He closed the office door. "My recollection, sweetheart, was that you bounced me."

"Maybe you deserved it, Bungee Man."

"I didn't come to apologize," he said. Dash knew he'd been right in emphasizing the danger of her situation. Besides, when he earned his wings, he had passed beyond repentance in the accepted human sense. Not that he was without flaw, but he didn't have to be judged by regular standards. In some ways, being an angel meant never having to say you were sorry.

"I can accept that. No groveling is required." A falsely innocent smile tickled the corners of her lips. "I assume you're here because you realized the error of your ways and you're ready to accept me as your partner.''

"I don't like this, precious. I'd rather have you and your cute little assets out of town and away from danger."

"Well, I'm not going anywhere until this case is solved."

"Then I guess I'm stuck with you."

"Like superglue." She stood and stuck out her hand. "Partners?"

He clasped her slender fingers. "Deal."

As quickly as possible, he broke contact. After last night's sloppy work, he wasn't going to let himself get distracted by her touch or the snappy way she looked or the fragrance of her perfume. He was here to do a job. That was all.

Since he'd goofed it and gotten her involved, he had to keep track of her. He figured it would be easier to protect her if he knew what she was doing. But that was all! No kissing, no touching and definitely no sense of lust.

Dash could handle the assignment. His willpower was strong. He'd never let himself get sucked in by a dame. That kind of thing had happened to other Avenging Angels, and the consequences were grim.

He tossed the posies on the desktop and lowered himself into a chair. "What's the latest scoop? You find anything?"

She told him about her strange conversation with Gary Gregory and the accountant's statement that Jack would let Hector get away with murder. As she talked, her eyes flashed vivaciously. "It sounded like Gary knew something," she said. "I thought of blackmail."

"That's a sharp observation, cookie." He pushed his fedora off his forehead. "Blackmail, eh?"

"The perfect crime for an accountant." She leaned back in her swivel chair. "Now it's your turn, partner. Tell me something about the crime. Let's stay with Gary as a suspect."

He shrugged. "Beats me. Why suspect the bean counter?"

"He's motivated by money, but he didn't inherit when Agatha died . . . unless he was romancing Sarah way back then in the hopes they'd marry and he'd get the house that way."

"Sounds too complicated," Dash said.

"Well?" She looked at him expectantly. "Do you have anything to add?"

"Don't rush me, kiddo. I'm not used to sharing."

"Not much of a nineties guy, are you?"

"Not a wimp, if that's what you mean." He frowned, unaccustomed to talking about his reasoning process aloud. Finally, he said, "Here's the thing about Gary. Roses."

"What about roses?"

"Not the flowers, but the chemicals he uses to grow them."

"I thought Gary was purely organic."

"Then you weren't paying attention last night when he was talking. He doesn't use any prepared treatments, but he has a regular laboratory where he concocts magic grow potions. Special stuff with long names. Stuff like oxyhydronitrogenous. I don't know exactly what it is, but it's a good bet that Gary's not killing aphids with kindness. Know what I mean?"

"Poisons." Liz grabbed her purse and took out the sheet with Gary's name at the top. She added the word "poison" to "blackmail" and "tablet." "Oh, yes," she said. "Gary also had a yellow legal tablet on his desk, just like the one I wrote my list on."

"Like the one you're writing on now? Like the ones that are all over this office?"

"Yes," she said, a bit defensively.

"You're not taking notes again, are you?"

"I have to, Dash. Or else I might forget something. But I'm being more careful now. I'm stashing my notes in my purse."

"Which you leave in your desk drawer when you wander around the office."

"I'll lock the drawer."

He leaned forward to check the desk and shook his head. "A two-year-old kid with a bobby pin could pick that lock."

"Fortunately, we have a dearth of two-year-olds in the office." She dug deeper in her handbag and produced the gun. "I've also brought this."

"It's not going to do much good in your purse. You need a shoulder holster."

"Swell plan," she said sarcastically. "You might not have noticed, but a loaded pistol isn't considered proper office attire."

"You want to be a private eye, you got to look the part."

She studied him carefully. From his snap-brim fedora to his polished wing tips, Dash looked like a detective. A Humphrey Bogart tough guy from the 1930s. "Like your costume?"

He spread his hands wide. "This is who I am. Take it or leave it."

She'd take it. Weirdness, arrogance and all, he was the most intriguing man she'd met in a very long time. Liz was glad to be working with him, to know that somebody else was on her side. "Dashiell Divine," she said. "Is that your real name?"

"Suits me fine."

"What did you mean, that first night when we met, when you said you were an angel?"

"Exactly what I said. An avenging angel. I'm on the side of justice, and I'm here to make sure the right thing gets done."

"That's quite a metaphor, Dash. You're poetic when you want to be."

"A poet? Don't make me gag."

She pulled the second sheet of paper from her purse. "I also talked to Sarah, and I made an appointment to go over to the house at one o'clock, supposedly to find a photograph so I can remember Agatha. I thought it might be a good time to search for the clue you said Agatha had left behind."

"That's the ticket. Now we're making some progress."

He rose from the chair. For a big man, she thought he moved with uncommon grace. No creaking joints. No lumbering limbs. He was as lean as a greyhound, built for speed.

"I'll meet you there, at Sarah's place. One o'clock."

"You know, Dash, as long as I'm searching for this object, it might help if you told me what we're looking for."

"Sure thing, sweetheart. It's a little statue, about eight inches tall. It's a falcon."

As he strode from her office, Liz was gaping. *The Maltese Falcon.* That was one of Bogart's most famous detective movies. Surely Dash was joking. They couldn't possibly be on the trail of the famous black bird. Or could they?

LIZ PARKED on the street outside Sarah's house at five minutes before one o'clock. Jack and Hector had not managed to show at the office, and she'd left a message with the receptionist that she could be reached at Sarah's house in case of an emergency.

As she approached the entryway, she looked around for Dash's car, but only saw a battered van with a bumper sticker that proclaimed, Woman Driver And Proud Of It. Liz was quite sure that statement didn't reflect Dash's personal philosophy. Was he late?

When she reached the front porch, he came up behind her. "Hello, sweetheart."

"Where'd you come from?"

"I was just floating around, waiting for you."

"I don't see your car. How did you get here? In a cab?" She recalled the incident at the park when they'd met. Sarcastically, she asked, "Or did you fly?"

He pushed the doorbell. "There's somebody else visiting Sarah. A couple of ladies."

"Sarah mentioned something about another meeting. I think they're from the battered women's shelter."

"The women who want this house," he said.

When the door opened, her ears rang with the echo of high-pitched female laughter. In contrast, Jack—who stood in the doorway—was red-faced and panicky. He looked like he'd been tiptoeing across flaming embers. Averting his gaze from Liz, he appealed to Dash. "You've got to help me, man. They're ganging up on me."

"Who is?"

"The shelter women. One of them is a feminist, the other is a nun." He pulled Dash inside. "It's been a solid ten minutes of men-are-jerks jokes."

"Sounds like fun," Liz said, gliding around the two males to enter the living room.

Today, Sarah was dressed in emerald stretch pants and a patterned turquoise and emerald overblouse with a matching scarf tied in her cascade of red hair. Though the outfit was conservative for Sarah, she was a peacock compared to her guests. One wore jeans and a T-shirt, the other was clad in a navy blue skirt and cardigan. Sarah introduced Marlena and Sister Muriel.

"M and M," said the sister as she beamed at Liz. When she looked at Dash and shook his hand, a curious expression illuminated her round face. Behind her wire-rim spectacles, her eyes widened. Her voice was a little breathless. "Don't I know you?"

"Not yet."

Her plain, unadorned hands clasped at her waist. "But I will come to know you, won't I?"

"You can count on it, Sister."

For some reason Liz couldn't explain, a peaceful silence spread within her. She had a sense that all was right with the world. But why? All she had witnessed was a first meeting between a private investigator who thought he was Bogie and a nun who worked at a battered women's shelter. Yet Liz felt strangely... blessed.

Beside her, Jack muttered, "Damn, how'd he do that?"

"Do what?" Liz asked.

"These females had their claws out and now... look at them! Three purring pussycats."

"Maybe you did something to set them off," she suggested.

"Me?" He tapped his broad chest. "You know that's impossible, Liz. In spite of the way I behaved last night, I can be charming. And I know how to handle women."

Dryly, she said, "Maybe your charm threatened them. Gosh, Jack, maybe you're just too sexy for a feminist and a nun."

"That's got to be it." He hitched up his loose-fitting trousers. He was dressed casually, apparently not planning to check in at the office. "How about some coffee, everybody?"

Marlena, the feminist, nodded. "Sure, that would be nice."

Jack flopped down in a Queen Anne style wing chair. "Sarah? How about it?"

When Sarah hesitated, he pursed his lips. His disgust was palpable. "Oh, I suppose you want me to get it."

"No, no, that's fine, dear. You stay right there." To everyone else, she said, "Jack has had a terrible day. We've been arguing about my intention to be married."

Sister Muriel turned to him. Her round little body stiffened, and it was obvious to Liz that the sister had a backbone of tempered steel. "Why would you object to the holy sacrament of matrimony?"

"Sarah's my cousin, and I need to look out for her best interests. I'm just not sure the guy really loves her."

Sarah defended him. "Jack really does have good intentions."

"Besides," Jack said, "ever since Sarah inherited this house, everybody thinks they deserve a piece. Even you. Am I right, Sister?"

"Charming," Liz muttered. She decided that right now was the best time to make an exit. "Don't bother with coffee for Dash and me. If you don't mind, Sarah, we'll just head up to the attic, find a photograph of Agatha and leave."

"That's fine, Liz." Sarah dug into the pocket of her overblouse and produced a large, old-fashioned key. "The attic is up from the second floor. There's a stair—"

"I know where it is," Liz said. "Once, when I was visiting, Agatha sent me up there to find some old records for OrbenCorp."

"All that paperwork is gone. Boxed up and warehoused at OrbenCorp."

"Where?" Liz asked. She knew there was no file storage room at corporate headquarters in downtown Denver.

"At the roasting and packaging plant in Aurora. That's where it belongs, after all. In the attic, I'm sorry to say, there's no organization to the storage. I can't tell you where the photo albums are located."

Liz took the key. "We'll find them."

She watched carefully as Dash bade a friendly farewell to the women and turned to her. "Let's go, precious."

He led the way to the front stairway but gestured for her to go first. She saw him exchange a wink with Sister Muriel before they climbed the stairs.

On the second-floor landing, she asked, "What was all that about?"

"All what?"

"There was something going on between you and Sister Muriel. Some kind of chemical reaction."

He chuckled. "You think I got the hots for a nun?"

"Of course not."

"What then? She's got the hots for me?"

"Never mind," Liz said as she fitted the key into a door at the end of the hall. Though she was certain Sister Muriel and Dash had some kind of connection, the very idea was ludicrous.

When she opened the door leading to the attic, they were hit with a blast of warmish stale air. Her nose wrinkled. "Yuck! Smells like death warmed over."

She hit the switch by the door, and the dim glow of distant bulbs shed light on the narrow stairway. As she hiked up, she told Dash to close the door behind them. "I don't think Sarah would appreciate having that stink through the whole house."

It was at least ten degrees hotter in the attic. The sloped ceiling at the eaves of the house was lined with pink insulation. The floor was unpolished wood. And the vast space, as large as the entire house, was filled with artifacts, the detritus of Agatha's life.

Liz sighed. "How are we going to find anything up here?"

"Welcome to detective work, sweetheart. This is the main job. Dull stuff. Digging through rubble. It's slow. It's boring. It's a pain in the neck."

"It might help," she said, "if you told me what we are looking for. And don't start that nonsense about the Maltese falcon."

"It's truth." Dash leaned against an old love seat. "Okay, maybe it's not a falcon. Maybe it's more like a painted bluebird made out of china. It's a hollow figurine with a little hole in the bottom."

"And why are we looking for it? What's the clue?"

"Right before Agatha died, she figured out what was going on. Somebody had tampered with the capsules she took every day for high blood pressure. They had done it over a period of months, gradually upping the dose of poison, allowing her body to assimilate the stuff, making her slightly sicker and sicker. Real slow. Day by day. Week by week."

As Dash spoke he felt the familiar anger building within him. He hated the injustice of murder. More than the death itself, he despised the deed. Whoever had murdered Agatha Orben had been cruel in their methods. The good woman had suffered unnecessarily.

Liz amplified his thoughts with expletives Dash, being an angel, could not speak. She ended with, "That sick, twisted son-of-a—"

"That's right," he said. "You see why I want to put this scum away? And the bird can help us do that. Inside the bird statue is tangible evidence, the kind of evidence that will convince a judge and jury that she was murdered. A capsule. It's one of the poisoned capsules this sleazebag fed to Agatha."

"We'll find it." Liz dug right in, checking out the cardboard boxes with inked notations on the sides describing the contents. She picked one up and shook it. There was a rattling and the rustle of crumpled newspaper. Liz carefully peeled back the tape and opened the box. "You'd like this," she said, pawing through the contents. "Looks like an entire box of ashtrays."

Dash watched as she sealed the box and meandered deeper into the dusty attic. With utter disregard for her tan slacks, she sat on the wood floor and checked the contents of a cardboard box marked miscellaneous. Again, she found nothing important.

After twenty minutes of digging through the attic, Liz was disheveled, but her dogged pursuit of the task at hand had not diminished one whit. She had an admirable streak of determination, Dash thought. Seldom had he encountered a mortal with such a firmly developed sense of justice. On some future day, he thought, Liz would make an excellent Avenging Angel. But that time would be a far day from now, way beyond his comprehension. And, by then, Liz might have changed. So much could happen. She might be married and have children.

A twinge of despair, almost painful, yanked at his angel heart. He had no right to think of her future. Or his own, for that matter. He moved from case to case. In a way, he was timeless.

She glanced at him over her shoulder. "Aren't you going to help?"

He'd already been through the stuff in the attic. That was the first place he'd looked when he was put on the case. Though he'd found nothing, Liz might have more luck. "I've already searched up here for the falcon."

"The bluebird," she said firmly. "It was a bluebird, not a falcon."

"Whatever. Anyhow, I already cased the attic."

"You searched? When?" Her blue eyes flashed with sudden comprehension. "Dash, are you telling me that you broke into this house and searched?"

"You might say that." He'd been invisible, of course. Gliding through the pieces of Agatha's life as quickly and easily as a breeze filters through a field of autumn straw.

"Breaking and entering? I can't believe you did that. It's illegal."

Not for an angel. "Yeah, I know."

Impishly, she asked, "Can you teach me how to do it?"

He groaned inwardly. "Listen, sweetheart, you're not going to need to know how to break and enter, or how to shoot a gun. You're not going to need any of this stuff because you aren't a private eye. This is your one and only investigation, and I'm going to be with you every step of the way."

"I could be a detective," she said. She sat on her heels. "I want to be one. Can't you hire me?"

Hire her? To be an Avenging Angel? "Impossible," he said. "No way. You wouldn't like the retirement plan."

"We're working together now," she pointed out.

"Just this once. I'm letting you help out because it's my fault you might be in danger. But—I've said this before, precious—I work alone."

"Why?"

He didn't have a quick answer for that question. He worked alone because he always had done it that way. And he'd always been successful.

"Why?" she repeated.

"When you have a partner, you got to watch out for them. A guy's got to protect his partner. Having somebody else around would make me vulnerable."

"But you'd also be twice as smart. Two heads are better than one. And I wouldn't mind an apprenticeship. Not at all. I'd do the boring, dirty work."

For an instant, he was swayed. Her eyes shone with eagerness. There was a note of clear, pure excitement in her voice, reminding him of the days when he'd first started as an Avenging Angel and had been optimistic about the prospect of righting all the wrongs in the world.

"Hire me," she said. "I'm ready for a career change."

But not ready to become an angel, he thought. Dash pointed to a box behind a steamer trunk. "There are the photo albums. You'd better pick one out."

Though she went to the box and opened it, she didn't drop her end of the conversation. "You know I'd be good, Dash. I really am a quick learner. And I jog, so I'm in good physical shape."

She pulled out a photo album and opened it. A snapshot of Agatha smiled at her. It must have been a formal occasion because she was elegantly dressed. Her silver hair was swept up, and she wore a lovely, sparkling necklace.

Dash peeked over her shoulder. "That's some jewelry she's got on. A lot of ice."

"Those aren't diamonds," Liz said. "Agatha never wore real gems. Her investments were in people, not jewels."

"Go ahead," he said. "Take the picture. Then we can get out of here."

"Excuse me, Mr. Hotshot Detective. But there might be a clue in these albums."

She was right, of course. Dash was surprised that he hadn't thought of that. Photo albums. Diaries. Notebooks. Those were all good sources for clues. Why hadn't he thought to check out the pictures? Was he losing his edge?

Liz flipped through another album and paused to study the neatly mounted photographs. "This is a company picnic. Must have been about six years ago, because there's Hector with his wife and son, Carlito. The boy was only ten or eleven in this photo. Nice-looking kid."

Dash peered over her shoulder and studied the boy's sullen expression. Handsome youngster, but there was a diffidence in his posture. Even at that age, Carlito looked like mischief.

"It's sad," Liz said. "They look so happy in this picture. Then came the divorce, and his wife and son left. Hector never talks about them. I don't think he ever sees Carlito."

"Why would Agatha save that photo?"

"She thought of the people at OrbenCorp as her family. Always remembered birthdays. Always made a charitable donation in all our names at Christmas."

Dash pointed to another photo. "Is that Sarah?"

"Hard to believe, isn't it?" Liz pointed and circled the plain face of Sarah Orben Pachen on the photograph. She wore no makeup. Her hair was dishwater blond. Her smile was shy. "She wasn't always flamboyant. A regular mouse when I first met her."

"She's wearing a cast on her arm," he noted.

"A little accident-prone, too," Liz said.

The door leading to the attic rattled open and Sarah called out, "Liz? How are you doing?"

"I found a picture. Be right down."

"Okay. You had a call from Hector. He wants to get together this afternoon."

"Thanks, Sarah." She glanced at Dash and whispered, "I can find out a lot from talking to Hector."

"You're right. We can. We," he repeated for emphasis, "can learn a lot."

"You're coming with me?"

"You got it, partner."

"Liz?" Sarah called again. "Are you coming?"

"Sure am." She flipped to the first photo and carefully removed it. Under her breath, she said to Dash, "If you come along when I talk to Hector, acting like my bodyguard, it's suspicious."

"What?"

"Suspicious," she hissed.

Liz closed the crate of albums, dusted off her slacks and headed for the staircase. "Let me handle Hector."

"Not a chance." Dash wouldn't allow it. If Hector Messenger was half as dangerous as Liz thought, Dash couldn't let her go to a one-on-one meeting. Not when Hector might know that Liz had just set out to be the latest incarnation of hard-boiled private investigator.

She paused at the top of the staircase, silhouetted in the dim light, and tugged the clasp from her tangled ponytail. Her long, soft hair flowed past her shoulders, and she raked her fingers through it as she descended the stairs.

Liz held out the photo so Sarah could approve. "Is it okay if I take this one?"

"Fine." Sarah barely glanced at the snapshot.

She hurried ahead of them, making it halfway down the staircase to the main floor before the front door slammed. Sarah paused. Her manicured fingers gripped the banister. She made a whimpering sound in the back of her throat.

"What's wrong?" Liz asked.

"It's Jack. He's being so difficult. Though he didn't contest the terms of Agatha's will when the lawyers read it, he's had second thoughts. He doesn't want Gary to have any claim on this house. Not Gary or anybody else."

"What about the shelter?"

"He'll block that, too. He was so nasty to Marlena and Sister Muriel." Half to herself, she muttered, "I'm trying to do the right thing. That's all."

Though Sarah wasn't being rude, she rushed them out the door and onto the porch before Liz had time to ask if she might use the bathroom to tidy herself up.

In the sunlight of an autumn afternoon, Liz noticed all the smudges and smears of dirt on her slacks. "I'm a mess."

"You want me to drive?"

"I said that I was messy, not insane. I'll do the driving."

They were on their way before he asked, "Where are we headed?"

"First we'll stop at my place so I can change into something more presentable. Then to OrbenCorp to talk with Hector."

Dash settled back in the bucket seat. Driving here and there. Asking questions. Making searches. Detective work was slow and tedious when he obeyed mortal restrictions. He could have flown from place to place, could have made himself invisible and followed each suspect until—during the course of their activities—they did something to betray their guilt.

But Dash couldn't leave Liz alone. He had to stay with her, to protect her.

"I was just wondering," she said, "do you work out of an office?"

"Sure do."

"And where's it located?"

"Over on Logan Street."

"I might just apply for a job. Would you give me a recommendation?"

"Forget it. You can't do what I do."

She scowled over the steering wheel. "Is that because I'm a woman?"

"Gender has nothing to do with it."

"I'll make you a deal, partner. If I crack this case, find the murderer and enough evidence to bring the killer to justice, will you recommend me?"

Dash thought about it. He couldn't imagine how, with her mortal limitations, she could accomplish that task. The case was months old. The only piece of evidence, the bird figurine, was so completely lost that Dash—with his supernatural angel powers—couldn't find it. And he was the best detective in the entire corps of Avenging Angels. There was no way Liz Carradine could accomplish the job.

"Will you?" she repeated.

It seemed harmless enough to agree. "Sure thing, sweetheart."

Immediately, the ethereal beeper in Dash's trench coat pocket sounded.

Chapter Eight

At the Denver Branch of Avenging Angels, Dash ran into Angelo standing just inside the front door. It was clear from the scowl on Angelo's face that Dash was being called on the carpet for one blessed reason or another. Dash scowled at him and drawled, "Angie, you got a problem?"

"I've reported you to St. Michael."

"How come? What's got your goat? For a desk jockey, you're kicking high."

"I don't intend to talk with you about this."

"What's the matter, Angelo? Computer on the fritz?"

"St. Michael's waiting upstairs. You're *his* problem, not mine."

Dash took a pack of Camels from the breast pocket of his jacket and stuck one between his lips.

Angelo groaned. "Really, Dash, must you try my patience? I wish you wouldn't smoke."

"We can't always have our wishes." Dash fired up his cigarette, inhaled deeply and exhaled. A gray cloud of smoke swirled toward the ceiling. "For example, I wish you wouldn't go running to St. Mike every time you have to sneeze."

"To sneeze?" Angelo's voice rose an octave. "This is considerably more than a sneeze."

Coolly, Dash said, "Nobody likes a snitch."

Instead of exploding in righteous rage, Angelo drew back. His gaze was speculative and amazingly calm, considering the provocation. "There's something very wrong with you, Dash. We've known each other for... forever, and I've always admired your work. But you don't have the same enthusiasm. You're slipping up on clues."

"Everybody takes a nosedive now and again."

"Not you. You were always the best." He rubbed his chin. "You need a change. Maybe a partner. Could be that you're suffering from burnout."

"Burnout?" Dash had to laugh. "I thought only the demons got burnout. Not us."

"Happens to the best of us," Angelo said.

Dash knew that Angelo was talking about himself. Recently, he'd had to discipline a guy who'd been around for a long time, and the punishment was nearly as hard for Angelo as for the offending angel. In a tired voice, Angelo said, "I don't know what to recommend for you. Reassignment is difficult. You don't have a singing voice, so the various choirs would be a mistake. And you'd be terrible as a baby-sitter for the Cherubs."

"So? Don't get on my case."

"You make it tough, Dash. You should have never suggested to that young woman that she could work here."

"That's between me and her. I didn't break any rules."

"You bent them." He stamped his sandaled foot and raised his eyes toward the heavens, seeking guidance. "What am I going to do with you?"

Dash puffed on his cigarette, slow and easy and not at all intimidated. "That's for Mike to say."

From the second-floor landing, a deep voice boomed so loudly that the glass in the chandelier tinkled. All the other Avenging Angels looked upward. "Dashiell!" It sounded like the voice of doom and judgment. "Dashiell, get up here! Now!"

Dash winked at Angelo. "Duty calls."

He whipped up the staircase and stood beside Mike. The saint was angry. His aura flared with a glowing nimbus of flame. "I've about had it with you, Dash."

"Yes, sir." Dash didn't smart off with St. Michael. Not only did he respect the man with all his heart, but Mike was the big boss.

"We don't work with mortals. Not ever."

"Yes, sir." Dash didn't say it, but he thought of the many occasions when he'd worked with the police. Several times, he'd arranged evidence for prosecuting attorneys. Though Mike and Angelo didn't want to admit it, times were changing.

"Why did you do it?" Mike paced on the landing, and his searing fiery aura trailed behind him. "Why did you tell Elizabeth Carradine that she could be your partner? You know better. Why'd you suggest to her that she could work here?"

"She's trying to solve the case herself. Won't back off. I need to protect her."

Mike glared at him. The full force of his radiant temper exploded with supernatural power. Few angels could endure the righteous wrath of St. Michael, the most forceful of saints, but Dash continued undaunted, "If she got hurt... If she got herself murdered because of something I did to draw attention to her, her death would be unjust."

"That's true," Mike said. His temper eased slightly.

"I can't just leave her hanging out to dry when there's a murderer at large."

"Protection is one thing," Mike said. "But you've gone farther than that. You hinted that she could work here, in these offices. Why?"

Dash gathered up all his courage. He thought about Liz. She was the one who suggested searching through the photo albums. She had arranged a plausible excuse to search at Sarah's.

Looking St. Mike in the eye, Dash said, "She's good. A natural detective. Having her here isn't a bad idea."

"What?" St. Mike roared. The very foundations of the building rattled as if in an earthquake.

"Hear me out, Mike. You're always saying you could use some decent help around this place. I mean, look around."

He gestured to the office floor below them. A couple of ladylike angels sat on opposite sides of a checkerboard, gazing upward at them with wide, unblinking eyes. Kiel sprawled on a chair in the corner, raking his fingers through his hair and looking anguished. Another young man floated lazily near the ceiling. It was the most unbusinesslike setting imaginable. "From what I understand, there have been time glitches on a couple of cases. Rumor has it that you even assigned a Cherub as an Avenger."

"A child," Mike said. "Not an infant."

"What kind of detective business is this? None of the avengers are hired on the basis of skill."

"True," Mike said thoughtfully. "Most of the mortals who show promise for this kind of work are corrupted on earth."

"Not only that," Dash continued, "but our training program was set up thousands of years ago. Nobody here understands how to work with lawyers."

"Lawyers," Mike said, "are always a problem. Don't even get me started on the screwups in the southern California offices."

"We could use a good secretary," Dash said. "Maybe even another operative."

"A mortal?" He scoffed. "Don't be ridiculous, Dash. We aren't exactly an equal opportunity employer here. You've got to be an angel."

"Why not? If she's good."

"Only once or twice—in the course of all history—have we needed to call in mortal assistance. Like that incident with King David and the footprints, of course."

"That was prehistory," Dash said. "That was the Dark Ages, when angels could still manifest and wouldn't be laughed off the street."

"The good old days." Mike sighed. His halo of fire ebbed to an ember glow. "Makes me nostalgic to even think about those golden times."

"We're coming up on a new millennium, Mike. Times change. We're working with cops more, and we've still got too many unsolved cases on file. You know it, and so do I."

"Be careful, Dash. You've been undercover too long. You're starting to behave like a mortal man."

Though Dash would have liked to shield the thoughts that flashed through his mind, it wouldn't do any good. St. Mike knew exactly how and where his mind was wandering. Ever since he was assigned to this case, ever since he met Liz, he'd been thinking that being mortal wasn't such a bad deal.

Sure, mortality meant you had to cope with pain, hunger and fear. You needed a job, an income, cash flow. There wasn't a lot of time for contemplation when you were mortal. But there were benefits, too. Like passion, like lust, like self-indulgence.

"Dash." Mike called him out of his reverie. "You know the rules."

"Yeah, I know chapter and verse. Take on too many mortal characteristics, and you're punished. If I mess up too bad, I get sent to the Fifth Choir."

"Don't get smug," Mike warned. "It's happened. Recently."

"But not to me," Dash said. "I'm good, Mike. I'm one of the few angels here who's suited to being a detective. My record is perfect. You need me."

"Pride," Mike said, "is a sin."

"Humility doesn't get the cases solved."

Dash braced himself for the burst of righteous fury that he expected from St. Michael. Like any good general, Mike wouldn't tolerate insolence or insubordination.

Instead, St. Michael frowned. "Don't screw up, Dash. I don't want to lose you."

"Yes, sir."

"Be careful with this woman. You're becoming attached to her."

"No lust," Dash said. "She's a beauty, all right. But I've got my lust under control."

"You bought a condom."

"A mistake," Dash said. "I thought it was a mint."

"She kissed you."

"Caught me off guard. It won't happen again."

"Be very, very careful." Mike's features softened. "I'm not worried about lust. But it looks to me like you might be falling in love, and that emotion is far more complex. There are procedures to be observed.''

"Got it," Dash said. Properly chastised, he left the offices. Instead of flying downtown and making himself invisible to observe Liz's meeting with Hector, he walked. He plunged his hands deep in his pockets. His strides were long. He needed time to contemplate Mike's warning about the sacrament of love and the proper procedure to be observed. Marriage. Love ended in marriage, an eternal bond between a man and a woman.

Dash shuddered. He'd never undergone that yoke. Though he couldn't recall his human existence before he became an angel, he knew from personnel files that he had not wed. And he had the feeling that he was missing something important.

He'd never sired a brood of children. *Go forth and multiply.* Wasn't that supposed to be an instruction for living? Somewhere in the rules and regs there was an indication that every being, mortal and angel and even devil, would have a mate. Part of the big picture, Dash thought. The union of male and female. Why hadn't it happened to him?

When he thought about Liz, with her long legs and sweet azure eyes, he got fuzzy inside. Though the memory of her did not blur the clear lines of good and evil that delineated his purpose, he felt his drive being slowed. His motivation to solve crimes softened because he was too busy thinking about her. This tenderness had to stop. He was an avenger, a warrior.

He thinned his earthly form to invisibility and soared to the fourteenth floor where OrbenCorp had their offices. Liz wasn't there yet. Nor was Hector, Jack or Gary. He sensed no danger in the corporate headquarters.

Swift as a beam of laser light, he flew to Liz's apartment and glided inside without taking solid form. She stood before the bathroom mirror and brushed her hair. Tawny highlights shimmered in her long brown hair as she stroked thoughtfully. Her blue eyes were soft and contemplative. Unguarded, she looked so lovely and sweet.

But he knew her better than that. He could be sure Liz Carradine wasn't thinking about fields of daisies and needlepoint projects. More likely, visions of detective work and mayhem danced in her brain.

He watched as she pulled her hair into a ponytail at the nape of her slender neck. Carefully, she fixed pearl studs into her pierced ears. She was humming tuneless snatches of song.

Too easily, he visualized what it would be like to wake up each morning and find Liz there beside him, warm and friendly in his bed. They would share a hot cup of java. They'd talk about their dreams. When she laughed, her amusement would lighten his heart. When she wept, he would comfort her.

No! He couldn't think this, couldn't even dream it. It was torture to imagine anything so unattainable.

But it didn't feel wrong. Love was a blessed emotion. Marriage was a sacrament. How could they be forbidden?

Confusion roiled within his chest. If he fell in love with Elizabeth, would he cease to be an angel?

In the blink of an eye, he soared away from her apartment. He needed contemplation. He needed to relax, unwind, to marshal the strength and wisdom of angels.

His powerful wings spread to their full span, he surged upward through the ether blue, higher than the rooftops of Denver, farther than the topmost floors of skyscrapers. He flew above the snowcapped peaks of the Rockies, seeking the radiant soul of the sun. As he ascended, higher and higher, separating from the earth, he sought peace. The singing of stars. The pure sensation of being one with the universe.

Beyond the horizon of earth, he departed from the atmosphere and ozone. In space, he found solace for his small worries. Surely, his little problems didn't amount to a hill of beans. Bogie had said that, and Bogart had been right. Not even a hill of beans. Dash rested, allowed his questions to float away. Far from earth he floated, weightless as a wish, ethereal as a prayer.

As a mortal, he would never fly. His life would be mundane and earthbound. He didn't want that. Never. Yet he felt a pull more compelling than gravity.

As quickly as he had flown, he returned to earth and materialized in the fourteenth-floor offices of Orben-Corp. The reception area was dark. Doors were locked. The offices had the air of total desertion that comes on Friday afternoon before the weekend. He went to Liz's office. She wasn't there. Nobody was there!

He glanced at the clock on the receptionist's desk. It was after five o'clock. Five thirty-seven.

The sharp edge of panic knifed through him. He had spent hours in contemplation. Not minutes. He had left Liz alone and unprotected, headed toward a meeting with Hector Messenger, a primary suspect in the case.

Where was she? Was she safe?

A terrible sense of dread knifed through his being. He'd lived through the major disasters of the twentieth century. Not only the small horror of unsolved crime, but he'd been in the Holocaust. In Chile during the massacres. He'd faced Idi Amin. He'd been in Vietnam. Of all that he'd seen, of all that he'd experienced, he'd never been as shaken as now, when he stood in Liz's office and stared at her vacant desk.

In solid form, he trembled in the darkened office. What was happening to him? He realized with terrifying certainty that he could not go on without her.

LIZ SLAMMED her car door. This afternoon had been nothing but one screwup after another. First, Dash had taken off with a promise to meet her at the office. Then he never returned. Typical irresponsible male behavior.

Then her meeting with Hector had to be postponed because Hector had to come to the processing plant where the raw coffee beans were warehoused before shipping. Muttering, she walked toward the vast, bland, square building with the OrbenCorp logo on the side. There was only one car in the parking lot, and she hoped it belonged to Hector. Otherwise, the entire afternoon would be a write-off.

Both Jack and Gary had been out of the office, and she'd spent the time from two o'clock to four-thirty sitting behind her desk, stewing in her own juices. Then she'd decided to come out here, to find Hector and confront him. But the traffic from town had been absolutely impossible.

Checking her wristwatch, she saw that the time was five forty-two. She was frustrated and angry. And hungry. She hadn't eaten since this morning. Why wasn't anybody where they were supposed to be? How on earth could she solve Agatha's murder if the suspects kept running off?

Liz marched up the concrete stairs to the office door beside the closed bays of the loading dock. If it was locked, she would just go home, have dinner and take a long soak in the bathtub while she considered the clues. Ever since she'd flipped through that photo album, Liz had the sense that there was something buried in the past that would yield a solution.

The doorknob twisted easily in her hand. The heavy metal door opened on soundless hinges. Good! Maybe Hector was here. Maybe she'd have a chance to talk with him.

She poked her head inside. The windowless office area was dark. Not promising. But a car was parked outside, and the door had been open. Somebody must be here.

Liz turned on the light switches beside the door. Unlike the posh corporate headquarters downtown, the processing plant with its warehouse area was barren and plain. The only decorations on matte beige walls were pictures the employees had tacked up. Family photos. Calendars. Liz called out, "Hello? Anybody here?"

Her voice made an eerie echo.

"Hector? Are you here?"

The only response was a faint hum from the air-conditioning system. It occurred to her that if Hector *was* here, they would be utterly alone. If he was the murderer, she needed to exert extreme caution.

In the back of her mind, she wished Dash was with her. She'd feel a lot braver if she had him protecting her rear.

Before taking another step, Liz opened the clasp on her purse and stuck her hand inside. Her fingers closed around the handle of her gun. She didn't dare take off the safety catch because she might accidentally shoot herself in the foot, but she held the gun ready. She curled her finger around the trigger.

Cautiously, she crept past the desks to the long, unadorned corridor that led to the warehousing and processing areas. That door was also open.

When she stepped into the warehouse area, she was met with the heavy aroma of fresh-roasted coffee from the processing area next door. The scent filled the air from the three-story-high ceilings to the smooth concrete floor beneath her feet. Though fluorescent lights were lit, the warehouse seemed dark and foreboding, piled high with the lumpish forms of raw coffee beans in burlap sacks.

She shivered. There was a prickling at the back of her neck, a sense that someone was watching her. Clearing her throat, she called out, "Hector? Are you here? Is anybody back here?"

There was a creaking from the wood pallets that were stacked beside the door. Rats? Liz shuddered, but she knew the warehouse was pest-free. Though plain and functional, this processing plant was perfectly sanitized.

From somewhere deep in the bowels of the warehouse, she heard a door slam. A frightened gasp escaped her lips. Her finger tightened on the trigger of her handgun. "Hector?"

"What?" came a response. "Who's there?"

"It's me. Liz."

She heard the sound of footsteps clunking on the concrete floor. Her heart slammed against her rib cage. She could feel herself begin to sweat as the footsteps came closer and closer.

And she saw Hector. His thick-shouldered silhouette appeared from behind a stack of wooden pallets. Though his face was in shadow, she knew that he was staring at her. His black eyes would be cold, hard and angry.

"Took your time, Liz."

"What?" She tried to banish the fear from her voice. But she might be staring into the face of a murderer. She knew the rumors about Hector's past. He'd been a mercenary. He'd been in Vietnam. Surely, he had killed before. He'd been a soldier then. But now? Had he murdered Agatha?

"I called Sarah's around noon," he said. "Told her I would meet with you here."

"I never got that message."

"You went to the office?"

"Yes."

He took a step toward her. "Did you talk to Jack or Gary?"

"No. They weren't there."

He came nearer. Only a few feet from her. His fists were clenched. The warehouse light reflected off his gold necklaces. A muscle in his jaw twitched.

Liz kept her hand in her purse, holding the gun.

"I wish you'd talked to me," Hector said, "before you told that damn bean counter, Gary Gregory, that I haven't been doing my job."

"I never said that."

"Come off it, Liz." He made a swift, slashing motion with his hand. "You told him I've been paying too much for the beans. You've been comparing figures."

"It's true, Hector. You're paying eight to ten percent more."

"You know nothing about this business," he snarled. "Nothing."

"Agatha told me to check your buy prices. To compare them against the buys of our competitors and the other coffee brokers."

"Agatha?" He wrenched his features into a pained grimace. "Never speak to me of Agatha."

Hector reached into his trouser pocket. When his hand emerged, he held a shaft. A button popped. A knife blade snapped out. The dim light shone against sharp steel.

Liz stifled the terrified scream that rose in the back of her throat. Would she have to shoot him? My God, could she do it? Her fingers tensed and trembled. Could she kill this man she'd known for eight years?

He turned away from her, plunged the knife blade into a burlap sack and withdrew a handful of raw coffee beans.

He thrust them toward her. "These are the finest beans in all Colombia. Of course, I pay more. I buy only the best. Agatha would have known that. Agatha would not have questioned my judgment."

He flung the beans to the concrete floor. "And I don't know where you got your figures. Sure, I pay more. Sometimes four percent more. But eight percent? Ten percent? No! It's not that high."

"It's on the computer," she said.

"Then the computer is wrong." His harsh gaze stabbed through her. "You are wrong. You all are. Even Jack. He wants me to buy cheap, not quality. And Gary is the same. Damn them! I miss Agatha. She knew how this business was supposed to run. She understood."

"I'm sorry, Hector."

"You—" He raised his finger, swift as the strike of a rattler. He pointed in her face. "You disappoint me, Liz."

He turned on his heel and paced away from her, disappearing behind the stacks of pallets and bags of coffee beans. She heard the door to the office area open and slam closed. He was gone.

Liz exhaled the breath she hadn't been aware of holding. Her finger twitched convulsively on the trigger. She tried to take a step, but her legs were paralyzed. "Oh, my God."

Now she knew what people meant when they referred to being scared stiff.

The door from the offices swung open. And she jumped. Had Hector come back? Was he going to kill her?

"No," Liz whispered. She wasn't ready to die.

She dropped her purse to the concrete floor, but she still held the gun in her hand. She raised her arm straight in front of her. She sighted down the barrel. "Who's there?"

"Take it easy, partner."

"Dash!" She flew toward him. Her arms circled his neck and she held on tight.

"Are you all right, precious?"

"Don't talk."

Instinctively, she sought his warmth, his reassurance.

When his arms gently embraced her, his nearness comforted her in a way she'd never thought possible. As he held her, Liz felt whole and complete, safer than she'd ever been in her life. Relief swept through her like a cleansing wind, blowing away the fear and easing the tension in her muscles until she felt limp and boneless. Liz doubted that she could even stand up without his support.

Gently, he patted her shoulders and smoothed her hair. "You're okay, Elizabeth. You're going to be okay."

Dash felt her heart hammering against him. The beat was rapid, fluttering. Her fear trembled through him, too. If anything happened to her, he didn't think he could stand it. He cared more for her safety than for his own. Her well-being meant more than all the celestial rules and regulations Angelo could throw at him.

"Hector was here," she whispered. "He left just before you got here. Did you see him?"

"No." Dash had flown. This was the fourth place he'd searched before he saw Liz's little red car in the parking lot. "Did he threaten you?"

"I don't think so. I mean, I don't think he meant to threaten me personally, but he was angry, and he had a switchblade knife."

An angry man brandishing a knife sounded potentially harmful to her health, but Dash didn't comment. Nor did he say a word about the gun in her hand. He was too grateful to find her in one piece.

"You're okay, Liz." He held her by the shoulders and reluctantly moved her away from his body. Her face was pale. But he didn't trust himself to hold her any longer. A prolonged embrace between them could lead to trouble. "You're okay."

"I know." She stood apart from him, swaying slightly. When she lifted her hand to brush her hair from her face, she realized that she still held the gun. Surprised, she stared down the barrel, turned the gun over her in hand.

When she gazed at him, the color had begun to return to her cheeks. "Do you believe this? I had the gun out. I was ready to use it."

Though her wide blue eyes still held the vestiges of fear, her mouth twitched into a smile. "Me! Mousy little me. Liz Carradine, the doormat, the secretary. Don't you get it, Dash? I was ready to shoot Hector."

"Yeah?"

"Just like a real private eye." She threw back her head. Her shoulders straightened. "Damn it, I knew I'd be good at this stuff."

Dash groaned. He wanted to read her the riot act. He wanted to tell her that the fear she'd experienced was nothing compared to real danger, to the sensation of death. But he didn't have the heart to give her a hard time.

Also, judging by the exultant look on her face, he didn't think his warnings would do any good. "Come on, precious. I'll take you home."

They walked through the offices, turning out lights as they went and snapping the automatic locks on the door.

Liz glanced around the asphalt parking lot, which was deserted except for her car. "How did you get here?"

"Does it matter?"

"I'm just curious. I mean, you keep turning up all over town, and you don't have a car. Either you're running up a gigantic bill in taxicabs or you're flying like Superman."

"You guessed it, sweetheart." He grinned. She didn't know how right she was. "Want me to drive?"

"No." She climbed behind the wheel and started her car.

"Why was Hector angry?"

"I needed to compare some figures with him. It looked like he was paying too much for raw beans. But he said he was paying more for better quality."

"Do you believe him?"

"I don't know." She swung her car out of the parking lot and aimed toward the highway. "But Hector was right about one thing. I didn't handle this situation well at all. I should have talked to him first instead of telling Gary."

"Why?"

"I guess Gary and Jack got mad at Hector. They aren't too concerned about quality. Especially not Gary. All he cares about is the bottom line."

Dash noticed, as she merged onto the highway, that Liz was driving faster and with more élan. She had a new sense of confidence that worried him. At the same time, he admired her spirit.

"As soon as I get back to my apartment," she said, "I'm going to write all this down and try to make some sense of it. Right now, I just have a lot of vague impressions."

"About what?"

"When we were looking through those photo albums, it occurred to me that the solution might be somewhere in the past. And now, with the stuff going on in the office—all this fussing about Hector and the beans—there's got to be a connection there." She frowned. "Or maybe not."

Dash leaned back in the passenger seat. "Tell me all about it. I'd like to know the history of these people."

"I'll start with Agatha."

Throughout the drive to Liz's apartment, she spoke of memories. Some good. Some not so good. The picture of Agatha Orben that emerged was one that coincided with Dash's impression. Agatha had been a good woman, dedicated to helping others. But she'd also been a smart businessperson. At times, impatient. At times, demanding.

Liz was still remembering when she parked behind the Victorian mansion where she had her apartment on the third floor. She unlocked the door. They ascended the stairs.

As soon as she opened the door to her apartment and glanced inside at the neat, pleasant decor, her words ceased. Her silence was sudden as a floodgate falling into place to staunch the flow of a river.

"What is it?" Dash asked. His gaze swept the room. It appeared to be perfectly normal.

"Somebody's been in here."

Chapter Nine

To the naked eye of any other observer, Liz's third-floor apartment would appear to be in perfect apple-pie order. But to her? She knew the instant she opened the door that someone had been inside. There were unmistakable signs. The fringe on the area rug was mussed. The miniblinds at the front window were closed.

Angrily, she marched to the south-facing window and placed her briefcase atop her wooden writing desk. The center drawer was not completely shut. The lid on her stationery box had been replaced upside down.

She turned, surveying the room. The magazine on her coffee table was skewed.

An intruder had been there. He'd read her magazine. His hands had flipped through the pages. Disgusted, she stormed across the room and lifted the magazine gingerly by two fingers. Holding the spine away from her, as if the magazine was a foul-smelling piece of garbage, she dumped it in the trash receptacle beneath the kitchen sink.

She spun around to face Dash, who had followed her into the kitchen. "I don't suppose you notice anything, but believe me—"

"I do," he said. "I can sense the presence of someone

else. And believe me, your intruder wasn't here for a friendly chat about recipes.''

Irritated, she rolled her eyes. ''What on earth do you mean? You can sense them?''

''It's a talent I have. A gift.'' He peered into her kitchen trash can and plucked out an aluminum can, which he set on the counter. ''Proof,'' he said.

She eyed him suspiciously. ''How do you know I didn't drink that soda?''

''Maybe you did drink it, but I guarantee that you're not the one who pitched the can into the trash.''

''Why wouldn't I be?''

He tipped his fedora back on his head and gave her a knowing grin. ''Lizzie, you're the type who recycles.''

She would have liked to snap at him, but Dash was right, absolutely right. Liz snatched the can from him. Never would she have thrown a recyclable aluminum can into the trash. But Dash had seemed to know it was there. How? How had he known?

Though she hated to think of Dash being the person who had crept into her apartment, her suspicions were unavoidable. She hadn't seen him all afternoon. After his beeper went off, he'd disappeared. Did he come back here? Did he break into her home?

He walked through the front room and pointed to the desk. ''The intruder was here.''

''Well, that's easy to see.'' Liz came up beside him. ''Look at the lid on my stationery box. The lilacs are upside down.''

''Anything missing?''

''I don't know.''

He strode across the living room and into her bedroom, where he pointed to the dresser. ''The drawers aren't properly aligned.''

"What were they looking for?" She pulled open her top dresser drawer. Her silky underwear and brassieres seemed to be in order, but she imagined the intruder staring at her intimate garments. Perhaps his fingers touched the lace waistband of her panties. As she looked into the drawer, everything seemed soiled.

She tried not to make a big deal about this intrusion. After all, a real private eye would need to be blasé about such things. But Liz was outraged and disgusted. The very idea that someone could sneak in here and handle her things was a loathsome violation of her privacy. She scooped out the contents of the drawer and dumped them in the hamper in the bathroom.

In the front room, indentations in the sofa indicated that someone had been sitting there. The pillows were slightly rumpled. Her imagination conjured up a picture of someone lounging comfortably. A man. A large, un-invited, faceless man sprawled on her sofa. Or perhaps he had a face. And a name.

She confronted Dash. "It wasn't you, was it? You came back here, let yourself in and sneaked around my apartment, didn't you?"

To her surprise, he gave her a respectful nod and a thumbs-up sign. "That's what I like to hear. Now you're thinking like a detective. Everybody's a suspect."

"Did you?"

"Not a chance, sweetheart. If I'd wanted to search the joint, I wouldn't have been so sloppy about it."

She agreed with his logic. "But I don't understand why somebody would come here. It's not much of a search, but were they looking for something?"

"The falcon," he said.

"Bluebird! It's a bluebird!"

"Whatever." He frowned. "But that doesn't make sense. Because I'm the only one who knows about that clue."

"Dammit, Dash! You can't be the only one!" She was nearing the ragged end of her patience. "You've got to be working for somebody. And this person who hired you has to have the information you've uncovered. Right?"

"Calm down, sweetheart. You're getting hysterical."

"Am I? And what does Bogie do when confronted by a hysterical female? Is this the scene where you slap my face and tell me you did it for my own good?"

"I would never strike you."

The seriousness of his statement stemmed the rising tide of her frustration. No matter how eccentric his behavior, she knew that—deep inside—Dash Divine was an honorable man. He would never hurt her.

Contrite but confused, she flung herself across the sofa, erasing the imprint of her intruder. "I'm sorry, Dash. I didn't mean to take it out on you. I'm just so angry."

"It's okay. Now you got the temper out of your system."

If only serenity were that easy. The residual outrage and sense of violation kept her heartbeat accelerated. A tension headache began to clang in the back of her head. "Why?" she questioned. "Why search here? Why would the murderer think I had a clue stashed here in my apartment?"

"He could have been waiting," Dash said. His tone was serious. "Maybe he wasn't looking for a clue. Maybe it was you he wanted."

"Waiting for me to come home by myself." The thought chilled her. If she'd come directly home instead of going to the warehouse, she might have found a cold-blooded killer sitting on her sofa, thumbing through her magazines.

And she recalled the incident in the park, when the jogger dressed in black had followed her, running at her pace, dogging her path. "I have something to tell you," she said. "I should have mentioned this before."

His gaze focused on her. "Go ahead."

"Well, you remember when I called Dr. Clark. And you got so, um, so angry."

"I remember."

"Right after that, I was running in the park, and there was a guy who followed me. He wore one of those baggy black nylon suits and a cap and he stayed back far enough that I couldn't see who it was. Anyway, I usually wouldn't think anything of it. Lots of people jog in the park. But this guy would speed up when I went faster. When I walked, he'd slow down."

"And this was before the dinner party?"

She nodded.

"So, even before we went there and your notebook was stolen from the car, someone might have suspected that you were investigating."

"Possibly." Her headache intensified. She hated to make mistakes, and not telling him might have been a big one. On the other hand, it was altogether possible that the jogger had no significance whatsoever. "I didn't think it was all that important. I might have been imagining—"

"I don't believe in coincidence."

She observed him closely, waiting for the outburst of rage, waiting for him to say that I-told-you-so she probably deserved. Instead, he seemed to be making an effort to control himself. A muscle in his jaw tensed. He reached into his pocket, took out his cigarettes, gazed at the pack longingly and returned it to his pocket. When he looked at her, a flame behind his eyes flared, then stilled.

"All right, sweetheart. You're the P.I., how do you investigate that coincidence?"

"Call Dr. Clark? Find out if he talked to anybody else?"

"Do it."

"But it's after hours on a Friday. How will I—"

"Are you a lady? Or a private dick?"

"There's a contrast for you!"

"This isn't funny, Elizabeth."

"You're right. Of course, you're right." She looked up the number, called the answering service and left a message for Dr. Clark Hammerschmidt to call her back.

In the meantime, Dash examined the edge of her front door, twisted the knob. He explained, "Your intruder picked both locks. You can see the scratches."

The break-in was too easy, she thought. Liz had always assumed that her apartment was fairly secure. But someone had entered and left without much difficulty. She might as well set out a welcome mat. *Pick the lock and come on in.*

"Tell you what, Liz. It's not smart for you to stay here, knowing that the killer can slide right in at any time. But there's a safe house that belongs to my office. It's kind of a distance away from town, but nobody will find you there."

She balked. "How far out of town?"

"Southwest. It's a classy setting near Roxborough Park."

"That's over an hour's drive." She rubbed at her temples, wishing her headache would go away. "I bet you'd like that, wouldn't you? I'd be safely tucked away, and you could investigate on your own."

He shrugged. "You can't stay here."

It was kind of a shame, he thought. He was just getting accustomed to the idea of having a partner, of having Liz as his partner. Still, taking her to the safe house was probably for the best.

"I have another idea," she said.

Her eyes narrowed in that sly but adorable expression that he was beginning to dread. "What?"

"I could move in with you."

Her suggestion knocked him for a loop. "You want to live with me?"

"Just until we catch the murderer. And I'm not hinting that it's condom time, either. We could do it as a strictly business arrangement. I'd pay my share for groceries."

"Actually, precious, I don't think so."

"But it's perfect." She marched into her bedroom, pulled a suitcase from the back of her closet and flipped it open on the bed. "Really, Dash. It's the only logical solution. That way I can still work on the case, but I'll be safely under your protection. So, where's your place?"

In a Logan Street office. On a handy church pew. Up in the galaxies. Angels didn't have places of their own. "You wouldn't like it."

"Don't worry if it's messy," she said, misreading his reluctance. "I understand how it is with bachelors. And if the clutter bothers me, I'll clean up. Otherwise, I can live with a mess."

"You don't understand..." How was he going to explain this?

Fortunately, at that moment, the telephone rang and Liz went to answer.

Dash followed her into the front room in time to hear her say, "Hi, Gary."

From her end of the conversation, he deduced that Gary Gregory wanted to stop by to discuss the situation with Hector. Liz told him that it was convenient and he should come right over.

She hung up the phone and looked at Dash. "Do you think it was Gary who broke in here before? Maybe I should call the police and have them do fingerprints."

"Don't bother," he advised. Though it was sometimes necessary to work with the police, he tried to steer clear whenever possible. It was a pain in the neck to explain who he was, to conjure up a fake driver's license and a fake address. "Whoever was smart enough to pick your lock would be smart enough to wear gloves."

"Good point." She charged into her bedroom and resumed packing. "You stay here in the bedroom while I'm talking to Gary, okay? If he tries anything, you can stop him."

Dash murmured his assent, but his mind was a million miles away. What was he going to do? Being truthful was always the best alternative. He should tell her again that he was an angel, and angels didn't have apartments.

That was the right solution, the smart thing to do. But he didn't want to tell her. He enjoyed having her relate to him as a mortal man. If she knew he was an angel, things would be different.

He touched the beeper in his pocket, half-expecting it to go off so Angelo could inform him that he was screwing up again. But the celestial summons was silent.

Dash was on his own. He needed to make his own decision.

In less time than he expected, the doorbell buzzed and Liz spoke through the intercom to Gary Gregory. Then she turned to him. "Go in the bedroom. Leave the door open a crack so you can hear."

He'd just settled in behind the door when he turned and saw Cherie, lounging on the bed amid Liz's half-completed packing. She batted her long fake eyelashes. "Problem, Dash?"

"You know it, babe."

"Now she wants to move in with you. I'd say you've got a very sticky dilemma on your hands." Her laughter trilled. "Honestly, you two are more fun than a soap opera."

"You could help me out," he said. "I'd make it worth your while."

"How?" Her eyes glistened with an avariciousness that was totally inappropriate for a Guardian Angel.

"You stay here and keep an eye on Liz while I go find myself an apartment."

"And what will you do for me?"

He gritted his teeth. "I'll talk to St. Mike about your potential as an Avenging Angel."

"Done," she said.

With a sigh, Dash turned himself invisible. He and Cherie slipped into the front room to observe Liz's meeting with Gary Gregory.

As soon as the accountant stepped inside, Liz offered him a soda, which he declined. "This isn't a social visit, Liz. You caused a tremendous amount of trouble with those purchase figures you showed me."

"Just doing my job," she said.

He sat on the sofa and popped open his briefcase. The first thing he took out was a yellow legal pad, and Liz felt herself stiffen at the sight of it. Was he going to confront her with her own list of suspects? Was he going to demand an explanation?

She was incredibly glad that Dash was in the bedroom, watching and listening. Even though Liz liked to think she could take care of herself, she didn't mind having backup, and she was confident that Dash wouldn't let anything bad happen to her.

Gary plucked a pen from his pocket protector and flipped through the sheaf of canary yellow pages. "I noticed that when you compiled your data, you only did comparisons for the last three months. Have you gone any further back than that?"

"No, I thought this was enough for a start."

He began removing manila file folders and scattering them around himself. His motions were jerky and stiff, like a chicken scratching for feed. His crest of hair twitched back and forth as he spread out documents on the sofa and coffee table. How convenient, she thought. Gary the birdman had brought his own nesting material with him.

"I talked to Hector," Gary said. "He went berserk, claiming that he's buying quality beans. What price quality, eh?"

"He has a point," Liz said. "And, apparently, Hector didn't realize that he was paying as much over cost as he was. He said it was only about four or five percent. Not eight or ten."

"Hector doesn't have a head for figures." He peered over the edge of his black-framed glasses and raised his eyebrows. "You know I've recommended you for his job. Several times."

"I didn't know that." Immediately, she felt more kindly toward this geeky accountant. "Thank you, Gary."

"In fact, this afternoon, when I finally talked to Jack, I mentioned that you ought to be the buyer."

What an irony! Just when she'd decided to dump OrbenCorp and become a private eye, she might be offered the job she'd always dreamed of. "What did Jack say?"

"He was too annoyed with Hector to respond."

"Typical."

"Jack didn't apologize for destroying my rosebush, either." Gary pulled his upper lip over the lower in that beaky expression, but there was nothing humorous in his look of barely suppressed rage. He was mad about that rosebush, and his features were contorted. He resembled a dark predator, a hawk. "The bastard," he muttered. "He had no call to do that. None at all."

Liz encouraged him to tell her more. "Do you think he's jealous?"

"Oh, yes. Oh, yes. He's envious because I've created a thing of beauty, my blue rose, and he's done nothing."

This guy had a one-track mind. "Actually," she said, "I was thinking that he might be jealous of your relationship with Sarah. You know, that you two are going to be happily married and all that."

"Maybe," he conceded. "I knew he'd be piggy about the house."

"And there's no reason for his possessiveness, especially since the house really doesn't even belong to Sarah. It's going to be a shelter."

He nodded disinterestedly. "I ought to quit right now. Today. That would serve Jack right."

"Why don't you?"

"Well, of course, I need the money. And I feel a loyalty to the memory of Agatha. She hired me and promoted me when no one else would."

"Why not?" Liz sensed that this was very important, that Gary might have a dark secret in his past, maybe even a criminal record that made him unemployable.

"This and that." He shrugged. "Anyway, my loyalty only goes so far, and I've just about run out."

"So you'd quit?"

"I should. I should. If I leave, Jack is in trouble. He's not much of a businessman. If I didn't watch over him every minute, he'd run this company right into the ground." Gary shuffled through his papers. "I seem to have forgotten my copy of the comparison figures. I don't suppose you have yours with you?"

She went to the desk where she'd left her briefcase. After unfastening the snaps, she rifled through the sheaves of papers and shook her head. "No, I left those numbers at the office."

"Oh, well. Then there's not much point in our conversation, is there?" He stood and started picking up the folders he'd scattered in every direction, then he turned to her. "We should get to know each other better, Liz. Maybe I'll take you up on that soda. Better yet, how about a coffee?"

"Sure, I'll perk some up."

When she went into the kitchen, Gary babbled about his care and treatment of the injured rose, and Liz found herself tuning out. How long was the birdman going to hang around?

"...extremely delicate," he said. "When bruised, the petals wither so pathetically. It's..."

He left his position by the sofa and went to her desk. While Dash invisibly observed, Gary opened Liz's briefcase and quickly perused the contents. He continued to talk while he searched.

And Dash wondered. What was he looking for?

Apparently, he didn't find whatever it was because he closed her briefcase and went to the kitchen. "I'm sorry,

Liz, I forgot that I'm supposed to be at Sarah's place in twenty minutes."

"I see." She'd already ground the beans and turned on the coffeemaker. "Well, you can have a rain check on the coffee. I do appreciate that you recommended me for the buyer job, Gary."

"Any time. Any time." In a second, he gathered up his stuff and was gone.

Dash materialized himself in the bedroom and came out through the door.

"Weird," she said. "I wonder what that was all about."

"He's definitely looking for something," Dash said. "But what?"

"I got a sense from him today that I've never had before. I've always dismissed Gary because he looks like a human egret, but today I had the feeling that he could be dangerous as a hawk."

"Good instincts," Dash said.

"And he said that Agatha hired him when no one else would. Is there some way you can check and see if Gary has a criminal record?"

"He doesn't," Dash said. "I did routine checks on all the major suspects as soon as I got started on this case. Apart from the usual traffic violations and divorce litigations, none of the principle suspects have criminal records."

"He might have changed his name," she suggested. "Gary is a computer whiz. There might be some way he's buried his past transgressions."

"Then we may never know," Dash said. But he was thinking of the super computer at the Logan Street office. Angelo was sometimes brilliant at computers. "But I'll see what I can find out."

"Great."

Her phone rang again, and she snatched it off the hook. It was Dr. Clark Hammerschmidt, returning her call. After she'd apologized for being so abrupt the other day, she said, "I just wasn't myself. I hope you didn't mention our conversation to anyone, did you?"

"I was concerned about your well-being," he said. "I could tell that you were terribly upset."

"Oh, you're right. And I'm so embarrassed. So, did you talk to Sarah?"

"To Jack," he admitted.

"I appreciate your caring," she said, then hung up the phone, gritting her teeth and making a mental note to never take a personal medical problem to Dr. Clark.

She looked at Dash and said, "He told Jack. Which means that Jack might have told Hector or Sarah or anybody."

"Why could you assume that?"

"Jack doesn't handle his own problems. If a copy machine in the office is broken, Jack calls a repairman. If he needs help with his golf swing, he makes an appointment with a pro. If he hears that his executive assistant—me!—is having a problem, he would probably punt it to anybody else."

"Bottom line?"

"The jogger might have been Jack. But it could have been anyone else."

"Are you protecting him?"

"No," she protested.

"So you don't have a thing going with the boss man?"

"Absolutely not."

"Good," he murmured. Her vehemence pleased him. "Okay, I'm going, Liz. Get yourself packed and I'll be back for you in an hour."

"One hour. You've got it."

Before he could leave, she called to him, "Dash?"

He swiveled, leaned against the doorjamb. "Yeah?"

"Thank you. I really appreciate being able to stay with you."

"Nothing to it, sweetheart."

"Dash," she called to him again. "I want you to know that you've made a difference in my life. It's good. And I'm grateful. I really... like you. What you're doing for me."

A strange warmth flooded through him. "Sure, okay."

"I mean it. I was always so dull. And now..."

"Elizabeth, you were never dull."

On the landing outside her apartment, he checked with Cherie. "You make sure nothing happens to Liz."

"I'll do the best I can." She pursed her ruby-red lips. "Of course, it would be easier if I could materialize and take on human form. I'm not much use if bad guys bash through the door with guns blazing."

"That's not going to happen. You just stay alert. If you sense danger, put the bug in her ear to get out."

"And where are you going to be?"

"I've got to find a place to live."

INVISIBLY, Dash whisked through several Capitol Hill area apartment buildings, looking for one that was vacant and furnished. After fifteen minutes of searching at the speed of light, he located a likely high-rise at the edge of Cheesman Park. On the tenth floor, there was an attractive apartment with a magnificent view of the mountains. On the main floor bulletin board, there was a notice that the apartment was available for sublet.

He whipped to the Logan Street offices and stood before Angelo's desk. "I need an in-depth analysis on Gary

Gregory. He's a computer genius who might have buried his criminal record.''

''Sounds like fun. I'll get back to you in three hours.''

Dash added, ''I also need a couple thousand dollars.''

''A bit much for petty cash.'' Angelo looked down his nose, enjoying Dash's predicament. ''Why?''

''Housing.'' Dash didn't have time for filing vouchers and forms in triplicate. He'd left Liz alone with only sultry Cherie as a guardian. Until she was safe, he couldn't rid himself of the fear that gnawed his belly.

''We have a safe house available,'' Angelo said. ''This is exactly the type of situation it's to be used for.''

''It won't work for this case.''

''And why not?''

Dash thought for a moment, then he said, ''I know how you feel about your computer, Angelo. Like it's a part of you. Like you're a team.''

''So?''

''That's how Liz is for me. She makes my brain work better and faster. She's helping me.'' Dash longed for a cigarette, but he didn't want to annoy Angelo. ''So that's why I want the cash. So I can keep her around. Please.''

''Please? You're being polite?''

''Guess so.''

''That's how it always is with you guys,'' Angelo nagged. ''Give me this. And give me that. The only time you're marginally civil to me, Dash, is when you want—''

''I don't have to do it this way,'' Dash flared. He was close to losing his temper, but he held back. ''I could conjure up the money, but I'm trying to follow standard procedure here.''

''Lighten up,'' Angelo advised. ''I'll give you what you want, but you have to listen to my advice first.''

In order to control the anger that was building within him, Dash thought of fleecy pink clouds at sunrise. He imagined harp music. He willed the tips of his fingers, which were prickling with the beginning signs of rage, to recall the softness of satin or angora...or the feel of Liz's long, smooth hair. For her sake, he had to calm down.

His voice was reasonably pitched when he said, "All right, Angelo. What would you advise me to do?"

"You're very unusual, Dash. I've never seen another of the avenging angels who had such a clear, unerring sense of right and wrong, combined with a natural skill for investigation." The swarthy angel, who had been sniping with Dash for decades, leaned across his desk. "Here's my advice."

Dash swallowed hard, determined not to be outraged by anything the supervisor said. "I'm ready. Tell me."

"Follow your heart."

Angelo reached into a pocket of his robe and produced a packet of money. "I'll get back to you about Gary Gregory. And where will you be staying?"

Dash gave him the address of the high-rise and sped away, wondering why Angelo had apparently changed his tune from the standard lecture about following rules. This was a kinder, gentler, less punitive message. Something was up. Dash could sense it. Office politics had never been his strong suit, but he could tell things were changing, adapting to the new millennium.

He materialized in the foyer of the high-rise and buzzed the apartment manager's office. He'd only been away from Liz for thirty-six minutes, but he was anxious.

Through etched glass bordering the door, he saw the manager, a tough-looking middle-aged broad, shuffling toward him. Though she was nicely dressed, the woman looked like she carried the weight of the world on her shoulders. She shoved open the heavy oak door. "What?" she demanded in a low, raspy voice.

"The sublet on the tenth floor," he said, pulling the wad of hundred-dollar bills out of his pocket. "I want it for a month."

"Not so fast, buster." But her eyes had popped wide open. Clearly, she was mesmerized by the crisp rustle of fresh money. "I got to get some info on you first."

"Okay, but I'm in a hurry."

Beckoning for him to follow, she dragged her emaciated body across the elegantly decorated, well-lit lobby toward her small office on the first floor. "Everybody's in a hurry," she grumbled. "Geez, you'd think every doggone minute was important."

To Dash, every minute *was* important. Every second away from Liz was like an eternity of worry.

The woman seated herself behind the desk and picked up a clipboard and a pen. Her cordial expression was pleasant enough. "Name?" she asked.

Dash answered with the standard data quickly until she got to the financial section of the form. "Place of employment?"

"DBAA," he said.

"Is that some kind of government job?"

"I'm an investigator," he said, fidgeting in the chair. "I investigate."

Her lower lip jutted in a frown. "How long you been there?"

"Forever," he said. "Over twenty years."

"You don't look that old."

"Looks can be deceiving, sweetheart. Can we fill this out later?"

"Can't give you the key until it's filled out." She looked at the form. "Okay. I need your bank, a major credit card and three references.

Great! He was an angel. He didn't have a bank or a credit card or any of the usual mortal trappings. Though he could conjure up those documents, it took time and effort to make sure all the records matched up. And he didn't have the time.

He pushed the wad of cash across her desk. "There's an extra two hundred for you."

Dash leaned back in his chair. "Do you mind if I smoke?"

Her mouth widened in a huge grin. "You smoke?"

"That's right."

She stood behind the desk. "We smokers got to stick together." She held out her hand. "Welcome, Dash Divine. You got yourself an apartment."

Chapter Ten

When he soared to Liz's street, which was less than three miles from his new apartment, Dash knew that something about him had changed forever. For the first time in his celestial life, he had a place to live, an apartment he could call his own. His own bed. His own bathroom. If he wanted, he could select his own pictures and hang them on the wall.

He felt settled, and therefore uncomfortable. For he was unaccustomed to the burdens of ownership. Until now, he'd been eternally free. An angel's wings gave him flight. His physical form was easily mutated into invisibility. He was not mortal and would live forever. Why, in the name of all that was holy, did he need an apartment?

For Liz. That was the answer that rang within him. He needed a place where Liz would be safe. Because she was of this earth, because she could die, because she could be hurt, he had to protect her.

Dash knew he was doing the right thing in thinking of her personal safety. But it wasn't natural for him. He hated to admit that Angelo might be right, but he felt like he was being domesticated. *Follow your heart.* Yeah? And was that going to lead him down the primrose path toward being a wimp, a wuss? A sensitive, nineties, politically correct whiner?

When he floated down from the clouds and glanced at her window, he saw Cherie give him the all-clear signal, and he breathed more easily. So far, so good. Liz was still safe.

He materialized on her street and reached into the pocket of his trench coat for a cigarette. Liz had asked him to cut down, but he was outside now, and he needed a moment to gather his wits.

If he continued his association with Liz, this was what his life would be—standing outside and smoking because she didn't like the smell of it. Women always wanted to change the men around them. He inhaled deeply. If only she knew how much she would need to change him.

He was so engrossed in his thoughts that, at first, Dash didn't notice the men who were standing across the street, waiting and watching. There were two of them. They were dressed in jeans, similar black jackets and baseball caps. The younger one slouched against the trunk of a tree, staring at the Victorian mansion where Liz lived. The other consulted a street map.

Dash stubbed out his cigarette, stuck his fists in his trench coat pockets and crossed the street toward them. He touched the brim of his fedora. ''You guys look like you could use some help.''

''Get lost,'' said the younger one.

But the other held out his map for Dash to see. In his other hand, he had a scrap of paper with Liz's name and address scribbled on it, then he pointed to the house across the street. ''Is this the place I'm looking for?''

Dash assessed the men quickly. He sensed danger about them, a potential threat. Their lilting Spanish accents brought to mind Hector Messenger and his travels in

South American countries. Why would they be looking for Liz?

The older man puzzled over the two pieces of paper in his hand. "I'm not sure if our address is right."

"Why wouldn't it be?" Dash asked.

"This woman who lives here, she's a secretary. And this is a big house, too magnificent for a mere office worker."

"Call her up," Dash said. "She can tell you if you're at the right place."

"I don't have her number," he said miserably.

"Where'd you get her address?"

"That's what worries me. I got it from this little blonde in her office." He made a twirling motion at his temple. "She was a little bit loco."

The younger man squared off in front of him. "We don't need your help, mister. You ask too many questions."

His partner advised, "Knock it off, kid. He can maybe tell us if this is the right house."

"Look what he's wearing, Jimmy. A suit can't tell us nothing."

Dash hated punks and bullies. This kid was both. Yet there was something familiar about him. "Don't I know you?" he asked.

"I never saw you before in my life."

"All your life? Well, I guess you'd remember," Dash said. "It hasn't been long since you were out of diapers."

"I'm old enough." The kid pulled a blade out of his jacket pocket and held it like a street fighter. "Take a hike, old man."

"Don't believe I will," Dash said. "It's a pleasant evening. I think I'll just stand here and chat with you two gentlemen. Apparently you're new in town."

When the kid made a feint toward him with the blade, Dash reacted. At lightning speed, he grasped the boy's knife hand and squeezed until the blade fell harmlessly to the grass beneath their feet.

"Who sent you?" Dash demanded.

"Not your business."

"I'm making it my business, punk. Now, you tell me who sent you or I'm going to tighten my grip." He exerted more pressure. His fingers were like a vise. "Tell me before I break your wrist."

"Hey!" His partner stepped between them. "There's no call for that. I'm sorry the boy was rude."

"Rude? The punk pulled a knife on me."

"But no harm done. Okay? We'll go. Okay?"

"Too late for that," Dash said. "Tell me who sent you. How do you know Liz Carradine?"

"We're not looking for her. Really. We want her to help us find somebody else. Okay?"

"Who?" Dash demanded.

Through thin lips, the young man said, "Don't tell him."

Dash tightened his grasp. He could feel the wrist bones grind together. The kid's face was pale. His eyes wavered with pain. Dash let him go.

Immediately, the kid dropped to his knees and scrambled to pick up his knife. Clumsily, he gained his feet, made a threatening motion toward Dash.

The older man stopped him. "Enough, Carlito! Let's go."

They ran to a late-model Chevy sedan and tore off down the street. Dash watched them leave. Maybe he should have questioned them further, but he had the answer he wanted.

Carlito. That was the name of Hector's son. The diffident ten-year-old boy in the photographs he'd seen in the attic had grown into a nasty piece of work.

Dash crossed the street and went through the performance of buzzing Liz's apartment and waiting until she let him in.

She met him at the top of the stairs with two suitcases packed. "Let's go, Dash. If I stop and think about what I'm doing, I'll never want to leave."

In minutes, they were in her car and headed toward Dash's new apartment. He glanced over his shoulder and saw Cherie lounging across the back seat. "Nothing happened," she informed Dash. "How come whenever you watch her, there's excitement? When I'm here, it's more quiet than a library at midnight."

"Luck," he said.

"What?" Liz asked, turning to glance at him. "What did you say?"

"Nothing important."

Cherie stretched out on the back seat. "I hope you found a nice place for us."

Dash hoped the same thing.

He fought with the door lock in the foyer of his brand-new high-rise home. Because he'd been in such a frantic rush, he hadn't tried the locks, hadn't even walked through the apartment that was supposed to be his place.

But Liz was impressed. "This is a very nice building, Dash. I didn't expect something so upscale."

"What? You thought I'd live in a dump?"

"Absolutely not. But you have such interesting taste. I expected something more...eclectic."

They rode the elevator to the tenth floor with Cherie providing a running commentary. "High-class building, Dash! I just love these mirrored elevators. Great for checking my stocking seams in the back. Do all the Avengers get apartments like this? I can't wait to be one of you."

Dash opened the apartment door and carried Liz's suitcases inside. There were two bedrooms, and he dropped her stuff in the larger one ''Here we go. Guest bedroom.''

"Very nice," she complimented. In fact, Liz thought, the place was *too* nice. It was more than clean The apartment had an unused atmosphere, like a show home. There were no smudges on the mirrors, no leftover newspapers, no dirty laundry.

In the front room, Dash opened the curtains on a magnificent view of a Rocky Mountain sunset. He swept his arm in a grand gesture. ''How about that? My view. I own that view.''

Liz settled onto the perfect fawn leather sofa 'You don't really live here, do you?''

Dash couldn't lie. It went against his nature. 'You're right, Liz. I rented this joint for a month, just for you.''

"I don't get it." Again, she felt a niggling suspicion about him and his mysterious employer and his apparent knowledge of events before they happened. "How did you know I'd need to leave my apartment?"

"I didn't. While I was gone, I found this place and made the arrangements to take it for a month.''

'You did that in an hour?''

"Am I amazing, or what?''

"Unbelievable," she said. "It seems to me, Dash, that you're involved in this case in a very strange way. You know of a clue that nobody else would know about. You appear and disappear without any visible means of transportation. You won't tell me where you work, won't give me any addresses. What's going on?''

He sat beside her on the sofa. "This is going to take some explaining."

Cherie stood at the door and waved goodbye to him. "Catch you later, big boy. I'm going to check out the rest of this place. Remember this— No lust. Not unless you've figured out how to get away with it."

She was gone.

Liz glared at him. "At least do me the courtesy of looking at me when I'm speaking. Are you working for one of the suspects?"

"No."

"Then who?"

"I'm working for Agatha herself."

"That's not funny, Dash. Don't even joke about it. Agatha is dead."

"Not really," he said. How could he explain the cosmos in a quick, easy lesson? He looked directly into Liz's blue eyes, the mirror to her soul. "Agatha is like me. She's an angel."

"Not that again." Liz bounded to her feet. With anger driving her steps, she paced across the thick beige carpet. "Maybe there really are angels. That's a possibility. But I'm doggoned sure that you're not one of them. You're solid in form. You're a private eye."

"There's a hierarchy," he said. "Rules and regulations for all celestial beings. Here's how it works, sweetheart, I happen to be assigned to the Denver Branch of Avenging Angels."

"Can't you be serious?"

"I've never been more dead serious in my life. Which, being an angel, is an eternity."

"This is ridiculous, and I'm not going to—"

"Be quiet and listen," he said. "Sit."

Reluctantly, she lowered herself into a chair facing the windows.

"I'm telling you straight," he said. "I'm an angel. Now, I'm not going to run through a series of cute miracles to convince you—like dematerializing and reappearing. Either you trust me enough to believe me, or you don't."

"Where are your wings? If you're an angel, you must have wings."

"I fly," he said casually. "That's how I found this apartment so fast. I flew, invisible, through the buildings in this area."

"Oh, Dash! You really can't expect me to believe this!"

"Yeah, Liz. I do."

With all his heart, he wanted her to heed his words and believe in him. If she was ready to accept him as he was, as an angel, there might be hope for honesty between them. And if there was honesty, there might be trust.

He couldn't change. She'd have to accept him as he was.

"An Avenging Angel," she said dubiously. "I thought you guys were supposed to have flaming swords and descend in a rage to whack off the heads of wrongdoers."

"Get with it, precious. We're in the twentieth century, not the Dark Ages. Now we work through the system. Like private investigators."

"Angel private eyes?"

"Here's what happened with Agatha. Just before she died, she realized that she'd been poisoned. And that's when she stashed the clue—a capsule that she hid in the falcon."

"Bluebird," she said.

"Whatever. Anyway, when she got to the heavenly realms, she raised a big stink about being murdered and not having the killer brought to justice. Since she was a woman who devoted her earthly life to good works, she had some pull. On her behalf, St. Michael contacted the Denver offices—"

"St. Michael?" Liz questioned.

"Patron of cops. He's my boss. That's who I work for. Anyway, he assigned me to Agatha's case." He turned his head and looked at her, willing her to accept his sincerity. "I got to admit that this case has been the toughest nut I've ever had to crack. The trail is six months old, and we've got four solid suspects with secrets in their past."

Still, he held her gaze. "And then, there's you."

"What about me?"

"From the first time I laid eyes on you, I thought you were the cutest little cupcake I'd ever seen. And you got spunk. You got fire. You're smart as a whip."

"I see," she said. "And this is a problem?"

"You bet your sweet petunias, it is. I've been having thoughts about you that I have no right to be thinking. I'm an angel. No matter how much I want to, I can't touch you. Lust is one of the seven deadlies." Within his physical shell, he felt his angel heart clench in a painful knot. "I can't let myself fall in love with you, Elizabeth."

"But *I* kissed *you*," she said.

"I was wrong to let that happen."

"Oh, I get it." Liz rose from her chair and stood unsteadily. "This whole elaborate story is a con job. You're trying to tell me that you're not interested in me. That's it, isn't it?"

"You got me wrong."

"Well, I've got to give you credit, Dash. This is the most creative excuse I've ever heard for not having a relationship. You're an angel? Oh, please. It would be a whole lot easier if you were honest and just said that you didn't want to get involved." She trembled. She clutched her hands together. "And what makes you think I'm even interested in a relationship?"

"Are you?"

She shook her head so furiously that her hair whipped across her face.

There was a tap at the door, and Dash went to answer.

Angelo stood there. He'd abandoned his angelic robes for an elegant Armani suit, tailored to flatter his girth. He strolled inside and went to Liz.

"Good afternoon. You must be Elizabeth Carradine." He tapped his chest proudly. "I'm Angelo."

"Oh, great! Not another one! I suppose you also work at the Denver Branch of Avenging Angels."

"As a matter of act, I do. Although I don't usually admit to it. Most people are so disbelieving."

"Really," she said. "I can't imagine why."

He turned to Dash. "I have information for you on Gary Gregory. I suspect that he might have altered computer records and created his current identity with an alias, but he did a thorough job of it, and I may never find the truth."

"If you're an angel," Liz said, "don't you just know the truth?"

"In this situation, I have to work through the mortal systems. There is, however, some indication of wrongdoing in Gary's past. But it's vague."

"What do you mean?" she asked.

"Let me put it this way," Dash explained. "If St. Pete was still keeping the records, there'd be a black mark by Gary's name."

"Good metaphor," Angelo congratulated him.

"So, what else did you get on Gary?"

"He used to work for an insurance company, and that's the same company he used to finance key-man insurance for Jack Orben and Hector Messenger. He might be taking a kickback."

"Or he might be passing on business to friends. There's nothing wrong with that."

"True," Angelo concurred. "Also while at the insurance company, Gary supervised malpractice insurance for Dr. Clark Hammerschmidt. In a particularly ugly case, he defended the doctor. Hammerschmidt owes him a favor."

Dash nodded. "So Hammerschmidt might have been working a cover-up for Gary while he poisoned Agatha."

"Or," Angelo said, "Dr. Clark Hammerschmidt might simply be incompetent. Actually, that's rather more likely. The doctor is essentially a good person with an unfortunate penchant for gossip."

"Thanks, pal. I appreciate your help."

"No problem."

Cherie chose this moment to drift lazily into the room, and Angelo perked up the moment he saw her.

She sidled over to him and introduced herself. "I'm a Guardian right now, but I'd be a great Avenger."

"Perhaps," Angelo responded. "We should talk."

He nodded to Liz and headed toward the door where he whispered to Dash, "Remember the advice I gave you in the office."

Follow your heart. But what did that mean? His heart told him to submit to the warm, protective feelings that arose when he looked at Liz. His heart told him that he could care for her in the way a mortal man cares for a woman. His heart wanted him to join with her, to make love to her.

Surely Angelo couldn't be condoning that unangellike behavior. Maybe he was hinting that Dash wasn't cut out to be an avenging angel, after all. This might be a setup. Angelo might have plans to get Dash reassigned.

But that couldn't be! Angelo, though sometimes an annoying stickler for the rules, was as honest as the day was long. Angelo wasn't capable of such devious behavior.

Dash turned to Liz, who perched uneasily on the edge of her chair. As he approached her, she jumped to her feet. "I need some time to think. I'll go to my bedroom now. Please leave me alone."

She closed the door and turned on the overhead light. An angel? Now they had come full cycle, she thought. Just when she was thinking that she could trust him as a private eye, he once again claimed to be an angel. It was a crazy story, and she didn't understand why he wanted to revisit that lunacy.

Liz wasn't gullible. If anything, she'd grown less likely to believe in fairy tales. *That's what this was—a fairy tale.* And a convenient excuse to avoid a relationship.

She unpacked in the clean, sterile apartment and stretched out on the perfectly unwrinkled bedspread. How did he happen to find this place? Did it belong to his office?

That had to be it. The apartment was another version of the safe house he'd talked about. And Angelo, who was at least as crazy as Dash, must be a co-worker.

Though Liz hadn't planned to fall asleep so early, she made the mistake of closing her eyes. Before she faded into unconsciousness, she imagined that she heard Dash's voice. He said, "Sleep well, precious."

And she felt a breeze, though the windows and curtains were closed. The balmy gust of wind, like a breath, lingered on her lips, then glided down her body.

Contentment spread through her, and she slumbered.

HER SLEEP was undisturbed, and she didn't waken until nine o'clock. Being an inveterate morning person, her spirits were renewed by rest, and everything looked better. So what if Dash wanted to pretend he was an angel? His excuses and delusions were unimportant. All that mattered was finding out who had killed Agatha.

She whipped into the hall and went into the bathroom to shower and change. Today was Saturday, so there was no need to report to OrbenCorp headquarters. However, she thought, it was a perfect day to sneak inside the offices and search.

As she stepped into the shower, her mind was active. Since Agatha's bluebird figurine had not been stored in the attic, there were two other places to search—the warehouse facility, where company records were stashed, and the OrbenCorp headquarters, where there was some storage space available. Though it was unlikely that Agatha's personal effects had been taken to either place, Sarah had mentioned records she'd cleared out of the house. The bluebird might have accidentally been packed with those.

All clean and ready to go, she strolled into the kitchen and found a pot of coffee already perked. But Dash was nowhere in sight.

Liz poured a cup and checked the refrigerator, which was mostly empty. There were, however, bagels. She toasted one, spread on cream cheese and strawberry jam and settled at the kitchen table to eat.

He strolled inside from the balcony. His long-sleeved shirt was rolled up at the wrists and his trousers were loose-fitting. No fedora, of course. This was the most casual attire she'd seen him wear, and she liked the look. He seemed less weird and more accessible. "Good morning, Dash."

His brown eyes were warm as the rising sun when he gazed at her. "Good morning."

"How's the weather outside?"

"Crisp." When he grinned broadly and chuckled, he looked about twenty years old. "I can't believe this. I rested in my own bed last night. I got up and here you are."

"Is that such a huge surprise?"

"Yeah, sweetheart, it is. Angels don't have homes. Usually, I just float."

"Well, let's not dwell on it, shall we? I'd like to proceed in solving the crime so we can both get back to our lives."

"You bet. Soon as you're ready we can visit Sister Muriel. I want to get the inside dope on Sarah and the house."

"Right," she said. "Sarah's only motive for murdering Agatha would be to inherit. However, if she's serious about turning the house over to the shelter, she'd know she wouldn't really inherit and would, therefore, have no motive."

"You got it, Liz." His smile was gentle and warm as a caress. "You're starting to think like me."

"I guess that makes both of us into good private detectives," she said. "Detectives, not angels."

"Still don't trust me?"

"Let's just say that I'm too old for fairy tales."

She grabbed a lightweight jacket and joined him in the front room where he had once again donned his patented Sam Spade trench coat.

They took her car, and Dash gave directions to the shelter where Sister Muriel currently worked. She came to the door when they inquired for her, and she stepped out on the wide veranda. Her smile at Dash was positively radiant. "I hope you don't mind staying out here. Many of our ladies are uncomfortable around men."

"I understand." Nothing infuriated his sense of justice more than the idea that there were strong men who would beat women and children. He would do anything to lighten the burden of the people who found a safe haven here.

Sister Muriel led them to a grouping of wooden outdoor furniture. "Now," she said, "how can I help you?"

Anxious to practice her interrogation skills, Liz answered, "We had a few questions about Sarah Orben Pachen."

"Yes?"

"Have you found her to be . . ." How to say this without explaining the whole murder scenario? "Difficult to work with?" Liz concluded. "Do you think she's in favor of the shelter or trying to block it?"

"Most definitely in favor." She cast a puzzled glance at Dash. "I thought you knew."

"No," he said.

"Then you didn't come here to offer comfort and solace to poor Sarah. I thought you were . . ."

"I am," he said. "But Agatha is my mission. Her death."

"Oh, dear. That doesn't sound good."

"I've come to avenge her death," he said.

"Dear me." Her voice was shocked, but her eyes twinkled behind her wire-rimmed glasses. "The world is changing so very quickly, it's hard to keep up. I never thought I'd see someone like you, Dash, with someone like you, Liz."

"What does that mean?" Liz asked.

"I think you make a perfectly lovely couple, but you're awfully different. Liz, you're a mortal woman. And, of course, Dash is . . ."

"Is what?" Liz demanded. "Dash is what?"

"Let's just say that as a human being, he's an imposter."

"Can we get back to Sarah?" Liz asked.

"Oh, yes, poor Sarah. She's determined to fulfill the terms of Agatha's will. And, of course, she has every reason to be sympathetic to our cause."

"Why's that?" Liz asked.

"Sarah was abused by her ex-husband. Rather badly so, but she seems to be healing." Sister Muriel frowned. "I hope I'm not talking out of turn."

"No, Sister," Dash said. "You've been most helpful. I'm grateful."

"Put in a good word for me," she said, rising to her feet.

On the way to the car, Liz shook her head. "She's nice, the sister. But definitely on a different wavelength. What did she mean, put in a good word? With whom?"

"A good woman," Dash said. "After all she's done, Sister Muriel is entitled to be a little eccentric."

"And I guess you're the expert on eccentricity."

He climbed into the passenger seat. "What's next? You got any ideas?"

"More searching. I can only think of two other places where the bluebird statue might be stashed away. The OrbenCorp headquarters. And the warehouse."

"Okay," Dash said. "Let's go."

Liz parked in the garage under the office building and they took the elevator to the fourteenth floor. On a weekend, the skyscraper, honeycombed with offices, had a deserted air. Their voices seemed to echo even in the elevator.

"The keys to everything are kept in the receptionist's desk, but I can get in there," Liz said. "After we check the storage area, we can make a thorough office-by-office search. Remember that Sarah said she'd given mementos of Agatha. One of the employees might have wanted the bluebird."

"The falcon," he said.

"Whatever."

But when she tried to fit her keys into the locked office door on the fourteenth floor, it was unnecessary. The door was already open. "Strange," Liz said. "I hope nobody else is here."

Inside, the office was dimly lit. The only illumination came from an inner office door that stood open. It was Liz's office. She reached into her purse and wrapped her fingers around the handle of her gun.

Dash went ahead of her, pushing the door wide. "Call the police," he said. "And let's get out of here."

"What is it?"

"You don't need to see."

She pushed around him. This was her office, dammit. She needed to know what had happened in here.

There was chaos in her narrow cubicle. File drawers were flung open. Manila folders and their contents were scattered on the floor and across her desk. In the midst of the clutter, she saw Jack Orben. He was facedown, lying motionless in a drying puddle of dark red blood.

Chapter Eleven

Liz closed her eyes. She heard a harsh ringing in her ears. Her mouth had that awful metallic taste of nausea. She felt like she might pass out, and she prayed that when she opened her eyes again, she would not see the blood.

As if from a distance, she heard Dash say that Jack had been shot. She heard Dash say that Jack was dead.

There was no escaping the facts.

When she looked down at Jack Orben, her boss for ten years and her sometime friend, she felt a cold revulsion. He was dead. All the breath had left his body. His skin would be clammy. His blood would be gelid. She probably ought to be weeping and mourning, but ice had formed at her nerve endings, numbing the sorrow.

This shell wasn't Jack anymore. Whatever he had been, the essence of Jack Orben, was departed. He was gone, vanished. His spirit had fled.

Liz placed her hand on her breast to feel the beating of her heart, a slow and heavy rhythm. Her vital pulse made a mockery of death. The real horror in this office was that Jack Orben had died too soon. He had been murdered.

And that fact made Elizabeth Carradine mad.

In a flash, the ice melted and poured from her like the

spring runoff from the mountains west of town. She shook herself. Tingling, she felt the stirrings of rage.

Unbidden, Dash took her hand and held it. His anger, identical to her own, joined with hers. Together, they communicated without speaking. Murder, the stealing of a life force, was unjust. The killer must be called to reckoning.

She turned to him. His elemental fury matched her own. "The person who murdered Jack also killed Agatha."

"Yes," he said.

"We've got to find them." She gripped his hand. His fingers, hot as fire, knitted with hers. "We've got to prove it."

"We will," he said.

And she believed him. His voice resonated with conviction. He knew what had to be done, and he would accomplish it.

He looked down at the body. "You never get used to this. To the injustice. I've seen battlefields where hundreds of young men were dead and dying. Victims. Lives cut short by violence. It never becomes easier to face the horror... and the rage."

"I feel it," she said.

He released her hand. "We should leave now. We can call the police from another phone."

"That's not the way it's done, is it? Aren't we supposed to wait for the police?"

Logically, he pointed out, "There's nothing we can do here. Jack is already dead."

"But it's not right to place an anonymous phone call and leave. Besides, the police will want to talk to you. They'll find your fingerprints here."

"Liz, I'm an angel. I don't leave fingerprints."

"Oh, I see," she said. With sarcasm, she disguised the deeper emotions that churned inside her. "And I don't suppose you have any identification papers, either. Being an angel must be difficult to explain to the cops."

"It is."

His tone and his expression were so serious that she almost believed him. Almost, but not quite. Liz was determined not to be sidetracked by any nonsense from Dash. And it seemed to her that every time he was confronted by a difficult human situation, he called up his angel excuse, like a rabbit out of a hat. What a bizarre ruse!

But that was his problem. If she was going to change her life, if she was going to move from being an executive secretary to a private eye, she couldn't run from the tough decisions. She needed to be solid, rational. Even now, even when she had been confronted—for the first time in her life—by terminal violence, she could not take refuge in tears or a fluttering heart, or turn to Dash and plead for him to handle the bad part of the investigation.

And this was the bad part. Jack Orben lay dead on the floor in her office. Could it get any worse? She took one long step away from Dash, flattening her back against a file cabinet. "I'm not ready to go yet. There must be a clue in this . . . what do you call it?"

"Scene of the crime."

"Right.

Fighting for detachment, she began to visualize a scenario. "Suppose Jack came into the office and surprised someone, a person who was searching through the files in my office."

"The same person who searched your apartment," he said.

"Perhaps."

"When Gary was in your apartment," Dash confided, "the little wimp conned you into leaving the room, going into the kitchen to make coffee. While you were gone, he shuffled through your briefcase."

"Why would Gary be looking for anything in here?"

"Beats me."

Carefully, she stepped around the body of Jack Orben and opened a file drawer. A handful of files had been yanked out, apparently scattered on the floor. In a glance, Liz knew what had been disturbed. "One of these files had Hector's price comparisons."

"Gary had no reason to take that," Dash said.

"Definitely not. Gary had a copy."

"And Hector?"

"I don't know why he'd take that file, either," she said. "The figures are on the computer. There's a record of the checks that have been cut and sent to the growers in South America. There's no reason for him to take my notes."

"But suppose Hector was in here, looking for the document so he would be prepared to defend himself. Jack surprised him. They fought. Jack was killed."

"That sounds as likely as anything else." She reached for the telephone on her desk. "I'm going to call the police. I'll stay here and deal with them."

"All right, sweetheart. If you insist. When you're done, come directly to the apartment."

"I will." She was a bit annoyed that he wasn't going to go through the police questioning with her. On the other hand, she needed to experience the official side of an investigation by herself. "And what are you going to do?"

"Search," he said. "For Hector Messenger. For the missing pieces to this puzzle. For the falcon."

"Bluebird," she said.

"Whatever."

FOUR HOURS LATER, an exhausted Liz rode up in the elevator to the sterile high-rise apartment Dash had tried to pass off as his own place.

Dash held the door open for her as she stumbled inside, making a beeline for the sofa where she collapsed. Her entire body felt limp, completely wrung out.

"You were right," she said. "Dealing with the police was horrendous. They kept asking me the same questions, over and over. They wanted to know where I was yesterday and last night and today."

"I know," he said. "They called here to verify that you were with me."

"I couldn't believe it! They considered me to be a suspect because he was murdered in my office."

"That's how it goes, precious. The person who finds the body is usually the person who put it there."

"But what a waste of time! They're going to be questioning everybody from OrbenCorp. In the meantime, Jack's murder is going to hit the newspapers and local television news."

"So what? A brief mention on page twenty-seven."

"Hardly that. Jack Orben was a big deal in town. He belonged to all the right clubs. He swung with all the right swingers. There's going to be a lot of sleazy publicity." She groaned. "I'm so glad to be hidden in this apartment. Nobody knows where I am."

"Nobody," he confirmed. "You take it easy, now. There's no place else you've got to go today. Nothing else you've got to do."

"You know what's really strange? I lied to the police. Before I got involved with this, I never even had a speeding ticket, and I sat there with a completely straight face and told the detective that I'd come into the office alone. I didn't mention you."

"If it made you feel bad, you didn't have to protect me. I can handle the cops."

"Well, excuse me, but I thought it would be easier to tell a little white lie than to fire off one of those angel stories." She fluttered her eyelashes and launched into a perfect ditz impersonation. "Like, you see, Officer, my friend Dash, like, he couldn't hang around for you. But, like, wow, you don't have to worry, 'cause he's an angel, and, like, he had to fly."

"Cute," he said.

"Not really. Not at all," she grumbled. "Did you find Hector?"

He shook his head. "He's not at his house. I asked the kid who takes care of his yard if Hector's been around, and he said he hadn't seen him since yesterday."

"He did it. Hector killed Jack," she said, pushing her hair off her forehead and staring at the ceiling. "I have it all figured out."

Dash leaned against the back of the chair and watched her as she slowly opened and closed her eyes. She stretched like a cat and sighed.

He knew she'd had a rough time with the police because he had been there, invisible in the offices while the interrogations had been going on. He knew that she'd been shaken, and he'd witnessed the moment of her transformation when she went from nervous to solid. At that moment, when she faced the cops and straightened her shoulders and answered their questions without the slightest quaver in her voice, he'd been endlessly proud of her.

And now, alone with her, he enjoyed watching her, having her with him at the end of a day. Usually, he would be alone, thinking. Sharing the case with her made all the difference.

"I like this," he said. "This talking back and forth. It kind of reminds me of what home life is supposed to be."

"Chitchat about murders?" She raised her eyebrows. "Instead of asking how was your day at the office, you'd ask about the police interrogation?"

"I like it," he repeated.

"What kind of home did you grow up in, anyway?"

Still, in a way, she agreed. When she was with him, she felt comforted and more secure. She liked it, too. To be perfectly honest, a predinner discussion of their progress on the murder case was far more appealing than the standard evening discussions her parents had about work at the office and trips to the grocery store and shopping for school supplies.

"Spill it," he said. "How come you think Hector's our murderer?"

"Here's my theory. He killed Agatha and Jack because he was taking some kind of payoff from the South American coffee bean growers. As soon as he knew we were going to find out, he took off. And now he's out of here. It's my guess that he's already left the country, could be anywhere in the world. We'll never find him."

"I don't think he's flown the coop," Dash said. "I've got a sense that he's still in town."

"You and your senses," she muttered. "We need facts, Dash."

"Here's a fact for you. Yesterday, outside your place, I ran into Hector's son, Carlito."

"Little Carlito? Do you remember that photo we saw in Agatha's attic? He was such an adorable boy."

"He's not so cute anymore."

"Why didn't you tell me?"

He shrugged. "I guess I didn't think of it. I forgot."

Though Dash had meant to share all his information with her, he still wasn't accustomed to reporting to anyone, not even a potential partner. He'd been a loner for a very long time, and change was hard. Keeping someone else in the picture didn't come naturally.

"What happened?" she asked.

"He and another guy were checking out your house. I think because they wanted to ask questions about Hector. And Carlito pulled a knife and—"

"A knife? Excuse me, Dash, but how could you forget a knife fight?"

"Nobody got hurt."

"This is going to stop right now." She tried to gesture emphatically, but she was so pooped that her hand flopped back on the sofa. "You are not to go anywhere or do anything without me. Understand?"

"And vice versa?"

"Right." She bobbed her head and yawned. "I'm so tired."

"You want dinner? I got Chinese, and I can zap it in the microwave."

"Maybe if I eat something I'll feel better. I'd like to make a run out to Sarah's tonight. I talked to her on the phone for a sec, but I'd like to see her before the news hits that Jack has been murdered and she's deluged with news media weirdos."

With groaning effort, she hauled herself off the sofa and over to the kitchen table where she plunked down in a chair. "Poor Sarah. This is her second close relative to die within a year. I feel so awful for her."

"What about you?" Dash said. "Agatha was your friend. Jack was your boss. I'm no kind of shrink, but I'd guess you're feeling some pain."

Her eyebrows knotted in a frown. "Right now, I'm so angry about the injustice of the whole thing that I can't feel anything. Maybe later." Softly, she added, "Maybe later, I'll cry."

Dash knew that she wouldn't call her attitude courage. But that's what it was. She was brave and tough. And he wanted more than anything to hold her close and give her his strength while she shed her tears.

She sat a little straighter in the chair. "At least planning the funeral won't be too overwhelming for Sarah. Jack had the arrangements made when he took out that key-man insurance policy."

"With Gary Gregory's friends," Dash said as he stacked food in the microwave. "How much was the policy for?"

"Two million dollars," she said. "It flattered Jack's vanity to think he was worth that much."

"And who gets the money? Sarah?"

"Sarah isn't a suspect anymore." She glared at him. "Remember? This morning with Sister Muriel? Sarah had nothing to gain because she's going to turn the house over to the shelter. Remember, Sarah was a battered wife."

"Therefore, innocent?" If only it was that easy, Dash thought. Unfortunately, being a victim didn't guarantee that you would never commit a crime—unless, of course, you fell under the jurisdiction of the Los Angeles Branch of Avenging Angels.

"Besides," Liz said, "Sarah doesn't get the insurance money. It goes into the company."

The microwave dinged, and he laid out a spread of half a dozen white cartons of Chinese food. "So? Who gets the company?"

"I'm not sure. Jack's stock shares are probably going to be parceled out. We'll have to ask Gary."

She dug into the cartons and loaded her plate while he sat back and watched. Again, he thought this was pleasant and comfortable. He liked being able to share dinner with Liz.

A voice in the back of his head warned that sharing— on a regular basis—might get real old, real fast. If dinner was a night-after-night affair, he might learn to dread it.

"When do you think they'll have the forensics workup on Jack's body?" she asked.

Dash felt a slow grin spread across his face. Her question wasn't the standard fare. Dinner with her would never be dull. "A coroner's report? They need to do the autopsy. And there's ballistics because he was shot. I'd guess Monday or Tuesday."

"I was just wondering," she said, "because the police confiscated my handgun. It seems I don't have a permit for carrying a concealed weapon."

Though he'd been there, watching over her, he asked, "They're not going to charge you, are they?"

"No, but they were very interested in knowing why I felt I had to take a handgun to the office. It was dumb of me to let them see it. But I started crying, and I dug into my purse to get a hanky, and there was my gun. Right there, in the middle of a murder investigation."

He nodded. It was pretty much amazing that the cops had let her go without filing major charges. "I'm surprised you're not in cuffs."

"I'm a fast talker."

"Yes, you are." He smiled again. The pleasure he felt in her company sank deep within him.

"I told the officers how scary it was—being a woman alone and all. And they bought it. Actually, they were fairly nice about the whole thing." She spoke with incredible sweetness for a woman who had just come face-to-face with her first murder victim and her first grilling from the cops. "And, you know, I'm lucky as sin that they didn't want to see those yellow pieces of paper I've been keeping my notes on. Those were in my purse, too."

"But not anymore?"

"On my way home, I tore them up into tiny pieces and tossed them in a trash can."

"Why? I thought that was your organization?"

"Too dangerous to carry that stuff around." She tapped her forehead. "It's all up here."

He preferred that method himself, but he didn't agree that all of her skill was in her head. It was also in her bright blue eyes that were so adept at observation, in her quick hands and in her warm heart, where she knew intuitively what was right and what was wrong.

She was made for this kind of work, he thought. She was made to be the perfect other half for him.

"Aren't you eating?" she asked. "Don't angels eat?"

"We don't need to," he said. "It's a pleasure, and I eat sometimes because I like the taste."

"Like smoking?"

"Same deal, precious. Angels aren't affected by time or disease or aging or bodily needs. Our physical forms are always the same, always perfectly functioning."

"You never gain weight?" She shoveled a forkful of chow mein into her mouth. "Never catch a cold?"

"That's why they call it heaven."

After she finished her dinner and splashed cold water on her face, Liz claimed to be ready for more action. "Sarah's place?" she said.

Being a detective was one thing, but he noticed how her eyelids drooped. Her posture was slouching instead of her usual shoulders-thrown-back pose. "Not tonight," he said firmly. "You need some rest."

"No, I'm fine. I've read enough crime novels to know that the best leads are found within the first forty-eight hours after a crime is committed."

"Tomorrow is soon enough. We can visit Sarah and, if you're up for the real boredom of detective work, we'll stake out Hector's house."

She eyed him suspiciously. "You're not just saying that, are you? You're not going to put me to bed, then go flitting off to do your own investigating?"

"No," he said. "Now that the police are involved, everything is complicated. As you pointed out, the coppers are going to be doing their own interviews and stakeouts. There's no need for us to bump heads with them at every corner." Dash had been through enough murder investigations to know better. "It's best if we leave them a clear playing field."

"But we could do it better," she said.

"You bet we could. And that's not because we're so slick," he said. "We've got the inside track on information."

"You mean Agatha?"

"That's right, Agatha the angel. You hit it right on the nose."

"Oh, Dash," she said with a heavy sigh. "When are you going to back off on this angel story?"

"Wish I could, sweetheart."

For the first time in his remembered existence, he envied mortal men. If he was mortal, she'd believe him. She'd trust him. If he was mortal, he would have no hesitation in founding a relationship with her, maybe making love to her. That thought was so delicious that he savored it for a moment. Making love to Elizabeth. Heaven took many forms, he thought, and this would be one of them.

"All right, Dash. You might as well tell me about it," she said as she headed toward the leather couch and stretched out on the cushions. "Have you been an angel for all eternity?"

"Only since the 1930s." He took the chair opposite the sofa and stretched out his legs to rest his heels on the coffee table. "I was an angel before that, but I wasn't assigned to the Avenging branch. There were a bunch of choirs and harps and tasks. I don't remember it very well."

"So, you've been a private eye since the 1930s." She grinned at the ceiling. "That's why you act like Bogart. His Sam Spade was the quintessential private eye of the time."

"I liked his style," Dash admitted. "Sam Spade was cool and smart and he always knew right from wrong. He wasn't scared to make the tough decisions, even when he knew it would hurt."

"Like you," she said.

"And you, sweetheart. You've got the instincts."

"Really?" She brightened. "Do you really think I've got a talent for being a private investigator?"

"I hate to say it, but yes. There's some skills you could brush up on. For instance, I've never seen you fire that gun you were dragging around. And your interview technique could use some polish. But you've got it, Liz. You understand justice."

"So I could do this work," she said. "Liz Carradine, private eye. Dash, you've got to recommend me at your offices."

"I already have. The boss—" he decided not to mention that the boss was St. Michael "—he actually looked as if he was considering the possibility."

"Then I've got a new career, the kind of job I've always wanted, something with excitement and adventure. Could I always work with you?"

"Count on it."

She lay back on the sofa and stared at the ceiling. "But there's this whole angel thing, isn't there? I mean, does everybody at your office think they're angels? Is that a job requirement?"

"Used to be. But things change."

"Let's have it, Dash. Get all this angelic weirdness out on the table."

"At my office, on Logan Street, the boss is always looking for good operatives. And he hasn't had much luck in recruiting from the ranks of the angels. They don't have an edge, if you know what I mean. Or they want to be Avengers for personal reasons." He thought of Cherie and her desire to take on solid form. "A lot of Guardian Angels think they can do this, but they can't."

"Guardian Angels?" She frowned. "So there are Guardian Angels, too?"

"And Ministering Angels, who work a lot in hospitals. And Cherubs. And Choirs. And Scholars who do inspiring. The heavenly host, you know. They're usually around when you need them."

"Strange that I've never seen one before you."

"Invisible," he explained.

"Let me have the whole story. I'm in the mood for a fairy tale."

During the next few hours, he told her what he knew about the ancient hierarchy of the angelic realms, the rules and regulations about sin, the limitations and the freedoms. Like flight. It was hard to put the sensation of flying into words, and while he talked, Dash realized that he could never give that up.

He needed to stay an angel. It suited him. It fulfilled his nature. But if he stayed an angel, could he stay with Liz? How could he give her up? And how could he stop being who he was?

"Now," she said, "tell me about yourself. What have you been doing since the 1930s when you decided to become as cool as Bogie?"

"You're tired, precious. You ought to go to bed."

"I want to hear. I'll try to stay awake."

But she lost the battle. He was barely through his war stories when her eyelids clamped shut.

He fell silent, watching her as she slept. The emotions that rose in his chest were almost painful in their intensity. He admired her courage and intelligence, and he adored the way she looked with her long brown hair spilling over her face. She was a beauty, all right. The curve of her slender waist entranced him. He liked her small, neat hands. And those legs! She had the longest, most graceful stems he'd ever seen.

He moved nearer to her, hovering above her. His mouth poised above hers, close enough to feel the warmth of her breath. Dash was so drawn to her that he could scarcely hold back. He longed to make love to her, to give her the most exquisite pleasure a man can give to a woman.

He had no right! If he touched her, if he had sex with her, the heavens would surely open and he'd be snatched into terrible retribution. But how could these emotions be wrong when they felt so right?

Caught on the prongs of a moral dilemma, he needed to go deep within himself to find the answers.

Gently, he scooped her up in his arms and carried her to the bedroom.

Still sleeping, she instinctively snuggled against his chest, and he groaned with his desire for her, for her happiness. And for his own.

When he stretched her out on the bed, he considered undressing her so she would be more comfortable as she slept. Immediately, he abandoned the idea. That temptation would be too much for him. He removed only her shoes, then gently covered her.

For most of the night, he stayed beside the bed, watching her sleep and wondering what would become of them.

Chapter Twelve

It was Sunday, usually Dash's favorite day of the week. Though the rules and regulations did not strictly require a day of rest, he liked to observe that idea, taking off one day for quiet contemplation. Usually on a Sunday he would fly, invisible, to several churches and listen to the choirs singing. Corny though it was, he enjoyed organ music, especially when the choir director threw out all the stops and blasted the music to the heavens.

He and Liz took a long stroll, passing several churches, and she asked one of those deep theological questions that had tortured humanity forever. "So, Dash, if you're really an angel, tell me a secret. Which religion is on the fast track to heaven?"

"I don't know."

"How can you not know?"

"I'm an Avenging Angel, Liz. A fighter. A warrior. All those decisions about the weight of sin are better left to the bureaucrats, the pencil pushers and the bean counters."

She laughed, and the sound of her laughter was sweeter to him than the combined singing of a dozen celestial choirs. "Are you telling me that there's a division of angels who do nothing but keep track of us mortals and tally up when we're dead to decide what's going to happen next?''

''It's computerized, I think. But I don't have anything to do with that.''

''You're crazy, Dash. But, God help me, I'm beginning to enjoy your craziness.''

When she easily looped her arm through his, he had to concentrate mightily to keep his desire for her at bay. When his arm brushed the side of her breast, he could feel a heavy excitement building within him. He patted her hand and disentangled himself from her grasp. ''I can't do this.''

''Can't do what? Hold hands?''

''If I touch you, I feel like I'm going to lose it, precious. My will is strong, but not that strong.''

''Well, all right. If you're going to be that way, let's get back to the case.'' A tiny frown tugged the corners of her lips. ''Or is there some kind of angelic restriction about working on Sunday?''

''It's not a hard and fast rule.''

''Lucky for us,'' she said wryly. ''Let's head out to Sarah's. If nothing else, I want to offer her my support in dealing with Jack's murder.''

When Liz parked her little red Honda on the street outside the house that had once belonged to Agatha, she was the fourth car on the street, not counting the three television news team vans. Members of the press and camera crews stood in clusters, talking among themselves. ''Must be a slow news day,'' she muttered. ''How are we going to get past this mob? It'll take a minor miracle.''

''No problem. Minor miracles are my business,'' Dash said. ''Let's go.''

"What do you mean, let's go? Do you think we can just stroll through these people? If they're hovering around Sarah like this, they're surely going to want to ask me questions. I'm the person who found Jack's body."

"Nobody will bother you," he said.

"And why not?"

He grinned broadly. "You're invisible."

"Oh, sure."

He came around to her side of the car and opened the door for her. "Stick close to me, precious."

Though she didn't believe for a minute that they had actually dematerialized, she couldn't explain how they were able to stroll casually past the several people who were drinking coffee in convenience store cups and chatting among themselves.

When they stood in the midst of a crew, Liz turned to a well-groomed television news reporter and asked, "Excuse me, but do you have the time?"

"He can't hear you," Dash said.

"That's impossible."

She reached over to tug on the sleeve of the reporter's navy blue blazer, but her fingers had no sensation. She couldn't feel the material. It was as if she could push right through him and he wouldn't know she was there.

"This is scary," she said. "Am I a ghost?"

"It's a trick of the light and energy forms," he said. "Come on, let's get moving. I don't like to do this for a long period of time."

"But this is amazing."

She jumped up and down. Though she was aware of her own physical movement, she didn't feel the pavement beneath her feet. "How can this be?"

"You want to investigate? Or do a tap dance?"

"I want to know how you're pulling this trick. It's got to be a trick of some kind. I can't really be invisible."

"Oh, ye of little faith."

He pointed her toward the door. When they stood on the stoop, she balked. "We're not going to walk through the closed door, are we? Because I don't know if I can do that without being completely freaked out."

"You're okay," he said.

He opened the door and ushered her quickly inside. As soon as she was in the foyer, Liz felt solid again. She had a sense of gravity she'd never realized before. What had happened out there? Had she really and truly been invisible?

"Ready?" he questioned. "Let's talk with Sarah."

"Was this like some kind of out-of-body experience?"

"It happened," he said. "Accept it and move on."

"You must have done this with mirrors or something. Don't get me wrong, but it's an illusion."

His eyes snapped into sharp focus. His voice was as harsh as a slap in the face. "When will you learn to trust me? Believe in me, Elizabeth."

"But I—"

"I am the only truth."

And that was what frightened her more than anything, more than facing Hector, than talking to the police. If she trusted Dash and believed in him, she would lose her distance. And she would be closer to him than she'd ever been to anyone in her life.

Liz turned away from him and called out, "Sarah? It's me, Liz."

"Liz?" Sarah appeared in the hallway leading from the kitchen. She rushed toward them and grasped Liz in a clumsy, one-armed hug.

Tears coursed down Sarah's cheeks. For a moment, she wept violently. Deep, gasping sobs shuddered through her body.

When Liz tried to comfort her by patting her on the shoulder, Sarah winced.

"What happened?" Liz asked. "Did you hurt your arm?"

"It's not important. Oh, I'm so glad you're here. This has been terrible, just terrible. First Agatha. Now Jack. What's become of our family? It's like there's some awful curse on the Orbens."

Liz knew it was nothing so dramatic. However, after having just passed invisibly through a crowd, she wouldn't doubt anything. "I kind of expected Gary to be here with you," she said.

"He was, last night. But now he's at the office, trying to put things in order. He says there's a ton of paperwork to be done."

Gary's behavior sounded cold and unfeeling to Liz. He ought to be here with the woman he supposedly loved. Quite obviously, Sarah needed company.

"This paperwork he's digging through," Dash said. "Does it have to do with Jack's death?"

Bleary-eyed, she nodded. "There's some kind of insurance policy, and Gary says the company needs the cash infusion to make up for loss of sales due to Jack's…" Her voice cracked. "His demise."

"I'm wondering," Dash said. "Do you happen to know who inherits the bulk of Jack's stock?"

Liz gave him a hard, dissuading look. How could Dash be so insensitive and unfeeling? Now was not the time to discuss the case with Sarah. She was distraught.

Still, Sarah answered. "His inheritance? I'm not sure. Probably his children from his first marriage. All I know is that Gary is executor of the estate. That's why he's so nervous about getting everything right. It's usually a lawyer who's appointed executor, you know.''

"Yes," Dash said quietly, "I know. Why did Jack choose Gary for the job?"

"Because he's good with money."

"I don't know the two men well," Dash said. "But they didn't seem to get along. Wasn't that why you were nervous about announcing your engagement?"

"What are you saying?" Sarah growled like a mother bear protecting her cubs. Obviously, she needed to cherish her memory of Jack. And to defend her fiancé, as well. "Sure, Jack and Gary had their spats, but underneath it all, they were friends, trusted co-workers."

"Of course they were," Liz said gently. "Now, let's go into the kitchen and make ourselves a cup of coffee, and you can relax." She frowned at Dash and placed her arm around Sarah, who winced with pain at the touch of Liz's hand. "Are you hurt, Sarah? What happened?"

"I've just been so upset, you know. I stumbled and fell and knocked my arm against the coffee table."

They sat around the kitchen table, and Liz found herself feeling troubled by Sarah's explanation of her injury. She'd once been a battered wife who covered her abuse by claiming to be clumsy. Was it happening to her again? Sometimes abused women were attracted to the same sort of men. Abusers. But Gary Gregory?

Liz didn't think the accountant had enough fire in his belly to lash out. Gary always seemed totally preoccupied by his roses or his figures.

When Sarah sat down, Liz reached over and took her hand. "We've spoken to Sister Muriel, and she told us why you are so in favor of turning this house into a shelter. Your first husband beat you."

Sarah's laughter was incongruous. It made a mockery of her pain. "Thank goodness, that's in the past."

"Is it?" Liz pressed. "Did Gary hurt you?"

"Oh, no." Her denial was too quick. "This was different. Gary didn't mean to hurt me. Last night, we argued, and he pushed me. Just to make a point, you understand."

"No," Dash said. "I don't understand."

Nor did Liz. Her politeness was forgotten in a flash of outrage. How could Sarah allow this to happen to her again?

"Gary's a good man," Sarah protested. "Oh, Liz, he's a wonderful man. I'd do anything for him. And I know he loves me. And he's never hit me. Never."

"Except for last night," Liz coldly reminded her.

"Last night, I don't know what got into him. He'd been answering police questions for hours. He doesn't have an alibi for the time in question. He was at home, working with his roses at the time when Jack was . . ."

"Jack was killed," Liz said brutally. "He was murdered. Shot in the chest. Did Gary kill him?"

"No!" She leaped to her feet so suddenly that her chair overturned. "Get out of my house!"

Liz started to apologize, but Dash shook his head. To Sarah he said, "Think about this carefully. Consider from every angle. Even if Gary is not a murderer—"

"He's not!" Her voice rose hysterically. "Get out!"

"Don't marry him," Dash advised. "He's not a good man. A good man never touches a woman in anger."

Sarah collapsed at the table, buried her face in her arms and wept. She repeated over and over, "Leave me alone. Leave me alone."

Dash took Liz by the arm and led her into the front room.

"We can't abandon her like this," Liz said. "There's no telling what she might do."

From outside, they heard the news hounds clamoring. Then the doorbell pealed. Liz opened it and ushered Sister Muriel inside. Though the small, tidy nun looked a bit frazzled, she managed a firm smile. "I came as soon as I heard the news. Where is Sarah?"

Dash pointed her toward the kitchen. "You're an angel, Sister. A Ministering Angel."

"One can only pray," she said, heading toward the kitchen. "Goodbye, children. And good luck."

After another bout of invisibility, Liz and Dash were in her car, heading north. "Is she really?" Liz asked. "Is Sister Muriel an angel?"

"Not yet, but she will be. She is a truly good woman. Sometimes, in small ways, a mortal being can be almost a saint. Those people have a special place in the hereafter. Like Agatha."

Liz drove steadily toward town, but she was unsure where they were headed. Though solving Agatha's murder was still foremost on her mind, she had to consider the distinct possibility that Dash was what he said he was. An angel.

But it was so hard to accept. He looked like a man. He was a handsome, strong, absolutely masculine man. He walked, talked and even smoked like a regular human being. But there were those minor miracles to consider. The invisibility, for one.

"Can you turn us invisible right now?" she asked.

"Why?"

"Because I want to see what it feels like again."

"You want more proof," he said. "Sorry, precious. It doesn't work like that. Either you accept what I'm saying or you don't. Trust me or not. It's no skin off my nose, precious, if you don't.''

"How about flying?" she asked. "Can we do that? Like Superman. Can you take me in your arms and fly to the mountains?''

"I've never mastered the skill of carrying somebody else," he said. "And I wouldn't do it for a gag. This is who I am. This is my existence.''

So it was up to her to believe or disbelieve him. Somehow, Liz felt like one of the children in the audience at *Peter Pan* being asked to clap their hands if they believed in fairies. When she was a little girl, she'd always clapped. But now? Now she'd seen enough of life to know that believing doesn't necessarily make it so.

"Where to next?" he asked. "We could take advantage of it being Sunday to make a search at the warehouse for the falcon.''

"The bluebird," she corrected. "Yes, we could.''

But the weather was perfect, and the skies were blue. The idea of digging through dusty old files at the warehouse was dismal.

"How about this," he suggested. "We can drive out to the warehouse, and I can search. I'll fly. It'll be done in minutes, not hours.''

"Tempting," she said. "And I do appreciate that you're not simply taking off on your own to search at angel warp speed." But did she believe he could do it? "Okay, Dash. Let's try that.''

It was a long drive to the northeastern end of town, and when she finally pulled into the empty parking lot and cut the motor, Liz climbed out of the car to stretch. She leaned against the hood, closed her eyes and turned her face toward the sun. "Okay, Dash. Go for it.''

She heard a whoosh beside her and felt a sudden breeze. When she opened her eyes again, he was gone. This angel stuff was more than a little unnerving. She closed her eyes again.

In a few minutes, he was beside her, straightening his necktie. "Nothing," he said. "A couple of boxes, marked Agatha, that had knickknacks. But no falcon."

"Then we're out of luck," she said. "Sarah said that she'd parceled out remembrances and mementos to family and friends, but I don't suppose she kept any kind of list."

"Probably not," he concurred.

"It seems like our investigation is going nowhere fast. We've got two major suspects—Gary and Hector—and no tangible proof." She tried to keep the disappointment out of her voice. "I guess we should just wait for the police to do their investigation and hope they pick the right one as Jack's murderer."

He got into the car. "Let's cruise past Hector's place. Maybe he's back."

She shrugged. "Maybe."

In northwest Denver, in one of the older neighborhoods that had been renovated and reclaimed by determined urban dwellers, they drove slowly past Hector's house. It was a small frame house, well-tended with a neatly clipped lawn and several fruit trees.

"There," Dash pointed. "That's an unmarked cop car. I guess the cops have got their own stakeout going."

"Then there's no need for us to hang around."

She returned to the center of town. On a beautiful late Sunday afternoon, there was an easy atmosphere on the city streets. Downtown, the Rockies baseball team was wrapping up the season of play at Coors Field. In the parks, people were strolling, jogging and sitting to read books. Autumn in Denver was a pleasant season, easy-going and calm.

They stopped for a latte and an ice cream, picked up deli food for dinner later, then returned to the apartment. They were pretty much compatible, Liz thought. She didn't feel the dating kind of urgency with Dash. He was different, easy.

At the apartment, she called her answering machine at home and listened to dozens of messages from people in the news media. And a couple of calls from people in the office. Then she heard the angry voice of Gary Gregory.

"Liz, you're fired," he snapped. "Sarah told me about your accusations, and I don't need that kind of disloyalty. Don't come in on Monday. We'll have your stuff packed and ship it to you. Goodbye."

She pushed the replay button so Dash could hear.

"I'm sorry," he said. "You're out of work."

"It was time to move on, anyway." She leaned back on the sofa. "To tell you the truth, I'm relieved."

"But you were there ten years."

"And could have been there another ten. Behind the same desk. Answering the same phone. And then I'd stay because I might as well. No, this is good."

After dinner, she took a long bath and retired to her bedroom, still pondering the case. There had to be something she was missing, some detail that was dancing around at the edge of her consciousness, just beyond sight.

Dash tapped on her bedroom door. "I came to say good-night."

"Come on in," she said. "I was just thinking about all the information we've gathered. I think there's a trail from the beans."

"The beans?"

He entered her room hesitantly. Though she was decently dressed in silky primrose yellow pajamas, he felt like he was intruding.

She sat cross-legged at the edge of the bed. "Here's what I think. Agatha suggested to me that I compare Hector's purchase prices for coffee beans with the prices paid by our competitors. That was after she was ill, but she might have had suspicions about his overpayments before that."

"And you think this was Hector's motive for murder."

"Dash, if the ten percent overpayments had been going on for several years and Hector was taking even half in kickbacks, his profit would be in the millions of dollars. OrbenCorp does high-volume purchasing."

"Good motive," he said. His gaze rested on the shimmering highlights in her long brown hair. He felt a heaviness in his physical body, a longing, almost a need.

"Then here's what happens next. I do the comparisons. I show the figures to Gary. Gary shows them to Jack. Jack confronts Hector. Hector kills him." She paused. "Are you following me?"

"Why would Hector kill Jack? He's still guilty of embezzling. Jack's death doesn't change the numbers."

"Nothing could change the numbers. They're all neatly recorded in Gary's nasty little computer."

"So why commit another murder? Being caught for a white-collar crime is far different than a first-degree murder charge."

"I don't know." She scooted back on the pillows and tucked her feet under her. "But I have the feeling I'm going in the right direction."

"Let's take it from Gary's side," he said, averting his gaze from her. She was far too beautiful to allow him to concentrate. "Gary wants to inherit the company. He romances Sarah. Kills Agatha. Then kills Jack. This leaves him as the executor of OrbenCorp and Jack's estate, as well as having Agatha's house when he marries Sarah."

"We can only hope that won't happen," Liz said. "I'd hate to see Sarah get stuck in another abusive relationship."

"Tomorrow," he said, "since you don't have to go to work, we'll look for Hector. We'll put in some real time on it."

"Okay."

She settled back on the pillows. Her blue eyes were soft and gentle as she gazed at him. Her voice was husky. "Have you used that condom yet?"

"I can't, Liz."

"I know, I know. You're an angel, and you can't touch me. But why? Is it so wrong to make love to someone you care about deeply?"

"I don't know," he said honestly. "Do you care about me?"

"I'm afraid so." The words came hard for her. She wasn't accustomed to making declarations of affection. "The way I feel about you is different than I've ever felt about any other man—or angel. We're so similar. We think alike. It's like we were made for each other."

"Yes," he said. "That's exactly what it's like."

He rose from the bed and turned out the overhead light. The only illumination came from starlight through the tenth-floor window, and the delicate glow permeated the room, softening the shadows and creating a mysterious intimacy.

When she looked at Dash again, his broad chest was bared. From what she could see, his body was perfect. The muscles of his chest bulged, his flat nipples were taut beneath the light sprinkling of dark hair.

She gazed into his eyes and gasped at the tenderness she saw there. His well-shaped lips whispered to her. "I love you. Elizabeth, I love you."

"Oh, Dash. I love you, too."

"For all eternity," he said.

"Show me," she urged. "Show me that you love me."

He came closer to the bed. "Lie down, my darling."

She reclined on the pillows. She raised her arms over her head in a posture of utter submission.

His hand glided above the surface of her skin, not quite touching. But she could feel the warmth of his caress. Her body yearned toward his hand. All her senses came alive.

Abruptly, he stood at the foot of her bed. "Elizabeth," he whispered. "Undress for me."

She sat up on the bed, near the pillows. Her gaze locked with his. With trembling fingers, she unfastened the buttons on her pajama top and allowed the two halves to part slightly. Before she removed her top, she wriggled out of the bottoms, sliding the yellow silk down her thighs and calves.

When she revealed her legs, she heard him catch his breath. "Beautiful," he said.

"A hot tamale," she said. Her voice was trembling. "A cute cupcake. A juicy, ripe tomato."

"A woman." His baritone voice deepened and resonated. "You are the most remarkable woman I've ever known. The only woman for me."

"Make love to me, Dash. Please."

She slipped the pajama blouse off her shoulder, yet held it over her breasts. Then she let go.

When she looked at him, he was also naked. His hips were narrow and his thighs were strong. His strong maleness was magnificent.

Though she held out her arms to him, he did not come closer. "Lie back on the pillows," he said. "Don't move."

She did as he asked, and again he came close to her. His hand hovered enticingly above her naked flesh. He lowered his lips, still not touching her, but breathing across her body, across her breasts. Her nipples hardened in response to him. Though she shivered uncontrollably, her skin was flushed and hot. She groaned with wanting him, needing him.

But as soon as her hands reached up and touched him, he darted away from her with quicksilver speed. He was invisible.

"Dash? Where are you?"

"Here," came his voice beside her ear. She reached for him, but he was not there.

Yet she could feel him all around her, enveloping her in a brilliant, luminous cocoon.

"Lie still, Elizabeth."

She stretched out on the bed.

"Close your eyes."

She did as he asked.

The pure sensations that shot through her body were unlike anything she'd felt before. Her skin was on fire. Her heart pounded heavily beneath her rib cage.

She parted her legs. She was moist with wanting him, slick with her desire for him. Never before had she been so aroused. The sheer pleasure caused her to moan.

Though she was alone on the bed, she felt his mysterious touch, his breath, his magic that heightened her senses. He was a wonder, a miracle.

A trembling, ecstatic release burst through her, and the most wonderful white-hot energy shivered across the surface of her body.

She was fulfilled, completed.

Quietly she murmured, ''I love you, Dash.''

''Elizabeth.''

He stood trembling and invisible at the foot of her bed. Though he technically had not touched her body, they had made love. He had broken the rules and awaited retribution, the swift strike of lightning, the flame of celestial rage.

Yet, the night was still, silent.

Dash felt no guilt for what had passed between them. He had not sinned.

Chapter Thirteen

The next morning they returned to Hector's quiet north Denver neighborhood and discovered that the police were no longer staking out his house. Liz and Dash hit the nearby convenience store for extra-large coffee and settled down to wait. After another cup of coffee and a half dozen doughnuts, it was almost noon and Liz had worked up the courage to mention the night before. Gazing at his rugged profile with wondering eyes, she said, "I enjoyed last night. Very much."

"So did I."

She bit her lower lip and cringed inside. Why was she so tongue-tied this morning? She might as well have offered the tired old cliché, was it good for you?

The weather was warm enough that they had the windows rolled down. All in all, she'd rather be jogging than trying to express the incredible feelings she'd experienced last night. But Liz needed to convey how much his lovemaking had meant to her.

"I've never felt so close. You were part of me. It was like my breath came from your lungs, it was your heart beating within me. Not my own."

He nodded briskly and looked out the window. "Mind if I smoke?"

"Oh, go ahead. Blow it out the window, though."

He struck a wooden match with his thumbnail, fired up a Camel and sucked hard.

She cleared her throat. "Listen, Dash, I'm trying to tell you that you are the most wonderful lover in the world, and that I meant it last night when I said that I loved you."

"I know. And I love you, Elizabeth. Last night was the first time, in all my eternity, that I felt so complete."

Her eyebrows raised. "The first time?"

"Yes."

"Dash? Are you telling me that you're a virgin?"

Diffidently, he straightened his shoulders. "You might say that."

"Well, either you are or you aren't. You can't be kind of a virgin any more than you can be kind of pregnant. And don't bother telling me that you've never made love to a woman before, because I won't believe it."

"Why not?"

"You're too good. The way you handled me was skillful, like a genius. If that was your first time, baby, I can't wait until you've got some experience under your belt."

She looked at him and grinned, but he was still staring out the window, paying more attention to his Camel than to her. "Why are you so distant this morning? You're like a stranger, like we hardly know each other."

Dash thought he'd been covering his confusion well, but he should have realized that Liz would see through any barriers he erected. He couldn't hide from her. Nor from what he'd done the night before.

And he didn't understand what was happening to him or to her or to them. Last night, they'd come together in an amazing way, more miraculous than flight, more filled with wonder than the resonance of a sweet heavenly choir.

Afterward, when he lay beside her, loving her with all his heart and every molecule of his being, he'd expected a summons from Angelo. He'd expected to see St. Mike materialize right beside him and condemn him. But that had not occurred.

And that gave him hope.

Could it happen again? Could he actually be allowed to touch her body? The thought of stroking her flesh and running his fingers through her hair was painfully overwhelming. But he wasn't ready to take that risk—not until this case was over and he knew she would be safe.

He could only draw one conclusion. The experience they had shared last night, the reverence for each other, wasn't wrong or sinful. He loved her, and love was a blessed state of being. He had done as Angelo said and followed his heart. Their passion was an expression of truth. But he feared it could not happen again without him seeking his own ultimate physical fulfillment.

And then . . . what?

"I'm an angel, Liz. Not a man. I can't promise you anything, I can't offer the future to you."

"My darling." Her eyes shimmered in the noon light. "Strange things have been happening. Odd phenomena. And if you want to believe you're an angel, I can accept that. But please, please, don't let it stand between us."

He flicked the ember off his cigarette and pitched the butt into the street. "You still don't believe me."

"I can't. Angels don't fit into my reality."

"Nobody will ever call you gullible, precious."

"I guess not."

He leaned back in the passenger seat and stared down the block toward Hector's town home. "We'll figure this out later. After the case is solved."

"Really?" She was alert. "Why do I have the feeling that after the case is solved, you're going to vanish like a puff of that damned cigarette smoke, and I'll be left alone?"

"That's how it usually happens," he admitted. "The transgressor is brought to justice, and my job is done."

"So you'd leave me?"

"No," he said. When he turned and looked directly into her eyes, he communicated the deepest intensity of his spirit. "Whatever it takes, I'll find a way to come to you."

She trembled. "You're scaring me, Dash."

"Me, too."

He pushed open his car door. "Let's walk. We can't sit here all day."

They strolled along the tree-lined street. A breeze rustled though the autumn leaves that blanketed the earth.

Shuffling along, she asked, "Have you ever seen *Peter Pan*? The play, not the movie?"

"Can't say as I have."

"Well, there's a part near the end when Tinkerbell, the pixie, is dying, and the only way she can be saved is if all the children in the audience clap their hands and say that they truly do believe in fairies."

She could feel him watching her as she tried to explain. "I remember clapping my hands so hard that I thought my palms would bleed. With all my heart, I believed. Then, after the show, I discovered that Tinkerbell wasn't real after all. She was just a spot of light, a bit of stage magic."

"And this has meaning for you," he said.

"It's like with OrbenCorp. I believed I could have the exciting, exotic job of buyer. But all I ever got to be was a glorified secretary for Jack. Now I don't want to believe in something I can't see or touch. Because I don't want to be so desperately disappointed again."

"And you'd be disappointed if I wasn't an angel?"

"I don't know. It is pretty exciting. How many women can say they're in love with an avenging angel?" She shrugged her slender shoulders. "But that's not what I'm talking about. I'm talking about love, the kind of love I have for you. It's strong and good and . . . eternal."

"Yes," he said. "That's how I feel, too."

"It's so wonderful that I'm afraid to believe in it. My heart would surely break if I couldn't be with you."

They circled around the block and down the alley behind Hector's house. Liz shook herself. She wasn't accustomed to revealing such personal insights, and her declaration of love left her feeling tense.

Back to the case, she thought. No more soul-searching for today. She asked, "How come the police aren't here anymore?"

"Most police departments can't spare the manpower for a long-term stakeout."

"Do you think Hector will come back here?"

He shrugged. "Maybe. Finding him is our best bet for right now."

Earlier this morning, she had called in to the blond receptionist at OrbenCorp. In a disguised voice, she'd asked for Hector and had been informed that he wasn't in the office today. She'd also placed a call to the warehouse. No Hector. Where had he vanished to? And why? Unless he'd murdered Jack, his disappearance made very little sense at all.

They were in the car for about an hour when Dash glanced into the rearview mirror and said, "Now we're in trouble."

"What is it? The police?"

"Carlito and his map-reading friend."

She glanced over her shoulder at a big, late-model Chevy sedan that was cruising extremely slowly and stopping at every other house while the guy in the passenger seat stuck his head out the window to check the address. "Maybe he knows where Hector is hiding. I'm going to ask."

She gunned the engine and pulled out into the street in front of Carlito's heavy sedan. Liz jumped out of the driver's seat and waved to him. "Carlito? Do you remember me? I'm Liz Carradine."

"Move it, lady."

She started toward him. "I really want to talk to you about your father."

Through the windshield, she watched as Carlito's gaze shifted from her to Dash, who had also disembarked from the car. The young man's jaw tensed. "Damn you!" he shouted.

Liz raised her hands in a placating gesture. "We're not going to hurt you. Really."

"Well, I'm going to hurt you and your friend, lady."

He leaned his arm out of the car window. In his fist, he held a revolver. It was an oversize gun, and it looked big as a cannon.

Liz registered that fact, pivoted and raced to her car. Moving at top speed, she dove into her seat and yelled, "Dash, get in! He has a gun! Get in here, right now!"

Dash poked his head in the door. "I'm going to take care of Carlito right now. I hate punks."

"Get in here!"

She heard a bullet smack into the rear of her car, and Liz stomped on the accelerator. Dash had no choice but to jump inside and swing his door closed as she squealed around a corner.

"Stop the car!" he ordered.

"I think not," she said, concentrating one hundred percent on her driving.

She was coming up to a stop sign. "Now what? *Drive right on through. Swerve if someone else is coming. Don't stop. Don't stop.*

But she wasn't accustomed to high-speed chases, so Liz tapped on the brakes. Half a second later, Carlito crashed into the rear of her little Honda with his big, heavy sedan. She could hear him shouting and laughing.

Liz glanced in her rearview mirror. "You think that's funny, do you?"

Dash urged caution. "Slow down. Let's get out and settle this."

Her fingers gripped the steering wheel. "The kid wants a chase, and that's what I'm going to give him."

She jammed the accelerator to the floor and took off at top speed. On the side streets, the little car blasted over potholes and soared over dips like a bucking bronco.

Though Liz was unfamiliar with this part of town, she knew there was a park with a lake somewhere around here, and she aimed in that general direction. Circling a park, she'd have more visibility, more chance to avoid obstacles on the road. At a stoplight, she swerved to avoid a collision. The Honda spun halfway around, but she righted it and continued on her rocket ship path.

A glance in her rearview mirror told her that Carlito had regained the space she'd gained with her first sudden spurt of speed. He was right on her tail. Why? The little creep!

After her second near accident, Dash ordered, "Park it."

"What? And get shot?"

"I'll take care of Carlito."

"Dash, this is not the time to try out your bulletproof vest. That's a real gun. Not an angel gun."

Liz knew she was going in the wrong direction, away from the park. The neighborhood had taken on a rural aspect. The little frame houses were farther apart. There were mailboxes at the edge of the road. Where the hell was she?

She made a frantic turn to avoid an elderly woman who was crossing the street with a bag of groceries. Liz swung the car too wide. Out of control, she careened along the road. Instinctively, she hammered on the brake. The Honda fishtailed, nosed into a ditch and came to a halt.

The engine was dead. Frantically, she tried to restart the car. "Oh, no! Dash, are you all right? Dash?"

He was out of the car. The sheer terror that rose in her throat was worse than anything she'd felt before. He was going to die. Dash was out of her car and striding toward Carlito and his partner.

She had to stop him. She flung herself out of the car. She was ready to throw herself in front of him to stop the bullet if that's what it took. If anything happened to Dash, her heart would shatter. He was more important to her than life itself.

"Stay back," he ordered.

"No! I can't let you do this!"

"Believe in me, Elizabeth. Stay back."

The power in his voice compelled obedience, and she halted.

The scene that unfolded on this quiet rural road was like a showdown from the old west. On one side, walking slow, was Carlito with the gun in his hand. Standing and waiting for him was Dash in his trench coat.

Carlito's older companion was shouting to him. "Don't do it, Carlito! We have other, more important things. Please. Get back in the car."

"I won't kill him," the young man said. "I'll just wing him. This guy in the suit is going to know who's boss."

He raised the huge gun, aimed and fired.

And Dash made a sudden grab, then held out his hand to show the heavy leaden bullet. He'd caught it in midair!

Carlito paled beneath the swarthy complexion that was so like his father's. He pulled the trigger again.

Again, Dash snatched the bullet from midair.

Liz could see Dash's fury. He seemed on fire with it. Sparks flew from his hands. He threw down the bullets. His body tensed. He seemed to grow larger and more powerful.

His clothing was transformed. Instead of his trench coat and fedora, he was clad in gleaming robes, so white that they were almost silver. Around his waist was a maroon cord. The color of a warrior, she remembered.

When he'd explained the hierarchy of angels, the maroon cord had that significance. A warrior. And that was exactly what Dash looked like. An all-powerful creature from another time and place. His dark hair lengthened from the conservative 1930s style haircut. His expression showed a terrible and magnificent ferocity.

Liz felt her breath catch in her throat. Dash was a phenomenon, a remarkable, eternal vision.

And then, in a sudden burst, he displayed his wings. They were massive. The span of shimmering feathers must have stretched thirty feet from tip to tip. And his wings were the most beautiful vision she'd ever seen. They spread in the afternoon sunlight, and the aura around him was intense as the sun itself or a star that had fallen to earth. With one stroke of his powerful wings, he lifted himself and hovered three feet off the ground.

He really was an angel!

In a sonorous voice, he said, "I will spare your miserable life, Carlito. For you are young and foolish."

Carlito threw his gun to the ground and fell to his knees. He was sobbing. His slim, boyish body trembled.

"Know this," Dash intoned. "I am vengeance. When you strike out against another, you strike out against me."

"I'm sorry," the boy cried out. "I'll be different. I'll change. I promise I will."

"I give you this to remember my fury." Dash lifted his hand, and the robes fell back, revealing a muscular forearm. He pointed, and a burst of light issued forth, touching Carlito on his hand.

The boy screamed.

Then, in an instant, Dash was standing there in his usual trench coat and fedora. He straightened his lapels and turned to Liz, who stared at him, slack-jawed.

She raised her hands and slowly she began to applaud. One clap after another after another. She banged her hands together hard. In her mind, she repeated the words she'd learned so long ago as a child. "I believe. I do believe."

Dash swept a bow in her direction. "Takes a lot to convince you, precious."

She ran toward him but stopped short before embracing him. He really was an angel. She really was in love with an angel.

"What's the matter, precious?"

"I don't know what to do. Should I kneel and beg for your forgiveness?"

"Yeah, sure," he drawled, "then you ought to kiss the hem of my trench coat."

She laughed and her tension faded. He was still Dash, the crazy detective who had captured her heart. But he was an angel, too.

"Come on," he said, "we need to talk to young Carlito and his friend."

Carlito was on his feet, trembling and speechless.

His partner stepped forward. Though equally awed, he was able to speak. "I apologize for my young friend. Can you help us?"

"It might be useful," Liz said, forcing the residual tremble of amazement from her voice, "if we knew what you were looking for."

"We are trying to find Hector Messenger, the kid's father. I am his uncle, the brother of Carlito's mother."

"I'm not sure that I understand," Liz said. "Why should a meeting with Hector's father be difficult?"

"Carlito ran away from his mother in Colombia two years ago, when he was only fifteen. He fell in with bad people, and we had given him up for lost. But Hector kept searching. Every time he was in the country, he searched for his son. And finally, Carlito came to me. He agreed to meet with his father, but he is fearful of being too easily discovered by local police. Do you understand?"

"I think so," Liz said. She glanced toward the young man, whose eyes were still wide and startled. "I'm sorry, Carlito, that you've had such a difficult time."

"I chose it," he said, straightening his shoulders. "But no more. I wish to start again, to make something of my life."

"So, what's the problem?" Dash asked. "How come you don't just pick up the telephone and call Hector?"

"We have need for caution," the uncle explained. "These bad friends of Carlito will kill us if they believe he wishes to betray them. So, we did not wish for Hector to be in danger.''

"And?'' Liz encouraged.

"On the telephone, I explained this to Hector. He wrote down an address and left it for me in a specified place.'' The uncle held out a piece of paper. "Here it is! We have gone to this place a dozen times, and we cannot find Carlito's father. You see, it says 9119 Jefferson.''

Liz took the piece of paper.

"I am not good with maps,'' the uncle said.

"I guess not,'' she said. "This says 6116 Jefferson. Number eight.''

She looked to Dash for instructions, but he was striking another match and lighting a cigarette.

"All right,'' Liz said. "Here's what we're going to do. You guys help me get my car out of the ditch, then you follow me. We'll find Hector.''

Carlito nodded. He gasped out the words, "Thank you.''

Still, she eyed him suspiciously. "You're not going to try something weird, are you? Not going to run away?''

"I will do as you say.''

As proof, he held out his hand. On his palm, she saw the mark Dash had left upon him. It was a small tattoo of a flaming sword.

BACK IN HER RED HONDA, driving to the address Hector had written neatly and the dyslexic uncle had read wrong, she blurted, "I was wrong, Dash. I'll never doubt you again.''

"That's a safe bet, sweetheart. Because angels never lie.''

"You really are an angel, a celestial being.'' Her eyes opened wide, and she released her disbelief. Unfortunately, the path she saw ahead of them was no less rocky. "This presents a whole new set of problems, doesn't it?"

"Guess so."

"And that Angelo person who came by the apartment, is he an angel, too?"

"That's right."

"And this office you work for on Logan Street. All angels?"

"Right," he said. "That's why I couldn't guarantee you a job there. Like St. Michael says, we're not an equal opportunity employer. You've got to be an angel."

"But you said your boss might be convinced. And your boss is a saint?"

"You got it, precious."

"Oh, damn." She looked up suddenly. "I shouldn't say that, should I?"

"It's your decision."

She wanted to become a professional private investigator, and the logical place to start was with Dash's office. Because she also wanted to work only with him as his partner. "Isn't there some kind of application I could fill out? Can't I be an honorary angel or something?"

"Up until now, I'd have said it was impossible. But things are changing, sweetheart. Faster than I ever imagined."

"There has to be a way..." The gravity of the situation was beginning to sink in. He really was an angel. When he'd said he couldn't promise to be with her, when he said they had no future, he meant it. Dash had obligations to another authority, the highest authority.

She was only a mortal woman—not even a saint. Liz felt very vulnerable and small. Her claim on him, her love for him, seemed unimportant in the grand scheme of things. She was only one insignificant person, and he carried the ultimate responsibility for justice and truth. He had powers beyond her comprehension.

"I liked it better," she said, "when I thought you were just a very eccentric man."

"Why?"

"We had a chance. I thought, maybe, with therapy and understanding, you could get over your delusions. I thought we could have a life together. And now? Oh, Dash, what are we going to do?"

"We'll find a way," he said. "Never give up hope."

She spotted the address Carlito's uncle had given them, and turned into the parking lot of a small, nondescript motel. She parked in front of number eight.

Sitting beside her in the car, Dash took her hand, and she again experienced the trembling fever that came whenever they were close. How could she live without him?

She fought back tears. "This isn't fair. I finally find the love of my life, and you're going to be taken away from me. I may never find you again."

"No matter what happens," he said, "we'll be together. Elizabeth, we're from different worlds. But we were made for each other."

She wanted to embrace him. "What would happen if I kissed you?"

"There's a good possibility the beeper in my pocket would go off, and I'd be called back to the office."

She reached her finger toward his lips, but she did not touch him. "My darling, I can't take that risk. If keeping you near me means I can never touch you again, that's what I will do."

"No, Liz. That won't work. I can't let you give up the pleasures of physical life. You're mortal. You need—"

"I need you. Only you, my dearest love." She blinked away the moisture behind her eyelids. "First we'll solve the case."

Stepping out of the car, followed almost immediately by Carlito and Jimmy, they stood on the sidewalk outside room number eight. Dash nodded toward the door. "Go ahead, Carlito. He's your father."

The young man raised his fist and knocked hard.

When Hector opened the door, his guarded expression turned to the purest joy. Slowly, he raised his hand and stroked his son's cheek. "Carlito," he whispered hoarsely, "I thought I'd lost you forever."

"My father, I—"

"I have missed you with all my heart."

When they embraced, Liz felt warm and cozy inside. No matter how much she disliked Hector, she recognized the depth of his love for his son.

Though it might have been appropriate to fade away and leave them to their reunion, there were questions to be pursued.

"Hector," she said, "may we come in? Only for a moment."

"Yes, please."

They settled around the nondescript room on chairs and on the side of the bed. Hector faced his son. It seemed that the father could hardly bear to take his eyes off his prodigal boy.

"Start at the beginning," Dash said. "Two years ago, Carlito took off and joined up with some bad people."

"That was when my search began," Hector said. "I was fortunate enough to be able to travel to Colombia frequently on business, and I used much of my time to search."

He reached behind his neck and unfastened the large gold necklace he always wore. He opened the locket and handed it to Liz.

Inside, on both sides of the locket, were small photographs of Carlito as a much younger boy.

"I showed the pictures to everyone I met," Hector said. "I tried to follow every lead. But nothing. I had no luck at all. I would have given up if his mother had not received occasional communication."

Hector frowned at the floor, then looked at Liz. "I wasn't doing a good job for OrbenCorp. I tried. But much of my time was occupied with my search. I told Agatha. Before she was sick, I told her of my problem and offered to quit so that she might hire another buyer. But she refused."

Liz nodded. That was very like Agatha. She'd been so understanding. "And that's why you sometimes paid too much for the coffee beans."

"No," he said. "I might have slipped once or twice, taking the highest price instead of negotiating. But I know coffee. And I know what is proper to be paid. My prices, a few percents higher, were for quality product."

"Hector, I did the figures myself. Consistently, you were eight to ten percent higher."

"Then your figures are wrong."

Dash pursued another line of questioning. "When was the last time you saw Jack?"

"We argued. On the day after the party." His gaze rested fondly on his son. "Then I received word that I must find another place, a secret place, to meet with Carlito. I left the address with the receptionist, and I have been here ever since."

When Dash spoke to Carlito's uncle, the man jumped nervously. "What?" he asked.

"Why were you outside Liz's house?"

"When we couldn't find this motel, I went back to the secretary and asked for the address of Elizabeth Carradine. It was a name Carlito remembered."

"And she gave it to you?" Liz said, aghast. "Just like that?"

"This girl at the desk," he said, "she maybe drinks too much of your fine coffee. She's a very nervous young woman."

If Liz had anything to say about it, she would also have been a very fired young woman. But Liz didn't have a say. She'd been fired herself.

Dash asked Hector, "Did you kill Jack?"

"No. I was sorry to hear reports on the television of his death. Jack was not a good businessman, but he had charm and humor. I enjoyed his company." As an afterthought, he added, "I will miss him."

Dash looked back and forth between Carlito and his uncle. "And you two? What do you know about the murder of Jack Orben?"

"Nothing," said the uncle.

Carlito shook his head. He looked so much younger than when Liz had first seen him. The attitude of rage had dissipated. There was still a rebellious spark behind his large, liquid brown eyes, but he had somehow regained an innocence. She supposed that a life-and-death encounter with an angel might have that effect on a person.

She nodded toward Dash. "We should go now."

He stood, tipped the brim of his fedora and smiled at the three men. His gaze focused on Carlito and he said, "Here's looking at you, kid."

"Thank you," Carlito whispered. He waved goodbye with the hand that had been tattooed, marked forever with an angelic reminder. The flaming sword of Dash Divine.

Chapter Fourteen

On the sidewalk outside the motel room, Liz savored the moment. Though she and Dash were still pursuing a murder investigation and still had the problem of how to create a lasting relationship when she was human and he was not, the newfound warmth between father and son gave her a sense that, at least for this moment, something was right in the world. Their happiness, no matter how elusive, brought pleasure to her soul.

Dash struck a match, lit a cigarette and brought her back to hard, tense reality. "I guess we know who our murderer is."

"Hush," she whispered. "Can you hear it?"

"Hear what?"

"There's a tiny click, the sound of something falling into place." Without pausing for breath, she continued, "Can you see it?"

"See what?"

"A flicker of light against the darkness. Hector and Carlito getting together, after so much struggle and pain, is a wonderful moment."

"Now who's the philosopher?" he asked.

She shrugged her shoulders. "The murderer is Gary

Gregory. It has to be, since we've eliminated everybody else.''

"Bingo," he said. "The little lady wins the prize."

"But I'm still not quite sure why. I mean, if Sarah dumps him, he'll be out of luck on the inheritance."

"Hector had the answer," Dash said. "The figures were wrong."

"But they couldn't be. I checked those figures myself for accuracy, and they came from…" Realization dawned upon her. "My figures came from Gary's computer records. Dash, that's the answer. He's been doctoring the figures all along."

"That's right, sweetheart. I think you've got it now."

"Gary is the head accountant at OrbenCorp. Nobody puts anything into the computer unless he okays the information. It would be simple for him to adjust the purchase prices that Hector gave him, adding a percent here and there. Then he would cut the checks for the amount Hector had given him. And Gary would pocket the difference."

"It's called embezzlement," Dash said. "And I'll bet if we can crack Gary's computer trail, we'll find that he has similar criminal charges in his background."

"It was almost too simple," she said. "All Gary needed to do was keep two sets of books. And Jack never verified the checks or invoices he signed. As long as his salary was paid, the figures bored him, and he'd sign whatever was placed in front of him. His signature was a rubber stamp."

"Agatha was about to put an end to it," Dash said. "She didn't know exactly what was wrong, but she was a sharp enough businesswoman to know OrbenCorp should have been more profitable."

"So she advised me to compare the figures." Liz felt the weight of the solution falling on her shoulders. "Gary would have gotten away with this forever if I hadn't done those comparisons, which meant Hector would see the numbers, and he would object to them and produce his originals."

"Unless Gary got the numbers corrected first."

"That's why he's at the office, working like a dog. He's covering his tracks."

"And that's why he came to your apartment and searched. That's why he went through your briefcase, even after you told him that you didn't have the comparison. He had to make sure he had every copy of the incorrect figures."

She and Dash were on exactly the same wavelength. She was feeding off his deductions and completing his thoughts. "And Jack. He must have gone to OrbenCorp after hours and found Gary in my office with the comparison figures in his hand. Gary couldn't give the computer printout to Jack."

Dash nodded and blew smoke into the air. "If Jack had the computer pages, Gary was caught. He couldn't let Jack know. He had to kill him."

"So," she said, "I guess the case is closed." Liz wasn't sure if she felt positive or negative about the ending of their investigation. Of course, she wanted Gary to be caught and convicted for the heinous crimes he'd perpetrated. But she didn't want her time with Dash to end. "What happens now?"

"We let the cops know what we've come up with. There are still a couple of loose ends, but—"

"I meant," she said, "what happens with us? Do you have to leave me?"

"I said it before, sweetheart, and I'll say it again." His gaze melted with hers in tender communication. "I won't leave you. I'll find a way to stay with you."

"How? Dash, I need to know. I don't want to lose you."

"We've still got a couple of loose ends to tie up on this case. First, I want to find out if Sarah was involved in Gary's scheme or if she's an innocent dupe he was using for his own ends."

"A visit to Sister Muriel?" she suggested.

"I think so." He liked that idea, and he sensed that the good sister might be able to offer a perspective he hadn't seen before. "Also, though I'm sure the cops can come up with enough to convict Gary on the murder of Jack, I want to see him punished for killing Agatha. We still need to find the falcon."

"Bluebird," she automatically corrected.

"Whatever. And another thing," Dash said. "It might be handy to have the originals on Gary's computer printouts for evidence. You wouldn't happen to have kept a copy somewhere?"

She shook her head.

"Think, Liz. Did you work on the figures at home?"

"Yes." She snapped her fingers. "Yes! I can't guarantee it, but I might have the rough draft that I threw away before I came up with the final copy. It's all scribbled on, but we ought to be able to read the figures."

"A trip to your apartment," he concluded.

They had a plan, Dash thought, and he wished that he could make it last for days instead of a couple of hours. After the case was closed, his beeper would summon him to the office. That was the usual procedure. If he ignored the call, the consequences would be grim. There were always the rules, the everlasting regulations, to be obeyed.

Despite his assurances to Liz, he had no idea what would happen next. They were in uncharted waters, turbulent seas that might overwhelm them.

There had to be a way to sail around the obstacles that confronted them. He couldn't leave her, couldn't forget the love that sang within him. There had to be a way.

When they pulled up at the shelter, Sister Muriel was outside on the veranda. It was almost as if she was waiting for them.

She beamed at Dash. "I was expecting a delivery of groceries, but I'm delighted to see you. Both of you."

As she glanced between them, her happy greeting faded. "Oh, dear me. You two are in love, aren't you?"

Liz nodded. "We are."

Sagely, the nun said, "That could be difficult."

"Got any ideas?" Dash asked. It didn't take a mind probe for him to know that Sister Muriel was not only a very good woman, but a smart one, to boot. She might see an answer where he failed.

Though his instincts for crime-solving were still sharp, his feelings for Liz had blinded him to the more philosophical side of life. He wanted to be with her. He needed her. In a celestial existence where physical needs had no relevance, he had never felt so out of control, so desperate.

He would risk anything for her. Even the dread condition of mortality. Quietly, he said, "I would give it up for her. All of it."

Liz protested, "Dash, I can't let that happen. You have important work to do. I won't stand in your way."

"If I can't be with you," he said simply, "I cannot go on."

Sister Muriel cleared her throat. "I do believe there might be an obvious answer, one that is directly under your noses."

They both looked at her, waiting and hoping.

"Love is not a sacrament," Sister Muriel said. "Love, though exalted, is only an emotion. But marriage? That's a blessed event."

"You think we should get married?" Liz questioned.

"If you're in love, that does seem to be the next logical step."

"But marriage," Liz said. "It's kind of sudden. I mean, there are invitations and flowers and cakes. And my dress. I don't even own a white dress."

"Those are the trappings," Sister Muriel said. "More important are the vows. Remember what they say. What God has joined together, let no one put asunder."

"No one," Dash repeated. Not man. Not angel. In his mind, he reviewed the myriad rules and regulations. There were definite cautions against sinning. No swearing. No lying. No lust. But he didn't recall a single footnote that forbade marriage. It was, as the sister had pointed out, a sacrament.

He dropped to one knee before Liz.

Sister Muriel cleared her throat. "Take off your hat, Dash. It doesn't look proper."

He clenched his fedora in his hand and gazed into Liz's beautiful azure eyes. "Marry me, Elizabeth."

"Just like that?" A gush of panic flooded her mind. She felt woozy. Was he really asking? Would she, could she, be married to an angel? Amid the turbulent confusion and doubt and hesitation, she knew what her answer must be. "I'll marry you, Dash. I'll always love you."

He stayed there, motionless, as if he was waiting. Then he stood and slapped his hat on his head. "This is a good sign. My beeper didn't go off."

"I'd be happy to arrange it," Sister Muriel offered. "I can contact one of the priests at the church nearby, and we can have the ceremony scheduled for later today. Shall we say in two hours? At six?"

"Six it is." A hot flush climbed Liz's throat. She was breathless, tense. "Could I get a drink of water?"

"Certainly, dear." Sister Muriel started toward the door of the shelter.

"Before you go inside," Dash said. "We had a question for you. About Sarah."

"Poor thing. It does seem she's made another mistake in judgment, doesn't it." She clucked her tongue against her teeth, making a disapproving noise. "I never did care for that Gary Gregory. It doesn't surprise me, not one little bit, to find that he's abusive."

"How deeply do you think Sarah cares for him?" Dash probed. "Does she love him enough to do anything for him?"

"I think not. She had done a great deal of therapy, you know. It was all at Agatha's instigation, but Sarah has been helped. And, from what she told me earlier today, she plans to end their relationship as soon as possible."

Weakly, Liz said, "Water?"

Sister Muriel took her arm and ushered her inside.

Liz was in such a frantic internal state that she hardly noticed the clean, attractive surroundings. She had a vague impression of polished woodwork and white walls and brightly colored but inexpensive paintings on the walls.

In the kitchen, which was gleaming clean, Sister Muriel introduced her to two women who sat at the kitchen table, sharing coffee and a quiet conversation. Then she asked, "Will tap water be all right?"

"Perfect," Liz said.

As soon as she tasted the cool, soothing water, Liz felt her temperature begin to ebb. The liquid washed down her throat, and she forced herself to swallow, to function normally. The dizzy sensation of vertigo faded, and she felt slightly more grounded.

Married? After all these years, she was going to be married. She'd found love, she'd found a companion for eternity. And she prayed nothing would interfere.

"Much better," she said.

"Quite a whirlwind courtship," Sister Muriel said.

"Quite."

Liz gazed through the window behind the sink at the blue skies, which would soon thin to sunset. Soon, very soon, it would be six o'clock. And she would be a bride.

Or else Dash might be snatched away from her. He might be forced to fulfill his angelic duties.

A sigh trembled on her lips. "I hope this works."

"Have faith," Sister Muriel encouraged. "In these difficult times, that is all we can do. But sometimes, that faith can change the world or move a mountain."

"Sometimes," Liz repeated. If only she could be absolutely certain.

Her gaze lit upon an object placed on the windowsill between a pot of blooming daisies and a green Chia pet. It was a small plaster statue of a bluebird perched on a brown tree branch. "Sister, where did you find that statuette?"

"It always makes me happy when I look at it. Such a cheerful bird. When I used to visit Agatha in her sickroom, the little bluebird was always there on the table beside her." Sister Muriel reached across the sink to pick up the statue. "After she died, I asked Sarah if I might have this. As a memento."

"May I take it?" Liz asked. "It might be evidence."

"Of course." Sister Muriel placed the bluebird in her hand. "If this cheery fellow can help you find and convict the terrible person who murdered my friend, you are most welcome to it."

"I'll try to get it back," Liz promised.

"If not, I won't be disappointed. Every day, it seems, my memories of Agatha grow stronger. Sometimes, I believe she is here with me, still encouraging, still doing her good works."

"Perhaps," Liz said, "she is."

On the porch, she held out the statue toward Dash. "Sister Muriel had this. As a memento of Agatha. Look, Dash. It's your falcon."

"Bluebird," he said.

He turned the cheap plaster bird over in his hand. There was a circular hole in the bottom that had been taped over. When he shook the statue, he could hear a rattling inside. Firm evidence, he thought. Finally, he could prove that Agatha had been murdered by someone who had exchanged her high blood pressure capsules for a dose of poison. With luck, there might even be a fingerprint on the capsule.

"This is almost all we need. Gary Gregory is cooked." He looked gratefully at the plump, pretty nun with the wire-rimmed glasses. "We have one more stop, Sister. But Liz and I will be at the church. Six o'clock."

As they drove away, heading toward Liz's apartment, Dash decided it was a good sign the church where the sister planned for the marriage ceremony to take place was named St. Michael's. A good omen. Or, possibly, a very bad one.

They barely spoke on the ride to Liz's apartment. Not only was the rush hour traffic difficult, but Dash was lost in contemplation. He truly could not imagine the consequences if he had transgressed. Angels who erred were often sent to the dread Fifth Choir, the celestial equivalent of Siberia. Avenging Angels were reassigned to less interesting positions. And, if he had blown it big-time, there was always eternal damnation.

Was it worth the risk?

He looked at Liz and knew the answer. She was his heart, she was part of the essence of him. To have her, he would risk eternal punishment.

When Liz parked behind her apartment, he hesitantly said, "About this marriage—"

"You've changed your mind," she assumed. "I agree that it's a big step—a giant leap—to be undertaken so precipitously. But I can't lose you, Dash."

"And I feel the same about you. I love you, Elizabeth. I want this marriage. I want it more than anything. We might be grabbing at straws, but we have to try."

"Oh, Dash." She wanted to kiss him, longed to draw comfort from his embrace. But it was too soon. They were not married yet.

They hurried up the stairs to her apartment, and Liz went directly to the trash container beneath the sink. She removed the magazine she'd thrown away when she thought it had been touched by an intruder. By Gary, she thought.

Beneath the magazine, there were coffee grounds, a disgusting orange peel and a few empty containers. At the very bottom, stained and crumpled, were the computer printouts she had used for her rough draft of the price comparisons.

Triumphantly, she said, "Here they are, Dash. These are originals, straight from Gary's computer."

He took the papers and turned toward the door. "Let's go, sweetheart. We've got a date at six."

"I want to change clothes." Though she didn't have a white, lacy dress, Liz did own a pale blue pantsuit with a satin collar. "I won't be a minute."

She went into her bedroom and stopped dead in her tracks.

"Guess again, Liz." Gary Gregory sat on the bed. In his hand, he held a very deadly-looking revolver.

She pivoted, but he was faster. He grasped her forearm and raised his weapon. The barrel of the gun pressed against her head.

"I was afraid you might try something," he said. "Even though I fired you, I had a feeling you'd come back to pester me. After all, you've seen the figures."

"But I'm not a computer," she said. "I couldn't remember. And without documentation, I couldn't prove—"

"Shut up, Liz." He guided her into the front room, keeping the gun close to her head.

Dash stood paralyzed, unable to help.

Gary ordered her to sit on the sofa and told Dash to sit beside her. "Don't try anything," he warned. "This gun is cocked and ready to fire. It's a hair trigger."

He ordered Dash to turn over the rumpled computer pages. As soon as he had them in his hand, he smiled. "Now I've got everything I need."

"Why did you kill them?" Liz asked.

"I felt really bad about Agatha, you know. She was, after all, the only person who would hire me after that embezzling charge—which I have since erased from the memory of every computer."

"Then why?"

"The money, of course. Raising my roses is expensive, and after I had that freeze in my greenhouse that nearly destroyed years of effort, I knew that I couldn't afford to go halfway. I needed the best that money could buy. So I started siphoning off money—small amounts at first. When the cash started getting bigger, I covered myself with key-man insurance."

"But Agatha was beginning to catch on," Dash said. "Is that it? She was onto you?"

"She had an inkling. I knew that as soon as she was out of the way, I could take as much as I wanted. Jack was so stupid. Even when I killed him, he didn't know why." Gary's beaklike nose protruded into Liz's line of vision. "And now I'll have to kill the two of you. And I want to make sure it's blamed on Hector. Better yet, on his thug son."

"It won't do any good to kill us," Liz bluffed with sheer bravado. She was so terrified that it took all her effort not to faint. "We have evidence. Hard evidence. One of the capsules, disguised to look like high blood pressure medicine, that you gave to Agatha."

"I don't believe you."

"It's true," Dash said tersely. He described the pill. "Might even have your prints on it."

"And where is this capsule?" Gary asked.

"If I tell you," Liz said, "will you let us go? I promise we won't help the police at all."

"Do you think I'm a fool?" He waved the gun in her face and pressed the barrel to her cheek. The cold metal stabbed into her skin. "You don't have any room to bargain. Either way, you're dead. But you do have one choice."

"What's that?"

"I can kill you slowly. Which is something I would rather enjoy doing." He raised his white eyebrows and stared at her with cruel intensity. "Or you can give me this capsule, and your death will be sudden and fast."

"You're insane."

"And you're deceased."

He cackled at what he must have perceived as humor, and she realized that he truly was crazy. Though he professed to have a logical motive for his crimes, she knew there was more. Dash would have called it evil.

Gary leered at her, enjoying the power he attained with a gun in his hand. "Now, Lizzie, what's it going to be? Fast or slow?"

"I'll get the pill," she said, playing for time. If she could move out of the line of fire, Dash could easily overpower this disgusting vulture who kept beautiful roses and terrifying secrets.

"Where is it?" Gary demanded.

"In my medicine cabinet. In the bathroom. I'll have to find it for you."

"Fine." Keeping the gun close to her head, he ordered, "Dash, you go first. Then, Liz, you follow. I'll be right behind you. Remember, Dash, if you make one false move, she's dead."

Dash rose slowly to his feet. Though he spoke not a word, Liz could hear him, as if he was speaking aloud. His voice instructed, "When you get into the bathroom, slam the door on him and hit the floor in case he starts firing."

She fell into step behind him, and Gary trailed her. She could feel the gun at the back of her head. Would this work? Would she be able to move fast enough?

At the bathroom, she slammed the door and dove.

Two shots crashed through the wooden door, but Dash leaped forward and locked it.

"We're okay," she said, somewhat amazed. "All right, Dash, do your angel thing. Whack him with a flaming sword."

"I'd like to take him alive. I want him to stand trial and be convicted for his crimes."

"Well, just knock him out. Don't you have a stun gun in your repertoire?"

"And how would I explain that to a judge?"

Gary was blasting at the door lock. In minutes, he'd be through the door. She had an idea. "I'll go through the window. There are enough ledges out there that I can climb to the roof."

"And then?"

"I might be able to sneak inside another apartment and use their phone. Just hold him until I get outside."

She was through the window and onto the ledge in a minute. Tiptoeing cautiously, she inched along the eaves until she came to a dormer. Carefully, Liz tried the window. Locked!

She kept going. The fancy architectural details made it simple to climb over to the other side.

Inside her apartment, she heard the bathroom door crack and slam open.

Gary's head appeared in the window. His crest of white-blond hair bobbed furiously.

Though she tried to duck, he spotted her and let loose a volley of gunfire. Where were her neighbors? Why hadn't anyone called the police? Where was a cop when you really needed one?

She peeked again and saw Gary shove himself onto the window ledge.

Dash's voice in her ear advised, "Hold on tight."

Liz braced herself.

The hot, vicious gust of wind came up suddenly, and Gary flattened himself against the eave of the house, clinging to her window frame. He tried to move, but the blast of air fought him. The gun dropped from his hand and fell three stories to the ground below.

Liz looked away from Gary to the pale blue skies and the western sunset. She couldn't say for sure, but she thought she saw wings, pearly white and powerful, stroking a tidal wave of air that rocked the shingles on the roof.

Gary lost his grasp and his balance. With a surprised screech, he fell back in space. He crumpled on the ground and lay silent.

Immediately, Dash was beside her. "Are you all right?"

"I'll live. How about Gary?"

"He's unconscious. His left ankle is broken."

"So he won't be going anywhere," she said.

She eased her way into her apartment and telephoned the police. But this time, Liz couldn't wait around for their questioning. She had a ceremony to attend.

IN ST. MICHAEL'S CHURCH, Dash and Liz—who had managed to change into her pale blue pantsuit and to drag a comb through her hair—stood before the priest. The only witnesses to their vows were Sister Muriel and three of the women from the shelter.

Despite his wildly beating angel heart, Dash listened to the words of the ceremony. If anything was to happen to separate them, he wanted every second branded on his memory. When Liz accepted him as her husband, saying a quiet, "I do," his joy was unbounded. Her love was better than flight, than invisibility, than any of the miracles of his existence.

And when it came his turn, his voice was strong. "I do."

From behind him, Dash heard the beautiful resonance of a heavenly Choir. He turned and looked up. At the rear of the church, in the choir loft, he spied Angelo, waving and cheering as if he was at a football game and not a solemn wedding ceremony. To his left was another cheerleader—Cherie in her leopard-skin robes. Behind them both, a celestial Choir was arrayed, and they celebrated the sacrament of marriage in powerful song.

"I knew you could do it," Angelo shouted. "Follow your heart. I knew you could figure it out."

Dash looked at the priest, who was speechless, staring at the miraculous manifestation in the choir loft.

But there was someone else at the altar. Dash's gaze fixed on a marble statue of St. Michael with his fiery sword held aloft. And the statue moved. It breathed. The fierce saint's eyes blazed and he offered a benediction. "I now pronounce you man and wife. Dashiell, you may kiss the bride."

Dash needed no more encouragement. He drew Liz into his arms. For the first time, he allowed himself to taste the honey of her lips. Her body was pressed firmly against him, and he reveled in the unfamiliar sensation. His fingers tangled in the length of her hair.

She was perfect, he thought as he ended their kiss, the first of a lifetime of kisses. He stroked her arm. With his finger, he traced the line of her jaw. He held her face in his hands and studied every angle and curve. "Here's looking at you, sweetheart."

This, indeed, was close to heaven.

After they had retreated down the aisle and stood on the church steps, accepting congratulations from Sister Muriel and her ladies, a well-dressed man approached.

Dash introduced him. "Liz, I'd like for you to meet Mike. He's a good friend and my boss."

"I've heard so much about you." She noticed that his necktie was exactly the same color as the maroon warrior cord that Dash had worn when he manifested as an angel. "In fact, I was thinking of asking you for a job. As an investigator."

"We're not quite that liberal yet," he said. "But I expect to be doing more consulting work with you in the future."

"Consulting work?"

"Frankly, I had hoped you and your husband might form your own private detective firm. After all, I can't really let him return to the agency. Nor do I suppose he would want to."

Dash nodded. He couldn't speak. His gratitude overwhelmed him.

Mike scratched his temple and grinned. "I would suggest the name Divine Investigations."

"Thank you, Mike," she said. "We'll consider it."

He nodded. "May your union be blessed with many children."

He walked away. He'd only gone a few paces when he vanished like a dream in the night.

She gaze at her new bridegroom. "When Mike said he wanted us to form our own agency, did that mean you've changed? Are you still..." She looked around to make sure no one was listening. "Are you still an angel?"

Without moving his lips, he sent a thought to her. "Yes, my darling. I am still an angel. Your angel."

"Well, I think we should get started on that blessing from Mike."

"Many children," he said. He reached into his jacket pocket, removed the fancy wrapped condom and placed it in her hand. "I guess I won't be needing this."

A police car squealed up to the curb of the church, and a uniformed officer jumped out and charged up the wide stone stairs to St. Michael's Church. "Dash Divine and Liz Carradine? We've just arrested one Gary Gregory for the murder of Jack Orben, and we have a few questions you might be able to help us with."

Liz linked her arm through that of her new husband, appreciating the very solid feeling of his body against hers. How had she ever thought her life was dull, mundane and routine?

"Please come with me," the cop said.

"You bet," Dash said. "We're there, Officer. And we got evidence that's going to make conviction a breeze."

So easily, he slid into his Sam Spade persona, the face he wore for the everyday world. And Liz smiled at him. She was the only mortal who knew all his secrets, including the very intimate detail that he wasn't anywhere near as tough as he acted.

He leaned toward her. Almost embarrassed, he dropped a kiss on her forehead. "You don't mind, do you, precious? We need to help the coppers whenever we can."

"No problem," she said sweetly. "I guess the honeymoon will have to wait."

"I've already waited several lifetimes for you to come along," he whispered. "A few hours more won't matter."

Without speaking, they exchanged eternal vows and pledged their love.

BRIDE'S BAY RESORT

UNLOCK THE DOOR TO GREAT ROMANCE AT BRIDE'S BAY RESORT

Join Harlequin's new across-the-lines series, set in an exclusive hotel on an island off the coast of South Carolina.

Seven of your favorite authors will bring you exciting stories about fascinating heroes and heroines discovering love at Bride's Bay Resort.

Look for these fabulous stories coming to a store near you beginning in January 1996.

Harlequin American Romance #613 in January
Matchmaking Baby by Cathy Gillen Thacker

Harlequin Presents #1794 in February
Indiscretions by Robyn Donald

Harlequin Intrigue #362 in March
Love and Lies by Dawn Stewardson

Harlequin Romance #3404 in April
Make Believe Engagement by Day Leclaire

Harlequin Temptation #588 in May
Stranger in the Night by Roseanne Williams

Harlequin Superromance #695 in June
Married to a Stranger by Connie Bennett

Harlequin Historicals #324 in July
Dulcie's Gift by Ruth Langan

Visit Bride's Bay Resort each month wherever Harlequin books are sold.

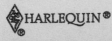

HARLEQUIN ®

MILLION DOLLAR SWEEPSTAKES

SWP-H296

Harlequin invites you to the
wedding of the century!

This April be prepared to catch the bouquet with
the glamorous debut of

For years, DeWildes—the elegant and fashionable
wedding store chain—has helped brides around the
world turn the fantasy of their special day into reality.
But now the store and three generations of family are
torn apart by divorce. As family members face new
challenges and loves, a long-secret mystery begins to
unravel.... Set against an international backdrop of
London, Paris, New York and Sydney, this new series
features the glitzy, fast-paced world of designer wedding
fashions and missing heirlooms!

In April watch for:
SHATTERED VOWS
by Jasmine Cresswell

Look in the back pages of *Weddings by DeWilde* for
details about our fabulous sweepstakes contest to win a
real diamond ring!

Coming this April to your favorite retail outlet.

WBDT

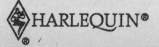

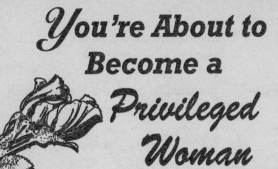

You're About to Become a
Privileged Woman

Reap the rewards of fabulous free gifts and benefits with proofs-of-purchase from Harlequin and Silhouette books

Pages & Privileges™

It's our way of thanking you for buying our books at your favorite retail stores.

PROOF OF PURCHASE
Offer expires October 31, 1996

**Harlequin and Silhouette—
the most privileged readers in the world!**

For more information about Harlequin and Silhouette's PAGES & PRIVILEGES program call the Pages & Privileges Benefits Desk: 1-503-794-2499

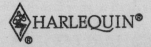

HARLEQUIN®